OUT

by

CHELSEA MILLER

This book is sold subject to the condition that it shall not, by way of trade or otherwise, be lent, re-sold, hired out, or otherwise circulated without the publisher's prior written consent in any form of binding or cover other than that in which it is published and without a similar condition being imposed on the subsequent purchaser.

The characters and situations in this book are entirely imaginary and bear no relation to any real person or actual happening.

First published in 1998 by Chimera.

Copyright © Chelsea Miller

CHIMERA

Out of Control published by
Chimera Publishing Ltd
PO Box 152
Waterlooville
Hants
PO8 9FS

Printed and bound in Great Britain by
Cox & Wyman Ltd, Reading.

OUT OF CONTROL

Chelsea Miller

A small insistent voice in her head suggested that maybe she didn't want to be untied. That maybe she liked being completely in his control, like this. That maybe she liked having to do whatever he wanted. Or whoever else was in the room. For all she knew, someone else could come into the bedroom, right now, and take her. More than one man. A whole string of them. Maybe even all the men in the office – the ones she'd cut down to size at a meeting, perhaps, the ones she'd humiliated in the past. They'd be more than happy to take the chance to be the ones in control, not her. They'd walk into the room, one by one – or maybe even three or four at a time. And then it would be their turn to humiliate her, to get their revenge for the way she'd treated them. They could do anything to her and she'd be powerless to resist, tied to the bed and forced to do whatever they wanted.

Chapter One

'It has to be one of the two Ws,' Simon said as he sat down, setting a pint before his best friend.

'Hm?' Marc looked at him, his grey-green eyes bewildered. 'What are you on about, Simon?'

'You. You've been in a dream all evening. I mean, I can't kid myself that my game has improved that much since last Friday night – and I thrashed you tonight, on the squash court. Nine-two. Come on, Marc, it's normally the other way round.'

Marc grimaced wryly. 'Yeah. Sorry. I know I didn't give you a good game.'

'Are you kidding? It's nice to win once in a while. Though I'd prefer it to be when you're concentrating, so I feel that I deserve it.' Simon grinned at his friend. 'So which is it then?'

'What?'

Simon rolled his eyes. 'Which of the two Ws? As in work, or women? It's got to be one of the two, to put you in this sort of state.'

'Both, I guess.' Marc took a sip of his pint.

'Want to talk about it?'

Marc looked round the pub; satisfied that no one from work was there to overhear him, he nodded. 'It's Sarah.'

'Sarah?'

'Sarah Ward. The new director of our division. The one I told you about, who joined the company about a month ago?' Even thinking about her made him hard. 'She's gorgeous, Simon.' His voice grew warm and appreciative.

'I've never met a woman like her.' He sighed. 'And she's completely untouchable, from those ice-blue eyes to that fabulous body she hides under a sharp business suit.'

Simon's brown eyes were sympathetic. 'And you fancy her like mad.'

Marc nodded. 'Though I hope to hell it doesn't show.'

'Trying to play it cool?' Simon guessed.

'Not so much playing it cool – more that I know better than to mix business and pleasure. You know the unwritten rule. Never sleep with a colleague – especially if she's senior to you. It just causes too many complications.' He grimaced. 'Not that I think she'd go for me, anyway.'

Simon privately doubted it. Most of the women he knew fancied Marc Dubois – who, quite apart from having a dynamic job in marketing and the vibrant personality and charm to go with it, looked like a Chippendale gone AWOL. He was the proverbial tall, dark and handsome man, with shrewd grey-green eyes and a mouth Simon's sister had once described as 'vulnerable, like a wounded puppy-dog', adding that it made a woman itch to kiss him. Women fell for Marc in droves; and if Simon hadn't liked his best friend so much, he would have been insanely jealous. 'So that's the woman side of it. What about the work?'

'That's Sarah, too.' Marc grimaced. 'I could murder her, I really could. She's making sweeping changes in the department – you know, the new broom syndrome.'

'Change for change's sake, you mean?'

'Yep.' Marc scowled. 'I wouldn't mind if she was making improvements, but she's not. She's doing it for the sheer hell of it, underlining that she's in charge. Her latest idea is that she wants everything to be much more disciplined.'

'Oh, yes?'

The teasing innuendo made Marc grin. 'Don't tempt me. I could quite happily haul her over my knee and spank her!'

'Except having her like that would distract you, make you forget why you were doing it,' Simon added, laughing. 'And then you'd be tempted to do something else with her.'

'Mm.' Very tempted. Once he'd bared her bottom, given her half a dozen hard slaps to punish her for being such a bitch in the office – then he'd want to bend his head to her reddened skin, soothe her with his mouth. And then some. It would take hours to finish what he wanted to do with her.

He grew serious again. 'I really don't know how to handle this, Simon. I've never had this problem with a woman boss, before. I mean, I like working with women – but Sarah's different.' He sighed. 'We had the mother of all rows, this afternoon. She'd been on a walkabout in the department – that's her buzzword for stalking round her little empire – and all of a sudden, my phone rang. It was her, summoning me for one of her little chats.' His jaw stiffened. 'You know what the office is like. I work with a team of women, and they like having pin-ups on their walls. Brad Pitt, David Duchovny, Antonio Banderas – from tiny pictures in the Sunday supplements to large specially posed calendars. There's a collage of them in one corner, labelled "sex on legs". I mean, we're a marketing department, a creative team. If they want pictures of their favourite hunks on the wall, it doesn't bother me. The way I see it, if they're happy with their surroundings, they'll all feel more relaxed and work better.'

'And Sarah doesn't see it that way?'

'No. She says that marketing departments need to be slick and stylish, and that having pictures everywhere is messy and tacky. She says the place needs to be cleaned up and a clear desk policy will be implemented forthwith.' He mocked Sarah's slightly upper-class and precise diction. 'God, she even objects to the basketball net my secretary has over her waste-bin!' Marc shook his head. 'If she has her way, everyone's going to be miserable. She'll take all the fun out of the office, and apart from making it a bloody awful place to work in, it'll halve our productivity.'

'Tell her.'

'I did. She wouldn't listen. She's sending round a memo, next week, telling everyone to take the pictures down, and keep to a clear desk policy. And you can guess who's going to have to deal with the fall-out. Ten women demanding what's so bad about their pin-ups and notices and wanting to know why they can't have framed photos of hubby or the kids and their cats and dogs on top of their PCs.' He grimaced. 'I don't see why the woman has to be so bloody difficult. No one's questioning her ability, the string of letters after her name or her high-powered career to date. No one's saying that she's too young to be in her role. And yet it's like she's out to prove herself.'

'Maybe she is.' Simon took a sip of his pint. 'It sounds like she's driving you mad, though.'

'Too bloody true. Half the time I'm torn between wanting to screw her silly, and needing to teach her a lesson.'

'What you need,' Simon said thoughtfully, 'is to be alone with her for a weekend. Just the two of you, somewhere nice and romantic. Screw her until you're both senseless. Get her out of your system – and then you can deal with her on a working level.'

Marc wrinkled his nose. 'Nice fantasy, Simon. Just her in my bed, all weekend. I could go for that. But you're forgetting a few things. Firstly, I don't sleep with colleagues

8

– and I bet she's even stricter than I am about that. Secondly, she doesn't fancy me. And thirdly, I've got an office to run.' He didn't add his fourth reservation: that spending a weekend in bed with Sarah Ward wouldn't get her out of his system. If anything, it would entrench her even more deeply.

'Yeah, well. Just a thought.' Simon drained his pint. 'Another?'

Marc shook his head. 'Better not. I'm driving,' he reminded his friend.

'Well, you would insist on moving out to the middle of nowhere,' Simon teased. 'Look, let's go out on the town, tomorrow night. Go to a club, have a good time, see what happens. You might meet someone to take your mind off work and Sarah Ward.'

'Thanks, but I'll take a rain-check,' Marc said.

Simon whistled. 'You really have got it bad.'

'Yeah.' Marc's smile was rueful. 'Ah, don't worry about me. I'll get over it. See you next Friday, at six thirty?'

'By which time you'll be back to normal and making me run around the court,' Simon said good-naturedly.

Marc left the pub; in the car, he switched on a tape of Bach violin concerti and turned the volume up, hoping that the music would relax him. He drove out of Leeds, taking one of the minor roads and then a narrow country lane to his cottage on the outskirts of a Dales village. Although most of his attention was on the road, part of his mind kept replaying Simon's suggestion. *What you need is to be alone with her for a weekend. Just the two of you, somewhere nice and romantic. Screw her until you're both senseless. Get her out of your system.*

Oh, yes. That's exactly what he'd like – to spend a whole weekend making love with her. A weekend of pure

9

unadulterated sex, with Sarah Ward. Underneath that ice-maiden exterior was one hell of a sensual woman, he was sure. Something about the curve of her lower lip suggested an inner wickedness. And she dressed too primly – as though she had to keep herself buttoned up, or she'd spiral out of control. He had a feeling she'd respond wildly to him.

He'd love her to be out of control with him, to fulfil that hidden sexual promise. Starting in the office. Supposing they were working late, on a Friday night, and he'd had to give up his regular squash match with Simon to meet a deadline... It would have to be something high-powered, involving just the two of them. The marketing strategy for the next year, he decided. Preparation for a presentation to the Board, something like that.

He settled back into the driving seat, still aware of his surroundings in the narrow and twisting lane, but with half of his mind on Sarah Ward. They'd be in her office. Her prissy, control-freak office. It was a shame, really – he'd love to sweep the papers theatrically from her bleached oak desk and take her across it. But as she kept rigidly to a clear desk policy, the only things on top of her desk were the leather blotter and the telephone. Even her filing trays were on top of her filing cabinet, rather than on her desk.

Still, they'd be on the same side of her desk, for once, working as a team instead of Sarah behaving like the imperious madam she was. He'd be animated, pointing out figures to her – and then their fingers would touch. Very lightly. The barest, tiniest contact of skin to skin... It would be electric. She'd turn to face him; and slowly, very slowly, the tip of her tongue would slick across her lower lip. Those ice-blue eyes would hold a question: and his mouth would answer it. On hers.

Yes. He could almost taste her. Her mouth would be warm and clean and fresh under his. And then she'd open her mouth to let him kiss her properly; his tongue would slide into her mouth, take possession. She'd close her eyes, tipping her head back, and he'd gently draw her to her feet. He'd loosen her hair, let it fall in soft waves to her shoulders. He'd remove her small round wire-rimmed glasses, placing them in her desk drawer for safety. Then, while he was still kissing her, he'd slide her jacket from her shoulders. The garment would land in a crumpled heap on the floor, but she wouldn't stop him. No. Because she'd be just as powerless to resist what was happening between them as he was.

And then he'd unbutton that prim white business shirt. Very, very slowly. The backs of his fingers would brush against the soft pale at the base of her throat; and then, as his fingers drifted lower, his mouth would drift lower, too. She'd arch her head back even further, offering him her throat, and he'd cover every inch of skin with his lips, nipping and teasing, arousing her. He'd linger in the hollows of her collar-bones, pressing the tip of his tongue to the pulse that beat hard and fast there; and then he'd drift lower, lower.

She'd be wearing white underwear. Except they wouldn't be just any old chain-store undies. She would be wearing Italian designer lingerie, silk and lace. Pure white, a couple of shades away from her skin-tone. Though her nipples would be hard, the rosy peaks obvious through the lace. He'd lower his mouth until he could suck her breast through the lace, making the material wet to increase the friction of his tongue against her sensitive flesh, give her more pleasure. Yes.

He'd feel her arch her back in response as he finished pulling her shirt from the waistband of her skirt. She

11

wouldn't protest as his hands slid up her back, unfastening her bra. And then he'd pull the lace away from her breasts, see the proud rosy tips tilting up to his mouth. She'd bury her hands in his hair, pulling him down, and he'd tease her, playing the tip of his tongue on her puckered flesh before taking a nipple into his mouth and sucking hard.

She'd be rocking her lower body against him, starting to simulate the thrusting movements of lovemaking; and he'd hitch up her skirt, pushing a thigh between hers so she could rub herself against him properly. He'd be able to feel the heat of her quim through their clothes; and it would drive him insane, thinking of the wet, creamy heaven between her thighs.

He wouldn't be able to stop himself.

He'd slide one hand up her thigh, brushing the soft flesh above her stocking welts – because, of course, a woman like Sarah Ward would wear silk lace-topped hold-up stockings, not tights – and then allow his hand to cup her quim through the thin silk of her knickers. He'd press his middle finger against her flesh, rubbing her clitoris through the soft material, until she was groaning and writhing and pushing onto him, the tone of her voice begging him to pleasure her.

And then, only then, he'd slide one finger under the edge of her knickers and enter her. She'd feel so hot and wet, so ready for him. He'd tease her, skate his fingertip around her clitoris, rubbing lightly as a butterfly's wing; and when she thrust towards him, he'd pull away, keeping the contact as light as possible. Teasing her. Tormenting her. Forcing her to tell him that she wanted him.

She'd tell him, all right. He'd touch her, push a second and third finger into her. He'd work her into the same state that he was in every time he thought of her, right on the edge – and then he'd stop. He'd smile at her, and ask

12

her what she wanted. And until that beautiful prim mouth told him what she wanted, very explicitly and very lewdly, he wouldn't touch her.

She'd resist at first. She'd refuse, say that she was going to restore some order to her clothes and they'd both pretend it had never happened. Then he'd draw the backs of his fingers down her cleavage, cup one breast and stroke the soft underside. She'd gasp and tip her head back; he'd continue to caress her, arousing her further, playing with her nipple and delighting in the way the areola puckered under his touch. And then he'd stop, ask her again what she wanted him to do.

It would be a game: to see who had the most power, the most self-control. She'd be good, very good – but he'd be better. Every time he'd break her resistance, touch her breasts or her belly or her mouth, and she wouldn't be able to suppress a shiver of desire. Yes, her mouth, he thought. He'd slide his glistening finger across her lips so that she could taste her own juices, the musky sweet-salt tang of her arousal.

That would clinch it.

She'd have to admit, then, what she wanted him to do. 'Marc. I want you to touch me.'

'Where?'

A pause. 'You know where.'

Another smile from him. 'You'll have to tell me what you want.'

'You *know*.'

'But you'll still have to tell me, if you want me to do it.'

Eventually, she'd give in. 'All right. I want you to touch me between my legs.'

Not good enough. 'How, precisely?'

Her eyes would glitter with a mixture of passion and anger, hot and icy at the same time. 'You know.'

13

'Tell me.'

'I want you to... to stroke my clitoris. With your—' a pause. 'Your hand.'

'My hand?' She wanted more than that. He knew. He knew exactly how she wanted him to pleasure her.

She'd shiver, seeing her thoughts reflected in his eyes, seeing her desire and its answer. 'With your mouth. I want you to use your mouth on me. I want you to make me come.'

Another pause; and she'd frown with annoyance. 'I told you.'

'You forgot something.'

Her turn to pause. 'I forgot something?'

'A little word beginning with "p".'

She'd close her eyes. 'Please.'

'Ask me properly.'

A sigh. 'All right. You win. Marc, I want you to lick me. I want you to lick my quim. I want you to suck my clitoris and put your tongue inside me. I want you to make me come. Please?'

He'd smile then, knowing he'd won. Knowing he'd made her ask him nicely – and he'd soon have her begging. Sarah Ward might have the upper hand in the day-to-day office life, but that was as far as it went. And then, very slowly, he'd pull her knickers down to her knees, haul her onto the desk, push her back to the hard surface and remove her knickers completely.

She'd look beautiful lying there. So lewd. Her shirt untucked and wide open, her bra undone and pushed down to free her glorious breasts, her skirt pushed up to her waist and those beautiful legs still encased in pure silk. He'd part her legs wider and stay there for a long time, just looking at her and taking in the sight, the way her intimate sex-flesh was every shade of pink from pale pearl

14

to deep vermilion.

And then he'd drop to his knees in front of her and bury his face in her pussy. He'd breathe in the scent of her arousal, a mixture of honey and seashore and musk and vanilla. The most beautiful scent in the world – the scent of an aroused woman. And then he'd taste her. He'd draw his tongue along the full length of her quim, exploring her folds and hollows. He'd tease the hard bud of her clitoris, flicking over it rapidly with the tip of his tongue until she thrust her fingers into his hair and urged him on. Then he'd take it between his lips, sucking harder as her passion rose.

He'd push his tongue deep into her vagina; her flesh would be like warm wet silk velvet against his mouth. He'd lick her again and again and again, until she was on the point of coming. And then – then, he'd lift his head, stand up, and unzip his trousers. He'd push his underpants and trousers down to his knees in one movement, and fit the tip of his erect cock to her entrance. Then he'd push into her, so very slowly – and she'd push back, lifting those long legs to wrap round his waist and pull him into her...

'Oh, Christ,' Marc moaned. He could see a gateway ahead of him; he pulled into it, suddenly desperate and not caring who might pass him on the road and see what he was doing. He switched off his engine and lights, thrust his seat back, and unzipped his fly, grabbing a handkerchief from his pocket at the same time.

Simon was right. He was in one hell of a state. He'd never had to pull off the road to masturbate over thoughts of a woman before. Never. And here he was, closing his eyes and tipping his head back against the seat, bucking his hips and tightening his grip and rubbing his erection at speed, just at the thought of sliding his cock into her warm sweet depths.

'Ahh! Sarah!' He couldn't help crying out her name as he came, wrapping the handkerchief around the tip of his cock just in time.

He remained there for a while, too shaken to drive on; then, finally, he managed to get himself back under control. He shoved the handkerchief back into his pocket, wiped the back of his hand against his forehead, and drove the last ten miles to his house.

'I've got to do something about it,' he said ruefully as he stripped off and headed upstairs for a shower. 'I can't keep on like this.'

But he found he couldn't concentrate. All weekend, thoughts of Sarah popped into his mind, interrupting whatever he was doing. Lewd thoughts. Thoughts of her spread across her desk, masturbating for him. Thoughts of her bent over a stool, her wrists tied to the legs of the stool with those soft silk stockings, her bottom tilted and her beautiful quim ready for him to take her. Thoughts of her kneeling before him like a slave-girl, looking up at him with a smile of pure wickedness before she opened her mouth and slid it over the tip of his cock.

He'd never masturbated so many times during a weekend – not even as a teenager at his randiest. The minute one of his fantasies popped into his head he had an instant erection: and he couldn't control his reaction. Whatever he was doing he had to unzip his fly and relieve himself, all the while wishing it was Sarah's hand curled round his cock, or her quim, or her mouth.

He couldn't get her out of his head. Whether his eyes were open or closed, he could see her. Imagine her, half-naked and posed invitingly for him. Imagine her on top of him, her beautiful breasts swinging by his face as she rode him. Her face tipped back, her back arched, her teeth bared and her eyes tightly shut as she climaxed, her voice hoarse as she called out his name.

By the Sunday evening Marc was feeling ravaged, out of control. Maybe Simon was right. Maybe what he needed was to spend a whole weekend in bed with her, turn her from an ice-maiden into the woman of his dreams. And then, once she was out of his system, he could deal with her at work. He could persuade her to let him run his department how he wanted. He'd done it well enough for the previous two years.

All he had to do was persuade her to spend some time with him, away from the office. A delightfully wicked plan formed in his mind. He knew he was on dangerous ground. If it didn't work, he would be out of a job.

On the other hand, the way things were going at work, he was very close to walking out in any case. And he had a feeling Sarah would enjoy what he had in mind. That 'don't touch' exterior was a smoke-screen, he was sure – hiding a woman with a very inventive and very sensual mind. She had a high-powered, high-pressure job; so she wouldn't necessarily want to be in control outside it. In fact, Marc thought, there was a very good chance that Sarah Ward was a sexual submissive. That she liked having the choices made for her, so she could switch off and just enjoy her body's response to a dominant man.

And he was going to find out. Very soon.

Chapter Two

'Come in,' Sarah called as she heard the knock. She looked up as the door opened, and blinked in surprise. Marc Dubois was the last person she'd expected to see.

He was the Head of Marketing – five years older than she was, with impressive qualifications, highly respected by the other directors – and they'd clashed horribly since the minute they'd been introduced. Sarah was uncomfortably aware that she found him attractive. There was something about his mouth that made her itch to touch it – or maybe to brush his straight dark hair back from his face, smooth her fingers over his skin, pull his head down to hers to kiss her. Maybe that was why she clashed with him so much, she thought. Because she wanted to keep a distance between them, and fighting him was the safest way to do it.

'What can I do for you?' she asked, her voice stiff.

'Do you have a minute, Ms Ward?' As usual, he was impeccably polite. Politically correct, too, always calling her 'Ms' rather than 'Miss'.

Part of her hated the formality; but at the same time she knew that she needed to preserve distance between herself and her direct reports. Using first-name terms was the first step to familiarity, and she couldn't afford to be familiar with someone like Marc Dubois. The minute she let him get close to her she'd lose that iron control. She couldn't afford to do that. She'd worked too damned hard to get where she was. 'I'm rather busy,' she parried.

'It'll only take a minute. Two at most,' he promised.

She sighed, and saved the file she was working on. God, if only he wouldn't smile at her like that. The worst thing was, he knew he was good-looking – but he wasn't arrogant with it. If only he'd been a cynical bastard, someone who rode roughshod over people, someone she could despise. But he wasn't like that at all. They'd had one hell of a row, the previous Friday, and it had been because he was standing up for his staff, fighting their corner. Marc Dubois was a genuinely nice guy – and that made him even more dangerous, in her book. 'All right. What is it?' she demanded, becoming imperious.

'I've come to apologise.'

Again, he caught her by surprise. She'd been intending to be haughty with him – but how could she after that beginning? 'Apologise?' The word came out almost as a croak.

'Yes. About Friday.' He shrugged. 'I went off at the deep end, and I'm sorry. I shouldn't have been rude to you.'

'I... That's all right.' She accepted his apology gracefully, almost tempted to apologise and admit that she'd been just as pig-headed and just as rude.

'I still think we need to discuss it, before you send out your memo. Talk about the situation objectively,' he said. 'Could you do that for me, please – delay your memo until we've had a chance to talk it through?'

God, God, why did he have to be so bloody charming? Why couldn't he have stomped about her office, demanded and raged, instead of being reasonable and talking to her in a way that made it impossible for her to refuse him? 'Yes,' she found herself saying, before her brain had a chance to jump in and object.

'Good.' Again, that devastating smile. Surely he must know what a weapon he had there, she thought. Unbidden, the thought of that mouth moving over her skin, pleasuring her, flicked into her mind; she shivered.

'Though I think we'd be more objective on neutral ground. Non-office territory, I mean,' he added.

She looked suspiciously at him. 'Meaning?'

'Meaning, why don't we have dinner together?'

'Dinner?' She was shocked. Was he chatting her up, asking her to go on a date with him?

'I enjoy cooking. Maybe you could come to my cottage on Friday evening – if you're not doing anything, of course – and I could cook dinner for you. We can talk properly then.'

He was going to cook for *her*? Christ, the man was full of surprises. 'I...'

'I thought a nice relaxing environment would help us discuss the matter. No strings. I live in the Dales and, somehow, things always seem more in perspective there than they do in the middle of the city. Away from the rush and the traffic,' he tempted.

'I... I'll check my diary.' She just about managed to still the tremor in her fingers as she removed her Psion from her handbag, switched it on, and checked her diary. Though that was just a front. Sarah knew full well that she had nothing arranged for Friday night. Weekends were always spent working, building her career and pushing herself to the very top. She didn't allow herself to have a social life. And she definitely didn't approve of socialising with colleagues, except for networking. She was his senior, not the other way round, so he would hardly further her career.

She'd tell him it was impossible.

'Yes, that's fine,' her mouth said, again working against her brain.

'Good. Seven o'clock?'

'I... Fine.'

'Is there anything you don't eat?' he enquired.

Thoughtful, too. Not taking anything for granted. 'Red meat,' she told him. 'Other than that, I like most things.'

'Good. I'll give you directions on Thursday,' he said. 'I can see you're busy, so I'll let you get on.' At her door he paused, turning to smile at her. 'Have a nice day.'

Sarah stared at the closing door in shock. Had he been teasing her? Was he taking the piss? Or... She sighed heavily, propping her elbows on her desk and cupping her chin in her hands. She'd just agreed to have dinner with him, at his place. A cottage in the middle of the Dales, he'd said – that meant right in the middle of nowhere.

What the hell had she just done?

Because now she couldn't shift the idea of his mouth on her skin. Of him arousing her with his lips and his tongue and those beautiful long fingers. Of him whispering words to her, words to shock her and excite her and make her lose her inhibitions. A soft, husky voice, murmuring endearments in French. Marc Dubois. An English mother and a French father, she guessed, who'd decided to live in England – according to Marc's personnel file, he'd been educated in London, both at secondary school and university. But Marc's Gallic side would take over when he made love.

She shook herself. Of course she knew his personal details – she knew those self-same details for all her direct reports. But only Marc got to her like this. Only Marc argued with her; the others, she was sure, said one thing to her face and another behind her back. That was a fact of office life. If you were near the top at age thirty, and a woman to boot, people would think you either slept your way up or were an ambitious bitch, happy to tread on anyone to get where you wanted, and they'd crawl to your face and stab you in the back.

It was one of the reasons why she didn't socialise. She'd

got where she was on the strength of her abilities – not because she'd slept her way there. She'd always stuck by the unwritten rule never to sleep with colleagues. She'd seen too many people make that mistake and lose a lot of ground because of it.

Though Marc Dubois tempted her to bend the rules. Not just bend them – shatter them into tiny pieces.

She squeezed her eyes shut, but realised her mistake almost immediately. Because without the sight of her office to distract her, she could see Marc even more clearly. She could see him kneeling on a bed in front of her, his grey-green eyes darkening with desire as he watched her. Watched her slide her hand between her legs and stroke herself, at his command. Watched her break her last taboo and bring herself to a climax in front of someone else...

She shivered, shocked to realise her hand was just about to hitch up her skirt and slide between her thighs. She never touched herself intimately in the office. Never. Christ. Her secretary could have walked in and seen her like that. Anyone could. Anyone looking through the glass window and the open slatted blinds could have seen her start to touch her breasts, her sex. Christ.

She'd have to find an excuse to cancel. She'd just have to.

And yet she knew that she'd go. She couldn't help herself.

The whole of Friday, she thought about ringing him to cancel. He'd taken the day off – she wasn't sure whether he'd had the day booked off for weeks, or whether he'd booked it immediately after she'd agreed to have dinner with him, and she couldn't ask Personnel. Even if they didn't ask her why she wanted to know, they'd gossip about her, speculate about why she was so interested in Marc

Dubois' leisure time, and she couldn't bear that.

Eventually, at half past five, she walked back to her city apartment and changed. He hadn't specified whether she should dress for dinner or wear something casual. It was at his house, so God only knew what he expected. Part of her was tempted to arrive in her business suit, say that she could only stay for half an hour...

She smiled wryly. Who was she kidding? She felt more like a teenager on her first date. It was ridiculous. They were going to talk business, and he was obviously cooking for her in an attempt to soften her up, persuade her to let his department stay a mess instead of bringing it into the twenty-first century, making it neat and slick and efficient. She could play the same game – and she'd play it better.

She showered quickly, forcing away the lewd thoughts that came into her mind. Thoughts of showering with Marc, of smoothing foaming gel into his skin and serving him like a maid, washing his back and sliding her hands down to his buttocks. Then turning him to face her, dropping to her knees and curling her fingers round his impressive cock. Stroking him, watching him arch his back as his arousal grew; and then dipping her head, letting her hair brush against his thighs before she opened her mouth and took the tip of his cock between her lips...

Getting dressed was just as bad. Whatever she put on she could imagine Marc taking off. She could almost feel his fingers, his mouth, against her bare skin. 'Get a grip,' she told herself savagely. 'This is business.' And the only reason she was wearing sheer silk lingerie was for her, because it made her feel good, she told herself. It had absolutely nothing to do with Marc.

Eventually she chose a pair of black designer jeans, a black cotton polo-neck sweater, and a pair of flat polished leather ankle-boots. Look but don't touch, she thought. If

Marc was hoping to sway her... Well, she could sway him. Maybe she'd flirt with him a little, try to reason with him.

'Liar,' she told herself softly. She wouldn't flirt with Marc to get her own way. She'd flirt with him because she wanted him. And that was precisely why she would make damn sure that the evening was as short as possible, and remained on businesslike terms. If she gave in to her baser nature, slept with him, she knew she'd regret it.

She took the map he'd drawn for her from her briefcase, grabbed her handbag and the bottle of white wine she'd put in the fridge to chill, and locked her front door behind her. Her car was small and sporty, sheer indulgence – the only 'flash' perk she'd allowed herself. The kind of car that most men she knew coveted: and she knew she looked good in it. Particularly when she had the top down and her hair loose and was wearing a pair of Ray-Bans, and her stereo was blasting out. *Boys of Summer, Walking on Sunshine* – music with a catchy tune, something summery and something she could sing to.

She ignored the small knot of men who gawped and whistled at her as she opened her car door. Part of her felt like leaning over and wiggling her bottom suggestively; on the other hand, she knew that would be asking for trouble, and she really wasn't that interested in them. Marc Dubois, on the other hand...

Swearing softly, she slammed her car door. She wasn't going to think about Marc. She was going to be cool and calm and businesslike.

So why had she left her hair loose? a little voice taunted her. Why was she wearing those figure-hugging jeans? Why was she wearing a provocative *chypre* perfume, so unlike the cool floral scent she wore in the office?

Scowling, she checked her mirror, signalled, and pulled away smoothly. Driving relaxed her; she switched on the stereo, pushed in the tape of soft bluesy-rock she often drove to, and followed Marc's directions.

They were excellent; at three minutes to seven she parked outside his small cottage. It was already dark, being late October, and the village had no streetlights, so she couldn't see what the place was like, but she had an idea it would be a chocolate-box type of place. Soft yellowy York stone, mullioned windows, roses round the door.

It suddenly occurred to her that she didn't know if Marc had a girlfriend. For all she knew he could be living with someone. His personnel file wouldn't give that kind of information. Maybe it was dinner *à trois*. But somehow, she didn't think so. However accommodating Marc's girlfriend or fiancée or wife might be, she'd draw the line at inviting his female boss over for dinner. Besides, Marc had said that he was cooking. Surely if he lived with someone, his girlfriend would do that?

Then something else occurred to her. Marc wasn't necessarily heterosexual. For all she knew, he could have a boyfriend. He could prefer making love with men.

But then again, she'd have known about it. No way would the office grapevine have kept something like that secret. There were no reports of liaisons between Marc and any of the women in the office, but that didn't mean he was gay. Maybe it meant that he had the same personal code as she did, and kept business and pleasure completely separate. And maybe, just maybe, he'd be prepared to bend those rules, tonight...

She climbed out of the car, grabbing the chilled wine and her handbag, and knocked on the front door. Her stomach knotted with excitement, and she cursed herself mentally. Honestly. This was purely business. What was the point of pretending otherwise? And yet every nerve in her body was taut and straining, expectant. Longing.

After what seemed to her like hours, he answered the door. 'Hello, Ms Ward. Thank you for coming.'

The formality she insisted on in the office somehow seemed incongruous, here. 'Call me Sarah,' she found herself saying, before she could switch her brain into business gear and be polite and formal with him.

'Sarah.' The word was like a caress; her nipples hardened involuntarily. And, from the brief flicker in his eyes, she knew that he'd seen.

Damn.

'Come in,' he invited, standing aside.

'Thank you.' She didn't trust herself to say his name. Instead, she stiffly handed him the bottle of wine. 'I didn't know what you were cooking, so I played safe.'

He unwrapped the tissue paper. 'Chablis. That's lovely – and it's chilled. Thank you, Sarah.'

He still hadn't enlightened her as to the menu. Sarah hated being in a position where she wasn't in control. She followed him awkwardly into his sitting room, and stopped dead. She wasn't sure quite what she'd expected – some kind of bachelor pad, maybe, a monochrome colour scheme and slightly shabby furniture – but it was nothing like that. The small room was beautifully decorated in rich blues and yellows: marbled blue paper below the dado rail and yellow paper with blue fleurs-de-lys above it. There were thick matching curtains at the window; an open fire with a silk Persian rug in glowing blues and yellows in front of it; and a pair of yellow two-seater sofas, low and comfortable-looking, with blue cushions scattered on them.

A framed print of Van Gogh's *Irises* hung on one wall, and a large pine-framed mirror hung over the mantelpiece, giving the illusion of extra space. Uplighters were set in the walls, and there was a good stereo in a corner of the room – currently playing some kind of classical music, soft and relaxing, although she didn't recognise it. And no television, she noted. Marc Dubois obviously had better things to do with his time than sit passively in front of the box.

She closed her eyes briefly as a vision of just what he'd do with his time flooded her mind. Making love, his lithe bare body stretched out on that beautiful Persian rug while his lover rode him, impaling herself on his glorious cock...

'Sarah?'

She suddenly realised he'd been talking to her, and she hadn't heard a word he'd said. 'Sorry. I was...'

'Mind on the office. I know,' he said softly. 'Can I get you a drink?'

She took control of herself. 'Wine would be lovely, thanks.'

He smiled. 'I'll be back in a minute. Make yourself at home.'

The minute that Sarah settled into one of the sofas, she knew she'd made a very big mistake. Christ. She should have checked him out properly before agreeing to have dinner with him. Or she should have cancelled. But this... this was all too tempting. She could imagine him pressing her back against these soft cushions, pushing one hard thigh between hers, and it made her quim pulse hard.

Because not only was his house beautiful: so was he. She'd never seen him in anything but a sober business suit, a coloured silk tie his only gesture towards the usual marketing man flamboyance. But in a pair of dark soft trousers and a cream cotton round-necked sweater, he looked fabulous. It set off his colouring to advantage – he'd obviously inherited his mother's fair English skin rather than his father's Gallic olive-toned complexion – and made him look positively edible. She was going to have her work cut out, just stopping herself from touching him. No way could she keep her fantasies in check. She knew that when she got home she'd have to dive for her vibrator, and it would take several hours to get him out of her system – or at least get herself back in control.

Things got worse when he returned. He handed her a glass of wine, and his fingers brushed against hers. Very lightly – but it sent her imagination into overdrive. She could almost feel him touching her much more intimately, and it strained her nerves almost to breaking point.

Deliberately, she was sure, he sat on the other sofa. 'Thank you for coming here this evening, Sarah.' And just as deliberately, he kept using her name. She knew that marketing types often did that, that using someone's name meant you were supposedly empathising with that person and making them feel like the centre of attention – but she couldn't help misreading his tone, imagining his voice growing husky with arousal as he said her name.

'That's all right,' she said, trying to keep her voice clipped. 'Thank you for inviting me.'

'Pleasure.'

God. That was worse. His smile. That beautiful mouth... She wanted to place her glass on the floor, crawl over to him and pull his head down to hers. Beg him to take her. Crudely, even – tell him that she wanted him to fuck her to paradise and back. She shivered, trying to steer the conversation to something normal. 'Your directions were very good.'

'I'm pretty much out of the way here, so they need to be,' he said quietly. 'Dinner should be ready in about ten minutes.'

'Oh. Thank you.' She cast around for a neutral topic. 'I like the music. What is it?'

'One of Haydn's baryton trios,' he told her.

'Bari—' She paused, not recognising the word.

'Baryton. It's something like a cello,' he explained. His lips twitched. 'Sorry. I like rather obscure music, I'm afraid – and I listen more to classical than pop.'

'It's very nice,' she offered. 'Relaxing.'

Conversation was slightly awkward until he ushered her through to the dining room. The room was as small as his sitting room, but just as impeccably decorated, with a thick carpet and glowing cherry-wood furniture. The walls were papered with a cream-and-green design she recognised as being a William Morris print, and there was a framed print on the wall she didn't recognise, though it looked Victorian. A man was half-crouched in the background against a hedge of may-flowers, draped in blue robes. A woman stood before him, reading from a book and looking back at him, her lips curved sensually and cruelly. The blue chiffon she wore clung to her body; although only her bare feet and her neck were revealed, she looked incredibly erotic.

'Burne-Jones,' he told her. '*The Beguiling of Merlin.*'

'Oh.' She flushed as she realised that she'd spoken aloud.

'And yes, he was Victorian. One of Rossetti's set,' he told her.

She suddenly remembered his personnel file. 'Your degree was in English, wasn't it?'

He nodded. 'I took a term's seminars on Victorian studies, too, as background. That's when I discovered Burne-Jones.' He grinned. 'But not the Haydn. That was Radio Three, on my way in to work one morning.' He spread his hands. 'Back in a minute.'

He returned with two plates; Sarah's eyes widened as he slid one of them in front of her. It looked incredibly professional. Either he was cheating and he'd raided Marks and Spencer's food department, or he was talented at more than just his job.

'Smoked salmon wrapped around fresh salmon mousse,' he told her. 'I made it this morning, so the flavours could mature properly.' He grinned. 'Next door's cat liked the trimmings, anyway. She was on my doorstep before I'd even put the salmon to poach in the wine. I swear she must have heard me open the fridge. I hope you like seafood?'

'Yes, thanks.' And he'd already asked her what she didn't like, she remembered.

It tasted even better than it looked. The second course was equally good, poached chicken breasts with a rich creamy tarragon sauce, served on a bed of spinach with tiny new potatoes and baby carrots. And the third course, a luscious white chocolate mousse served with out-of-season strawberries, was to die for, she thought. God. A man who was good at his job, nice-looking, cooked like an angel... What else would he do well?

Being half-French, of course he'd be skilled in the sensual arts, as well. He could probably keep her in orgasm for hours. She fought to keep her pulse under control at the thought.

By the time he brought the coffee through, Sarah had managed to relax. Marc had kept the conversation on a light and friendly level – not mentioning the subject that had already caused so much friction between them – and she discovered that she liked his company. He was witty, charming... and very skilful at drawing her out. Part of her was annoyed by it, but she was enjoying herself too much to be sharp with him.

Eventually, she yawned and glanced at her watch, her eyes widening in shock. 'Is that the time? Marc, it's been a lovely evening – thank you – but I need to get up early tomorrow.' She didn't need to tell him why. Both knew it was to do with work. 'I'd better go.'

'You're over the limit,' he told her. 'You've drunk nearly a bottle of wine, and the mousse was laced with kirsch. Look, I have a spare room. Why don't you stay? No strings.'

'I...' Sleep in the same house as him? Lie in bed, knowing that only a wall separated them, and how easily she could go to him, crawl in beside him and arouse him to fever pitch with her hands and her mouth? God. It would test her control to the limit.

On the other hand, he had a point. She was over the limit. 'I could call a taxi.'

'You could. But it'd be easier to stay here, wouldn't it? My bathroom has a lock on it, and you could be up early in the morning, without having to break off from your work tomorrow to come and pick the car up.'

He'd got her there. She hated wasting time. 'All right, thanks.' She paused. 'We haven't talked about the department yet.'

He shook his head. 'You look tired – and so am I. Let's talk over breakfast.'

Breakfast. With him. It sent her imagination back into overdrive. Sitting in his kitchen at the scrubbed-pine table, wearing his bathrobe – enveloped in his scent, just as she'd been enveloped by his body the previous night – while he wore just a towel wrapped round him. Sharing croissants, feeding each other and licking off the buttery flakes from each other's bodies, before making love again in the shower...

'I...'

He squeezed her hand gently. 'Relax, Sarah. No strings. I'll respect your privacy.' He stood up. 'Come on. I'll get you a towel and show you where everything is. I think I've got a new toothbrush somewhere, too.'

He thought of everything. She was impressed. And yet part of her wanted to throw caution to the winds, tell him that she'd be happy to use his toothbrush. Why balk at that intimacy, when she wanted to do all kinds of lewd things with him?

She shook herself, and followed him into the hall.

Once he'd shown Sarah to the spare room, Marc went downstairs and did the washing up swiftly, trying to keep his libido in check. The CD playing in the kitchen was a Roberto Alagna collection; he switched it off, knowing that the tenor's melting voice always made him think of making love. And that particular track, from Bizet's *La Jolie Fille de Perth*, was one that really put him in the mood. Soulful, yearning, passionate – and just when the woman he wanted so badly was in his spare room. It made his cock throb.

And she'd looked glorious. Wearing that figure-hugging outfit; he'd barely been able to keep his hands off her. The jeans and sweater had emphasised her curves, rather than hiding him; and she'd worn her hair loose. It had taken the tiniest jump of his imagination to imagine that hair spread across his pillow. Particularly as she hadn't been immune to him. He'd noticed her nipples hardening the moment he opened the door – and it hadn't been because it was cold outside. It was one of the mildest Octobers for years. No; it had been because she wanted him just as much as he wanted her. And she knew he knew that.

What was he doing? That vulnerable look on her face, when they'd been talking over dinner... He'd wanted to kiss her right there and then, kiss away all the pain. He was almost tempted to give up his plans for the weekend and have a blazing row with her in the office instead.

Behind the cool and sophisticated façade, it seemed that Sarah Ward was as human as the rest of them. She'd loved the white chocolate mousse he'd made for her; he'd hardly eaten any of it, consumed by erotic thoughts of her as he watched her eat. He could imagine peeling that black sweater from her, unhooking her bra and then smearing those beautiful breasts with the sweet creamy confection. He'd have eaten more than his fair share then, licking it from her skin. Daubing a trail of it down her stomach. And then smearing more between her thighs, letting the sweetness of the confection mingle with her juices before he licked her clean – bringing her to orgasm several times in the process.

A shiver of pure lust rippled down his spine. Cool it, he reminded himself sharply. Let her wait. Don't even walk in that direction, yet. Wait until she's soft and sleepy, more likely to respond. Then act. He smiled wryly. Call it off, indeed. If anything, seeing her in casual clothes had made things worse, had made him want her so much more. There was no way he could back out now.

Chapter Three

Sarah lay back against the pillows. To be so near and yet so far – it was driving her insane. She was sure that Marc wasn't indifferent to her. Something in his eyes had given him away when he'd looked at her: a dark and soulful gaze, almost yearning. He'd been scrupulously polite, friendly even – but she wanted more than that. Much more.

It must be the wine, she told herself. She hadn't noticed how often he'd refilled her glass – until he'd reminded her that she was over the limit, and she'd realised that there were two empty bottles on the table. That was it. She was tipsy. That was why she had had the sudden urge to barge into the bathroom, pretending she didn't know he was in there, and knowing full well that her appearance, naked, would make him act. Make him take her.

She was lying, she thought wryly. She wasn't that tipsy; she never drank enough to lose control. It wasn't the drink putting ideas into her head: it was Marc's proximity, coupled with too many months spent celibate. When she'd showered she'd been able to smell his clean fresh scent, and it had aroused her. Now, lying in his spare bed, she couldn't stop thinking about his body lying next to hers. On top of hers. Inside her...

'Oh, God.' She forced her thoughts away from Marc to her surroundings. The room was nothing like she'd expected. The floorboards were bare and polished, with a single silk rug beside the bed; the dressing table, wardrobe and bedside cabinet were all pine, as was the large cheval mirror opposite the bed; and there was a large double bed with a wrought-iron headboard, thick pillows and a warm duvet with a white *broderie anglaise* cover. The lamp on the bedside table was also wrought-iron, with a white pleated lampshade. The walls were painted white, and there was a pine-framed picture of white irises on one wall. The curtains were filmy muslin, and the whole room had a romantic feel to it that really appealed to her.

If she'd known that Marc Dubois was like this...

She smiled wryly to herself. In that case, she would never have accepted his invitation to dinner, because she'd have known just how dangerous he could be to her. He could make her control crack – more than crack. Shatter completely.

She closed her eyes, snuggling under the duvet. There was something about the feel of cool white cotton sheets against her skin, something that made her stretch and luxuriate in it. She could imagine Marc lying there beside her, his arm curved possessively round her waist and his face buried in her shoulder as he slept. And then she'd wake him, rubbing her bottom against his groin and teasing his cock into hardness. He'd murmur sleepily as she turned to face him, cupping his face and kissing him; then he'd react, kissing her back and stroking her breasts, sliding his hand between her legs.

Yes. Sarah gave a small moan of pleasure and pushed the duvet back. She slid one hand between her thighs, cupping her mons veneris and letting her fingers rest lightly on her quim, feeling the heat of her arousing. Slowly, infinitely slowly, she parted her labia, gliding her middle finger up and down her musky divide. And then, when her finger was wet and slippery with her juices, she slicked it over her clitoris and began to rub, arching her back and tilting her pelvis up to the strokes.

Marc finished clearing up in the kitchen. He'd heard the bathroom door click twice: once when she'd gone in, and once when she'd come out. With any luck she would be in bed now. And he'd seen the way she'd looked at him over dinner, so he knew she wouldn't be sleeping, despite the glasses of wine she'd consumed.

He walked swiftly upstairs, carrying a glass. He stripped off in the bathroom, showered and cleaned his teeth. Then he tucked a towel round his midriff, filled the glass with water, and went to Sarah's bedroom.

He knocked on the door and walked in.

Sarah whipped her hand from her groin, shocked at being so nearly caught masturbating – especially by the man whose body had driven her to such erotic thoughts. She pulled the duvet up to her neck. 'Marc!'

'Sorry to disturb you. I thought you might like a glass of water,' he said solicitously.

She flushed. Could he guess what she'd just been doing? Could he smell her arousal in the air, that tell-tale sweet-salt musky aroma? Could he see it in her face, the guilt and the pleasure combined? 'I... Thank you.'

He bent to place the glass on the bedside table; she couldn't help licking her suddenly dry lips. God, he looked so good, just with that towel round his waist. His skin was smooth and pale, his chest dusted with a light covering of dark hair that arrowed down over his midriff. His muscles were good, too – not from gym workouts, she was sure, but some other exercise. Squash, maybe... or making love.

To her surprise he sat on the edge of the bed and stroked her cheek with the backs of his fingers. 'Sweet dreams, sweet Sarah,' he said softly, bending his head to kiss the tip of her nose.

Her pupils dilated. Unable to help herself she tipped her face up for another kiss. He regarded her for a long, long moment, and then at last he lowered his face again, brushing his lips so very lightly against hers.

She slid her hands round his neck, burying her fingers in his hair. It felt good; clean and thick and springy. She urged him on and his mouth opened, his tongue probing against her lips until she opened her mouth to give him the access he wanted.

He certainly knew how to kiss, she acknowledged. Even if she hadn't already been wet from touching herself, she would have been ready for him within seconds of his kiss. Sure, strong, passionate... God, he was good. She wanted him to use his mouth elsewhere, bring her the ultimate pleasure.

She gave a small murmur of pleasure as he pulled the duvet down, baring her breasts. 'Yes,' she murmured as he broke the kiss and trailed his mouth down to her throat. 'Yes.' Her nipples felt hard, almost painful; she needed to feel his hands on them, his mouth. 'Oh, Marc,' she moaned as the tip of his nose traced a path down her cleavage. She could feel his warm breath against her skin, and it was driving her mad. 'Yes. Do it.'

Slowly – enough to make her dig her fingers into his scalp to hurry him up – he opened his mouth over one breast, sucking on its hard rosy tip. She moaned as his teeth grazed her sensitive flesh. With her previous lovers she'd had to insist on more foreplay; with Marc, she could hardly wait. She wanted to feel him inside her. She wanted to feel him filling her, stretching her. Now.

She tipped her pelvis upwards and was frustrated to feel him laugh softly against her skin. And then she felt cold air against her. She opened her eyes, shocked. He'd moved away – he wasn't even touching her! 'Marc?'

His face was grim. 'Sarah, you're my boss. I can't sleep with you.'

'But—' She was even more shocked to feel her eyes filling with tears. 'Marc...'

'I'm sorry. I took a liberty. If you'd be kind enough to forget it, I'd appreciate that.'

Forget it? With her sex empty and aching, her nipples throbbing and her entire body aware of his? 'I...'

'I'd better leave,' he said. 'Because if I stay here I won't be able to stop myself.'

'Stop yourself what?' The question was out before she realised she'd spoken.

'Making love to you, Sarah. Using my mouth, kissing and licking you all over. And I mean all over. Starting at your beautiful white throat.' As he spoke it was almost as if he were doing it, she could imagine it so strongly. 'And then your breasts. And then down over your thighs, to the curves of your knees, your ankles. Your toes.'

She closed her eyes, moving sensuously against the sheet. 'And then what?'

'And then back up your legs. I'd part your thighs and lick my way along your beautiful quim. I'd suck your clitoris, and then I'd push my tongue into you as deeply as I could. I'd lick you and lap at you until you didn't know what day it was.'

Sarah's moist lips parted. 'And then?'

'And then I'd turn you over and start on your back. Your shoulders. All the way down your spine. The backs of your knees.'

'Oh, yes.' Her moan was involuntary.

Marc didn't seem fazed by her reaction. He didn't seem angry, excited; from the way he spoke, it was as if he, too, were lost in some erotic dream, she thought.

'And then?'

His voice grew husky. 'And then I'd prop you up over some pillows, tilting your pretty little rear towards me. I'd stroke you. And then I'd use my mouth on you, touch your forbidden places until you were begging me to take you.'

'And then?' She held her breath in torment.

'And then I'd take you. Give you pleasure – and take just as much in return.'

She opened her eyes to look at him. His pupils were dilated, and there was a slight flush across his cheekbones. Her gaze travelled downwards; it was obvious to her that he had one hell of an erection under that towel. He felt the same as she did. That same strong, urgent need.

'Then do it,' she said softly. 'Do it.'

Marc looked at the woman lying on the bed. Bloody hell, she was even more beautiful than he'd imagined. Her skin was so pale, so creamy. No doubt it was soft and fresh-tasting, too. Her body was perfect: generous firm breasts, a narrow waist, softly flared hips. The perfect hour-glass figure. That, combined with the fair hair spread on the pillow in waves and the wicked curve of her mouth, was devastating. It took him every ounce of control not to touch her, just to talk to her and tell her what he wanted to do with her.

It was working even better than he'd hoped. She was receptive enough to his words. He could see her arousal in the taut line of her body, her erect nipples, the slight flush on her face. He had a feeling she'd be more than receptive to his deeds. When he made his next set of suggestions, she'd agree to them. And then... Then, she'd be his.

'You're sure about this?' he asked. 'Because once I start, I won't be able to stop. I won't be able to get enough of you.'

'I'm sure,' she nodded.

He smiled and dropped his towel, noting how her eyes widened when she saw his erection. Past lovers had told him that he was well endowed: and he knew exactly what to do with it, too. Slowly, he climbed onto the bed beside her, kneeling over her and bending his head. He kissed her throat, licking her skin and glorying in its clean fresh taste. A pulse beat hard under his tongue; she was as excited as he was. This was going to be good for both of them, he knew.

'Licence my roving hands,' he murmured.

'Hm?'

He smiled wryly. 'Just quoting. Showing off.'

'Don't talk. Kiss me. Touch me.'

'Always in control?' he asked. 'Or will you let me take control, this time? Humour me, let me please you?' He pulled back to watch her face, her eyes.

She stared back at him; he could see her internal battle. She didn't want to let her subordinate in the office – even though he was hardly in a junior position – be her superior in bed. It went against the grain, letting her direct report have the upper hand. And then the sensual side of her nature took over; she suddenly looked so wanton, so desirable, that he almost came from looking at her.

'All right,' she said finally.

'All right what?'

'I'll humour you. You're in charge.'

He bent his head to kiss her properly. Her mouth opened beneath his, and again she let him explore her. And then, just as he'd told her, he kissed her all over. He moved down over her throat, noting the way she tipped her head back into the pillows and arched her back as his mouth drifted down to her breasts, over her abdomen. She tilted her pelvis, demanding. He teased her, moving down to caress her left thigh and bypassing her quim. She made a moan of mingled disappointment and pleasure: disappointment, because she wanted his mouth on her sex, but pleasure, because she loved what he was doing to her. Cherishing her.

In the morning she'd hate them both. She knew that. But right now she was going to enjoy everything he did to her. She arched her back as he licked the hollow of her ankles. She couldn't help a murmured, 'Yes. Oh, yessss,' as he switched legs, starting with her toes.

God, he was good. And how had he guessed that she wanted him to take control, so she could lose herself? Then she remembered that he'd done her job as well as his own, for the four months between their previous marketing director leaving and her appointment. Yes, he knew what the pressure was like, the constant need to make decisions – and make the right ones, because the wrong ones would have an instant impact on the company's profit and put your job on the line. He knew what it was like to have people expect so much of you, expect you just to click your fingers and make things right.

Now, he was giving her the ultimate freedom. The freedom not to choose. He was making the choices for her. And she loved every second of it.

She could feel his breath, warm against her quim, and moaned again. His hands pressed against her inner thighs and she spread her legs wide, bending her knees so that her feet were flat on the mattress. She almost came at the first stroke of his tongue along her musky divide; as he began to lick her in earnest she lifted her hands to grasp the headboard, her knuckles growing white as she fought to keep control.

It was so good, so good. The way he lapped at her, flicking rapidly over her clitoris until her sex was melting, then plunging his tongue as deeply into her vagina as he could. Sarah found herself rocking her hips, pushing her sex hard at his face, wanting more. And then, at last, she felt the warm spirals of her orgasm start, moving from the soles of her feet; it gathered momentum as it moved up through her calves, her thighs, making her legs shake. And then – sheer bliss – it exploded in her solar plexus. She came so hard she saw stars.

'And that's just the beginning,' she heard Marc say.

Deftly, he flipped her over onto her stomach. True to his promise, he started on her back, kissing his way down her spine. He licked the dimpled hollows at either side of the base of her spine, then bit gently at her buttocks. Sarah pushed her throbbing mons hard into the bed, groaning into her pillow as his mouth travelled down one leg, lingering at the sensitive spot at the back of her knees, then down again to her feet... and up her other leg.

He pressed his body against her for a second, and she groaned; his cock was hot and throbbing in the groove of her buttocks. She wanted him. Oh, how she wanted him.

'Marc. Take me,' she murmured hoarsely.

'Hup,' he said softly in reply, urging her to her hands and knees. He placed a couple of pillows under her stomach, then gently pressed her shoulders. In response, Sarah sank down so that her bottom was tilted towards him.

Marc stroked her buttocks. The light circling movement of his fingertips drove her wild. She wanted him inside her. She pushed her bottom back towards him, widening her stance.

'In good time,' he murmured against her skin. With shock she felt the tip of his tongue probe the rosy pucker of her anus.

'No!'

He held her down, easily stilling her struggles. 'Easy, easy. You're going to like this,' he promised.

The very fact that he was holding her against her will made her quim throb even more. God, she thought, am I some kind of pervert? It's one thing letting him do what he wants, but it's quite another, enjoying it when he makes me do it.

Marc resumed the gentle kisses, his tongue lapping her intimately. She could imagine that proud thick cock – the one he'd pressed so gently against her, letting her feel its heat and mass – nudging that forbidden entrance, and she was shocked to find that she liked the idea. It was something she'd never done, something she'd always thought vaguely disgusting: but she wanted Marc to do it. She wanted him to take her in every possible way, and then some.

'Yes,' she sighed. 'Yes.'

He paused for a moment. 'What?'

'Take me.'

'Not good enough,' he teased her. 'Tell me properly.'

'I – I want you to slide your cock in me.'

She fully expected him to do it; but he didn't. He moved so that the tip of his cock was pressing against her sex. When she tried to push back, force him to enter her, he moved back too, keeping just the lightest contact between them. 'Tell me,' he said.

There was a slight edge to his voice, as if he were ordering her. Part of her fought against it. Who the hell was he to order her about? She was his boss! But part of her, a deeply sensual part she'd buried under her career for too long, loved it.

'I want you,' she murmured.

'So many words. Less is more in marketing, remember. Tell me.'

If that was the way he wanted to play it... She arched up, removing the pillows and flinging them to one side, and rolled over onto her back so that she could face him. Well, if that was how he wanted to play it, then she'd do it by the letter. 'Fuck me, Marc. Please.'

The sudden flush on his face told her that she'd said exactly what he wanted to hear, the way he wanted to hear it, and she almost laughed. Yes. It was incongruous, the office ice-maiden using such earthy terms: but exciting, too. For both of them.

He didn't move. She arched her back, tilting her pelvis and spreading her thighs. 'Please,' she murmured. Surely he could see how wet she was, how badly she wanted him? Why wasn't he doing it? Did he want her to beg?

It struck her. Yes. Of course he did. She remembered him telling her that he was going to make her beg him. He wanted complete control, didn't he – reversing their usual day-to-day roles? 'Please,' she said softly. 'I'm begging you, Marc. I want you to fill me. To fuck me – to Paradise and back.'

He moved then, dipping his head down to kiss her hard; as he fitted the tip of his cock to the entrance of her sex, she wrapped her legs round his waist, pulling him closer. He sank into her easily, up to the hilt. He stayed there for a moment letting her get used to the feel of him, his thickness and length – and then he started to move. Long, slow, deep thrusts that had her in orgasm right from the first; and he kept going, taking her to another peak, another.

She tipped her head back against the pillows and gave a little bubbling moan of bliss. She wanted this to go on for ever. For ever. And then she felt his body tighten against hers; a moment later, as her inner sparkling lit again, she felt him pulse inside her. He fused his mouth to hers and she kissed him back with abandon, wanting him.

When he finally slipped from her he rolled onto his back, tucking her into the curve of his body and resting his hand lightly on her hip. Sarah was content to lie there quietly, her hand resting on his chest and her fingers tickled by his rough dark hair. He made no attempt to talk. Eventually she drifted into sleep, sated by his cock and lulled by the beat of his heart against her hand.

Some time later, Sarah woke to find Marc stroking her body; while she'd been asleep he'd obviously switched off the bedside light, because the room was now in darkness. She remained still, letting him caress her. He played with her nipples, lightly brushing her skin with his fingertips, and she couldn't help arching up towards him.

He chuckled and bent his head to kiss the tip of her nose. 'You're awake, then?'

'Mm,' she murmured.

'Sarah. I've been lying here having all sorts of wicked thoughts.'

'Oh, yes?'

'Yes.' He kissed her lightly. 'I don't know what it is about you. The way you smell, the way you taste, the way you feel... but I'm hard, just thinking about you and what we did.' He took her hand, placing it over his erect cock. She tightened her fingers around the hard rod, rubbing it lightly, and he groaned. 'Sarah. I want you again. I want you now.'

'Then why don't you do something about it?' she asked lazily.

'Because I... I want to go further, this time.'

She stiffened, remembering the feel of his tongue against her anus. Was he intending to lubricate her there, to enter her?

'Later, perhaps,' he said, making her flush as she realised that she'd spoken aloud. 'But now... you said, earlier, that I was in charge.'

'Yes,' she whispered uncertainly.

He rubbed his nose against hers. 'Trust me. You'll like what I have in mind.'

She paused for a long while; finally she agreed. 'All right.'

'Good.' He turned away from her for a moment; he hadn't switched the light back on, so Sarah had no idea what he was doing. She heard a soft brushing sound that could have been a drawer opening, then a faint rustling.

It's a bit late for condoms now, she thought, but said nothing. Anyway, condoms wouldn't have been appropriate. Marc had told her that he wanted to go further with her – further than bringing her to a climax with his mouth and his cock. So what did he have in mind? He'd said, too, that he wasn't intending to bugger her. Yet. So did he want her to use her mouth on him, to fellate him to orgasm?

He turned back to her, and she tensed slightly, but he merely bent his head to kiss her lightly. 'Sweet Sarah.' His hands slid along her arms, his thumb rubbing in small circles over her skin; then she felt something around her wrist. Something soft, brushing her like gossamer.

'Marc?'

'Shh. Trust me.'

When he lifted her arm, bringing it up to the headboard, she realised what he was doing: tying her wrists to the bed. He was using something like a silk scarf. But what would a silk scarf be doing in the drawer of the bedside cabinet in his spare room? Unless he'd planned it all from the start...

46

Before she could protest he had tied her other wrist to the headboard, and was kissing his way back down her arm, starting at her wrist. He licked the hollow in the crook of her elbow, and she shivered with pleasure. So what if he had planned this? She was hardly in a position to criticise him. She'd been masturbating over thoughts of him, after all, when he'd knocked on her door to bring her that glass of water. It had been an excuse, yes, but a thoughtful one.

And then she stopped thinking as he kissed her mouth, then crawled down the bed, kissing and caressing her as he moved. She made no protest as he tied her ankles to the footboard; although he tied her firmly he made sure her bonds weren't too tight. And she had to admit, the idea made her wet. To be tied up, completely at his mercy, unable to resist him. She might be a pervert, but she liked the idea very much indeed.

'Sarah.' He stroked her face with the backs of his fingers. 'Sweet Sarah. One more thing?'

Fully expecting him to slide his cock against her lips, she murmured her assent and opened her mouth. She was shocked when the anticipated contact did not take place. Instead, she felt more silk trailing against her face, then across her eyes. He was blindfolding her.

'Marc, I—'

'Shh.' He silenced her with a kiss, then resumed tying the blindfold. When he'd finished she heard the click of the light.

'What are you doing?'

'I want to see you,' he said. 'Do you know how desirable you look, Sarah? Your beautiful creamy flesh, your hair spread over the pillow, your wrists and ankles bound with black silk scarves?'

So she'd guessed right. She shivered. 'Why have you

47

blindfolded me?'

'Because now you'll have to concentrate with your other senses.' His voice was sensuous and inviting. 'Taste. Touch. Scent.'

'Hearing? Or were you going to put earplugs on me?'

He chuckled richly at the waspishness in her voice. 'Sound, too. In fact, we might as well start now.'

She felt him climb off the bed, and panicked. 'Marc? You're not leaving me like this?'

'Only for a minute or two, sweetheart.'

She lay still, counting rapidly in her head. *Mississippi one, Mississippi two, Mississippi three*... Finally, she heard the door click again, heard a series of clicks that meant God only knew what, and felt the mattress give under his weight. A couple of moments later she heard a rich tenor voice and realised that he'd fetched a portable stereo. She didn't recognise the voice or the song, although it sounded French to her.

'I was listening to this downstairs,' he explained. 'It's a piece of music that... Well, it affects me. I had to turn it off in the end, because it made me think of you upstairs, all warm and soft and curvy.'

'And?'

'And you're even more beautiful than I expected,' he told her huskily, making her shiver with delight. 'That's why I wanted you like this. So I can watch you. So you have to concentrate on something other than sight – and I can see your beautiful face as you come, again and again and again.' He paused. 'Of course – I might not be the only one.'

'What?'

'I might not be the only one,' he repeated, the caress in his voice reflected in the way he traced the curve of her breasts with his forefinger. 'What would you say, Sarah, if someone else were here in the room with us? Someone silent, watching us – someone you couldn't see?'

Her muscles tensed. 'Someone else?' she croaked.

'Doesn't the thought excite you?' he continued. 'Think about it. You'll never know for sure that we're alone, right now. For all you know, someone could be standing at the foot of the bed, seeing your beautiful legs spread and tied – and what's in between. Your beautiful quim, already puffy and shining with arousal. That beautiful deep vermilion furrow, so rich and so inviting.' He shifted so that he was kneeling between her thighs, she judged. 'Inviting, Sarah – inviting me in. You feel like warm wet velvet when you're wrapped round my cock. And you look good, too.'

'I... Is someone else here, with us?'

He laughed. 'You'll have to guess, won't you? But doesn't it excite you, the thought of exposing yourself to someone? He – or she – will be able to see everything. Everything, from the way your warm soft quim moulds to my body as I enter you, to the way your breasts swell when you become aroused. From the way your nipples harden and stand out to the flush on your face and the way you bare your teeth when you come. You don't have to do anything to give that person pleasure: just *be*. That's enough.'

She shivered. She was completely at his mercy now. She'd trusted him... Had she been wrong? Was he what she'd thought him to be, an inventive and exciting lover – or was he some kind of maniac who'd tricked her?

'So let us melt, and make no noise,' Marc whispered.

'What?'

He chuckled. 'Showing off again, my sweet. I was quoting Renaissance love poetry at you, trying to impress you. Ah, Sarah. I just want your body to melt into mine.

Let yourself go. Trust me – see how good it's going to be for both of us. I want you fluid and soft beneath me, Sarah.'

'Beneath you?' There was a touch of ice in her voice.

'You can't be anything else, in your current position,' he reminded her. 'But yes, later, I want to see you ride me. I want to see you straddle me and lower yourself onto my cock. I want to see you throw your head back in abandon and touch your breasts and rub your mons against me. What goes around, comes around.'

The words were spoken lightly, but Sarah had the uneasy feeling that they contained a threat of some kind. She hadn't worked it out yet, but she would.

'Stop thinking,' he commanded softly. 'Just be.' He drew his finger along the length of her quim. 'Mm. Warm and wet,' he told her. 'Your mind might deny it, but your body can't. You're enjoying this, Sarah. You're enjoying being helpless for once – not having to make decisions, not worrying about what you should be doing. Because I'm in control right now. I'm making the decisions for both of us.'

She swallowed. 'And why should I trust you?'

'This does,' he told her, brushing the soft underside of her breast and squeezing her nipple gently; a shaft of pleasure lanced through her. 'And this.' She felt him lean over her, and then the tip of his tongue touched the throbbing pulse in her neck. 'And this.' He shifted back again, cupping her mons and teasing her clitoris. 'And this.' His finger skated down to the entrance of her sex and penetrated her. 'Tell me you like what I'm doing to you.'

'I...' Her throat was dry.

He added a second finger, and her arousal flooded through her. Yes, he was right. She was enjoying it; the feeling of being helpless and submitting to his will.

'I like it,' she said quietly.

'Good.' He leaned forward to kiss the tip of her nose, and continued pistoning his fingers in and out of her. Sarah felt her climax rise through her body, bubbling like some cauldron – but he didn't stop. He merely laughed with pleasure at her reaction. 'Oh, Sarah. You look so incredible when you come. Just imagine how our friend is enjoying the view.'

She didn't rise to the bait; she couldn't. All she could concentrate on was the way he touched her, the way he skilfully coaxed a second and third climax from her. And then, while her quim was still rippling, he eased his cock into her, lengthening her orgasm and taking her on to the next plateau.

Chapter Four

The next morning Sarah woke and started to stretch, with her eyes still closed: then she realised that she couldn't. She couldn't move at all. She opened her eyes and suddenly remembered where she was and what she'd done with Marc the night before. She was still tied to the bed in his spare room. She glanced up at her wrists. They were tied to the bedstead with two black silk scarves. A glance at her ankles told her that they, too, were tied to the bedstead with two black silk scarves.

She digested this in a moment of shocked disbelief. What the hell was Marc playing at? Why had he left her tied up like this? And where the hell was he? Her only consolation was that he'd removed the blindfold at some time while she'd been asleep.

The blindfold. She was annoyed with herself when she realised that just the thought of it made her sex pool. What he'd done with her, the previous night, tying her up and blindfolding her, exposing her intimate places for his enjoyment – and even hinting that someone else was watching them – wasn't the kind of thing she usually did. Bondage wasn't one of her kinks. Yet she'd wanted him to do it. She'd wanted to him to go further, too.

Had they been alone? Or had there really been someone else sitting there, watching the way he'd teased her nipples and fingered her sex, then finally pushed his cock into her? Watching the way she'd reacted to him, her body quivering and her sex growing hot and moist?

She shivered at the thought; as soon as he'd started

touching her she'd been incapable of all rational thought. Now she was on her own, and her mind was back to its usual quick state, able to deal with anything – and she wasn't sure what she felt. Part of her hated the idea of being exposed to a stranger like that. It was degrading, humiliating, being touched by a man purely for someone else's amusement.

At the same time, part of her was incredibly excited by the idea. To be part of a show, the reaction of her body to the skilful touch of her lover turning her watcher on, too. To know that the more lewdly she acted, the more her audience would enjoy... himself? Herself? Themselves? Marc hadn't been specific about the sex or number of people in the room besides them. Had there been anyone else there at all?

He'd played music, so it had masked the sound of anyone else's breathing. But then again, she'd been in no state to concentrate on anything but the way Marc had touched her. The way he'd teased her breasts, her hardening nipples. The way he'd talked to her, telling her how desirable he found her. The way he'd stroked her quim, trailing his finger along its length and dabbling in her wetness. The way he'd penetrated her with a finger, adding a second. The way he'd made her come – and then, finally, eased his cock into her. And kept thrusting, again and again and again, bringing her to a second and a third climax before he finally came himself. And continuing again, once he'd rested and his cock was back to full hardness, taking her again and again until she was sobbing his name, tugging at her bonds and her body bucking with a mind-blowing orgasm.

She swallowed, aware that her sex was heating again. God, what was wrong with her? One of her colleagues – a junior colleague, at that – had tied her up and screwed her silly, making her lose count of the number of times she'd come. And now, even the thought of what he'd done to her was making her wet, wanting him again. Wanting his hands and his mouth and his cock pleasuring her again and again and again. Where was her famed self-control, her iron will?

And where the hell was he? Why had he left her like this? Why hadn't he untied her?

A small insistent voice in her head suggested that maybe she didn't want to be untied. That maybe she liked being completely in his control, like this. That maybe she liked having to do whatever he wanted. Or whoever else was in the room. For all she knew, someone else could come into the bedroom, right now, and take her. More than one man. A whole string of them. Maybe even all the men in the office – the ones she'd cut down to size at a meeting, perhaps, the ones she'd humiliated in the past. They'd be more than happy to take the chance to be the ones in control, not her. They'd walk into the room, one by one – or maybe even three or four at a time. And then it would be their turn to humiliate her, to get their revenge for the way she'd treated them. They could do anything to her and she'd be powerless to resist, tied to the bed and forced to do whatever they wanted.

They could stand over her, masturbating and covering her body in their creamy fluid as they came. She'd be forced to watch them as they smiled and laughed, rubbing their cocks, their balls lifting and tightening and then the pearly semen arcing from the tips of their cocks, spattering against her skin, the warmth of the fluid soon cooling on her body. And then they'd use their fingers to scoop up the sticky tangy mess, smear it over her mouth so that it trickled down her face, over her neck, coating her skin with a sheen of white. They'd make her lick her lips, taste their offerings.

Or maybe they'd push their cocks into her mouth, making her take them as deeply as she could and commanding her to suck them harder, harder. They'd be insistent – not viciously so, but forceful, demanding, making her submit to them. They'd come in her mouth, forcing her to swallow the pearly fluid and demanding that she recounted the subtle differences of taste and texture between each man.

Maybe they'd do it more than once: the first time they'd do it without a blindfold, so she could see whose cock she was sucking, and the second time they'd cover her eyes with a silk mask that blacked out the light, and make her guess who she was fellating by the taste of his come. For every guess wrong she'd be sentenced to a punishment.

Punishment. Yes. That would be a much more subtle pleasure. She wouldn't know precisely what they were going to do to her, but she'd have a pretty good idea. She'd be face-down, her creamy-white buttocks presented invitingly to them. They'd stroke her soft skin, almost preparing her. And then she'd hear the sharp swish of a cane through the air, hear the crack of the pliant bamboo against her flesh, and feel the line of fire across her buttocks. A sharp, tingling pain that eclipsed every other feeling, then slowly melted into a different kind of pleasure, a deeper and darker and ultimately satisfying throb.

Or maybe they'd use a whip, and she'd hear the sharp crack of the leather caressing the air as it fell on her naked skin, a snaking line of pain and pleasure combined. Or maybe they'd make it really personal and use their hands, making her guess whose hand had just left a red imprint on her white skin and doubling the punishment when she guessed wrong.

And even when she could guess right, maybe she'd guess wrong on purpose, provoking longer and deeper punishment, until her buttocks were smarting and her sex was weeping with desire and her nipples were so hard that they, too, hurt, a sharp ache of pleasure echoing the sting of her buttocks.

And then they'd use her displayed sex, kneeling on the bed and taking her one after the other, until she'd lost count of how many different cocks had filled her. Or maybe they would use their mouths on her, lick her to the point of climax and then stop, watching her struggle against her bonds in her desperate need to come, but unable to do anything about it. They'd make her beg them – make her talk dirty, refusing to touch her until she'd told them in very explicit terms exactly what she wanted them to do to her. They could tease her clitoris with their tongues and their fingers, making the hard little knot of nerves pulse and twitch – but again, stop just before she came and make her beg for release.

They could use a large thick dildo on her: showing it to her first, making her gasp at the size and wonder if she'd be able to take it all. But she would. Her mouth might protest but her sex would react in just the way they wanted, her labia swelling and her juices flowing just at the idea of being filled by something so big. They'd tease her with it, push just the tip in and piston it rapidly in and out of her, the fattest part of the tube rubbing against the narrowest part of her sex. And then, when she was moaning and rocking her hips, almost at the point of begging them to fuck her with it properly, they'd slide it all the way in. One of them would hold her labia apart while another pushed the thick tube into her; and another would video it, the lens zooming in to show her quim flexing round the dildo as she climaxed.

A second orgasm would follow, and a third. They'd make her come again and again and again, until she was yelling and rolling her head from side to side, completely abandoned to pleasure and not caring that they were watching her at her most intimate and unguarded. Then finally, when her whole body was quivering, they'd remove the dildo and make her lick the hard plastic tube clean of her own sweet-salt juices...

She shivered. Christ, where had all those images come from? It wasn't the kind of thing she normally thought about. Had Marc slipped something into her drink? Some kind of drug, some stimulant to affect her libido? Or was it her unaccustomed position, being forced to do exactly what someone else wanted her to do?

Whatever, she knew she was aroused. Painfully so. Her nipples almost hurt; she could see how hard they were, rosy peaks rising sharply from the soft curves of her breasts. And her sex ached. She wanted to push her hand between her legs and rub herself to a swift climax, push her clitoris hard against her pubic bone until her quim flexed and the sweet nectar flowed. Or jam three fingers into her sex, push herself to the limit and beyond.

But, as she was tied spread-eagled to the bed, she could do nothing. She couldn't even squeeze her thighs together to ease the ache. She was completely helpless, completely turned on – and she had to wait until Marc decided what to do next. Whatever and whenever that might be.

'You bastard, Dubois,' she muttered. 'Where the hell are you?'

It was sheer torture, lying there, with all these vivid pictures in her mind and not being able to do anything about it. What scared her more was how easily those pictures had arrived. She'd never thought of herself as the submissive sort, in work or in play. Now, she wasn't so sure. That vision of the men in their office taking her one at a time: she could imagine something far more graphic. Herself, taking more than one of them at a time.

She'd be kneeling on the bed, wearing a stretch lace navy teddy – black was far too obvious – with the top pulled down to expose her breasts, a pair of matching lace-topped hold-up stockings, and navy stilettos. She'd be astride one of them, his cock embedded deeply in her sex, the lace of the teddy's gusset an extra friction against his cock.

At the same time, another man would be kneeling by his shoulders, and she'd be sucking his cock; his hands would be wound into her hair as he urged her on, tilting his pelvis towards her as she took him as deeply as she could, sliding her mouth up and down his shaft. A third and fourth man would be beside her on the bed, squeezing her exposed breasts and rubbing her nipples while she rubbed their cocks, curling her fingers round their thick shafts and masturbating them in perfect synchronisation. And a fifth man would be kneeling behind her; he'd be pulling the lace teddy slightly to one side to expose the cleft of her buttocks. He'd watch as the other man's cock slid in and out of her quim, glistening with her juices. Maybe he'd dabble there himself, anointing his fingers with her nectar and then lubricating his cock with it. Then he'd rub his cock in the groove of her buttocks, judging her rhythm before fitting his lubricated cock to the tight ring of her anus, letting her push back onto him until he was embedded deep in her forbidden passage. And she'd be moaning as she sucked the man in front of her, wanting more – her words unintelligible as she had her mouth full, but her meaning very clear to them...

She squeezed her eyes tightly shut. No. That wasn't her. She wasn't like that. She was Sarah Ward, and she was in control – not some sleazy tart so desperate for sex that she'd let any man, any number of men, do what they wanted to her and beg them for more. The minute Marc Dubois untied her she'd flay him alive for what he'd done to her.

Liar, the voice in her head whispered. If anything, she'd wanted him to go further. She'd wanted him to do more than just slide his cock into her sex. She'd wanted him to make her suck him while his cock was still glistening from her juices, so she could taste herself on him as she licked her way down his shaft. She'd wanted him to turn her over, have her kneeling with her head resting on her bound wrists, and redden the cool creamy surface of her buttocks, his hand raining slaps on her soft flesh until her sex was weeping for him, swollen and puffy and...

She swallowed hard. And just where had that idea come from? She'd never played those kind of games, ever. She'd read about it in a couple of cheap paperbacks, but the idea had done nothing for her, and she'd ended up throwing the books aside, half-finished.

Before she could think about it any more, the door opened and Marc walked in.

She lifted her chin. 'Untie me, you bastard.'

'And good morning to you, too,' he said coolly. There was a slight glint of amusement in his eyes. 'Did you sleep well?'

'Tied up like this?' But she must have done. When Marc had finally finished making love with her, the previous night, she'd fallen asleep within seconds, drained from the long series of orgasms he'd brought her to. She hadn't woken until this morning, until – whatever time it was. There wasn't a clock in the room, so she had no idea whether it was seven or eleven. From the light filtering through the curtains, she suspected it was nearer the latter.

'Tied up, just like that.' He smiled at her. 'Good morning, Sarah.'

'Just untie me, you bastard.'

He shook his head. 'Oh, no. No, no, no. Particularly when you ask like that.'

'All right. I'll ask you nicely,' she said through clenched teeth. 'Please untie me, Marc.'

'No.'

Her temper snapped. 'What the hell are you playing at?'

'I'm not playing at anything,' he told her quietly. 'I'm deadly serious, believe me.'

'So why have you kept me here like this?'

'Because you need someone to teach you a lesson.'

'A lesson?' Involuntarily, she thought of the spanking she'd been fantasising about, and her sex throbbed. She coughed to cover her confusion. 'What sort of lesson?'

'You've been behaving very badly at work,' he said. His voice took on a kind of silky quality, she thought. 'Very badly. And behaviour like that needs to be punished.'

'You're punishing me?'

'Not at the moment.' He spread his hands. 'But I will do.'

'What you're doing is false imprisonment,' she told him crisply. 'It's illegal.'

'Really?'

'You know bloody well it is.'

He smiled. 'Well, last night you agreed to being tied up. You didn't make a fuss then. If anything, you virtually egged me on once you realised what I was doing.'

She flushed. 'That was last night.'

'You're making quite a fuss about it now.'

'Are you surprised? How would you feel if someone tied you up and refused to let you go?'

He grinned. 'That isn't the issue, at the moment. And

your body doesn't seem to be quite so anti the idea.' He nodded at her prone figure, and Sarah was horribly aware of the erect state of her nipples. Her fantasies had aroused her, and it was very obvious to him.

'What are you planning to do with me?' she demanded.

He shrugged. 'Don't panic. I won't lay another finger on you, until you ask me to. Until you beg me to, to be precise.'

'Untie me. Please.'

'No.'

She swallowed. 'How long are you going to keep me here like this?'

'As long as it takes for you to admit that you're wrong about the office.' His voice grew husky as he added, 'And to admit to your true nature.'

'My true nature?'

'That you're a submissive, at heart.'

She scowled. 'I am not.'

'No? If I touched your quim, right now, I think it would be wet. Very wet. Because you're turned on by this, Sarah. You like being helpless. Just as you liked me talking to you, last night, telling you that someone was watching everything I did to you and the way your body reacted to the way I touched you. It excited you, didn't it?'

'No.'

'Such vehemence. And we both know you don't mean it. I can see how aroused you are, Sarah.' His voice was like melted chocolate, and it turned her on even more, to her intense annoyance. 'Your nipples are hard for me – I bet you're aching for me to touch them. Caress them, squeeze them, make that pleasure even sharper for you. You'd like me to use my mouth on you, suck you and lick you. To use my teeth on those hard little peaks, balancing that fine line between pleasure and pain.'

'I would *not*.'

'No?' His lips curled with amusement. 'So you're not in the slightest bit excited. I wonder why your sex looks like someone's painted you with honey then? Glistening and sweet, ready for me to touch you and tease you and taste you. That's a figment of my imagination, is it, Sarah?'

She scowled again. 'You bastard. Just let me go.'

'No.'

'You'll have to let me go by tomorrow night. They'll miss me in the office on Monday. And you.'

'Not at all.' He shook his head. 'I have the week booked off as holiday.'

'Well, *I* haven't.'

'I'll ring the office on Monday morning and tell the personnel department that you're staying with friends, in Cumbria, but you've come down with the flu and won't be in for the rest of the week.' He shrugged. 'No one will question me.'

'You'll never get away with it.'

'Won't I?' Marc smiled. 'We'll see on Monday morning, won't we?'

'Untie me,' she demanded again.

'No.'

'You bastard.'

'Temper, temper.' He wagged an admonishing finger at her, then turned away and left the room.

Sarah watched him go, shocked. Surely he wasn't going to leave her there like that? He couldn't. But that seemed to be precisely his intention. To leave her there. Alone. And still tied...

Chapter Five

She wasn't sure how long it was before the door opened again. It could have been minutes; it could have been as much as an hour, or even longer. She was glad he hadn't decided to desert her; at the same time, his appearance made her even angrier because she realised how much she was dependent on him.

'I'll have to remember that you're not a morning person,' he said, grinning at the obvious fury on her face. 'Next time I see you in the office at half past seven, I'll put up a riot shield before I ask you if you want a cup of coffee.'

She was tempted to swear at him, tell him where to go – but she knew that that was just what he was angling for. So she said nothing, and turned her head away.

'Hey, Sarah.' He sat down on the bed beside her and stroked her cheek with the backs of his fingers. 'I was only teasing. Lighten up, will you?'

She turned back to him, giving him a cold stare. 'It's a bit difficult when you're kept prisoner.'

'Prisoner? We've been through this, Sarah. You agreed to being tied up.'

'Not for this long, I didn't.'

He didn't argue with her; instead, he set the tray he was carrying on the bedside table. There was a pile of fresh hot buttered croissants on the plate. The smell made her realise just how hungry she was.

'Breakfast,' he said. 'I thought you might like some croissants and orange juice. I was going to bring you some coffee – but that'd hurt if I spilt it on you.'

Her eyes narrowed. 'Untie me, and it won't matter if you spill it.'

He shook his head. 'We've already discussed that, Sarah. I'm not untying you until you agree to leave me to run the office as I want to – and admit that you're a submissive, at heart.'

'No way.'

'Well then. You've made your choice. You'll stay here until you change your mind.' He leant over to pick up a croissant from the plate, then took a bite. 'Want some?'

She made no reply; he merely smiled and continued eating. Bastard, she thought. Callous, selfish, unprincipled – no, that wasn't quite right. He wouldn't have planned this if he didn't have principles, principles that she was going to compromise. He wasn't selfish, either, because he wasn't doing this just for his own amusement. He was trying to do his best for his staff.

But callous, yes. Eating in front of her like that, when he knew she was hungry. When he knew full well that she hadn't eaten or drunk anything since the previous night – and the amount of alcohol she'd consumed, even though it wasn't that much, had been enough to make her throat dry. Orange juice would be just perfect to quench her thirst. But until he untied her she couldn't even touch it.

'Sarah. Sulking's not going to help, you know.' He sounded almost like a kindly uncle. Though there had been nothing remotely avuncular about the way he'd touched her the previous night. 'You must be hungry, and these croissants are good.'

She couldn't resist the barb. 'Make them yourself, did you?'

'No. I bought them ready-to-heat at the supermarket, yesterday morning. I didn't squeeze the orange juice myself, either.' There was a trace of amusement in his voice. 'Why don't you just give in, Sarah?'

'No.'

'You'll find life so much easier if you do.'

The threat hung in the air, unspoken. What the hell did he have in mind? she thought suddenly. Was he planning to beat her, whip her until her buttocks were striped and stinging, so she finally submitted to him? And then what? When she told him that yes, she was submissive at heart, what would he do then? What new delights would he introduce her to, refined sensual practices she hadn't even dreamt of?

And why was there a corresponding throb in her sex at the idea? Angry both with him and with the direction her thoughts were taking, she turned her face away from him again.

'Suit yourself.' He continued eating and sipping orange juice; her stomach growled, loudly enough for him to hear it, and she flushed.

'When are you going to stop fighting me – and yourself?' he asked softly.

She turned her head back to stare at him. God, don't say he was a mind-reader as well? 'How do you mean?' she fenced.

'I think you know. And you'll tell me later.' He broke off a piece of buttery croissant. 'Now, I'm not intending to starve you. You need to keep your blood-sugar levels up.' He ran the tip of the croissant along her lower lip, leaving tiny flakes of pastry on her skin. 'Eat,' he commanded, his voice quiet and yet compelling.

Sarah resisted him for just long enough to show she wasn't doing it to obey him, and opened her mouth. Again he teased her with the pastry, brushing it against her lips in the same way that he might tease her with his cock. Her colour heightened as a lewd thought popped into her head, of Marc fingering his own cock to full hardness and then feeding it between her lips. Damn, what was wrong with her? A flaky pastry was hardly a phallic symbol. He was just feeding her some breakfast, that was all. And yet she couldn't get the picture out of her mind. Marc Dubois kneeling before her on the bed, and herself on all fours: and his fingers curved round his long hard shaft, gently brushing its tip against her open lips...

She allowed him to feed her a bite of croissant, and noted that he took a bite immediately afterwards, eating from the place where her lips had touched. He'd said he wouldn't lay another finger on her until she asked him to, so this was the nearest he was going to get to touching her. And she wasn't going to ask him. Of course she wasn't.

Despite her resolution, her sex heated. The way he was feeding her, letting her take tiny bites from the rich delicious pastry, was incredibly sexy. She could imagine the picture they presented: herself, still naked and spread-eagled on the bed, reaching up to take a bite from the pastry, her breasts thrusting up slightly as she lifted her head. And the good-looking dark-haired man, still fully clothed, teasing her and making her stretch higher for it. Watching her with desire, staring at her mouth and imagining it closing around something more substantial than the croissant, something thicker and heavier and—

She shivered. Now was definitely not the time to be thinking anything like that. Not if she wanted to win this battle. And she couldn't afford not to win. There was more than just their day-to-day office life at stake here. She forced herself to think only of the food. But it was hard. He could have brought her cereal, toast, fruit – anything less erotic than croissants. She suspected he'd chosen them deliberately, knowing that the buttery pastry would be left in tiny flakes around her lips and she'd be forced to lick them, just as she'd moisten her lips in desire.

The worst thing was, she was still turned on. He was right: being tied up and helpless excited her. She was completely at his mercy. Any moment now, he could stop feeding her breakfast and take her, make her do anything he chose. No matter how lewd, how obscene, how unlike her normal behaviour, she'd be forced to do it. She'd have no choice. He could push the croissant into her and suck it out again, eat the confection soaked in her juices. Or even make her eat it herself, with her juices like syrup on the pastry...

Again she shivered, and tried to think only of the fact that she was having breakfast. She didn't meet his eyes, afraid he could see the struggle in her face and knew exactly what she was thinking. Well, he wasn't going to get away with it. She wasn't going to let him win.

When they'd finished eating the croissant, Marc held a glass of orange juice to her lips. She sipped gratefully; the liquid was refreshing and just what she needed, after the previous night. She drained the glass and he refilled it from the plain crystal jug, letting her drink a second glass. He managed to let some of the liquid spill over the rim of the glass, so that it ran down her face and throat and onto her breasts. She scowled at him, knowing he'd done it on purpose. With her hands tied she couldn't wipe away the sticky liquid herself – she'd have to ask him to touch her. Well, she wasn't going to. She was going to put up with the faint discomfort.

He smiled at her. 'Oops.' She didn't dignify his comment with a response; it just made him grin all the more. 'Sarah. Surely you don't want to stay there like that all day, sticky with orange juice?'

She still refused to answer. She had a nasty feeling that if she asked him to clean her up, he'd take it as meaning that she wanted him to touch her again. He wouldn't use a cloth to clean the sticky juice from her skin; he'd use his mouth, licking her throat and the swell of her breasts. And then he'd be tempted to work on her erect nipples, teasing them with his tongue and blowing on her spit-slicked skin to make her gasp with pleasure. He wouldn't stop there, either; he'd travel downwards, caressing the soft undersides of her breasts, nuzzling over her ribcage, across her abdomen, then finally between her parted legs. He'd lap at her, teasing her clitoris from its hood, then flicking his tongue rapidly across it until she was writhing, struggling against her bonds as she came, her quim flexing madly and wanting him to fill her, to fuck her again...

She closed her eyes. 'Go away, Marc.'

'If that's what you want.'

She was shocked to feel the mattress spring back as he stood up, then hear the soft click of the door. He really had gone. He'd left her alone with her thoughts, her fantasies – still covered in crumbs and sticky orange juice.

She hadn't expected him to take her at her word. She'd expected him to argue with her a bit more, then let her go. It looked like he meant it: he was going to keep her there until she did what he wanted. Well, she thought, opening her eyes again, he was going to have a long, long wait. Her will was just as strong as his – wasn't it?

Marc walked downstairs and picked up the telephone in the hall, dialling a familiar number. The line rang for a long time before the receiver at the other end was picked up and a bleary voice muttered, 'Hello?'

'Heavy night last night, was it?'

'Huh? Oh, Marc. Yeah.' There was a pause. 'Uh, are we supposed to be playing squash, this morning?'

Marc chuckled. 'No, Si. Strictly Friday nights only, even

though we missed last night. But I do need to see you, at my place.'

'Why?'

'Remember our conversation, last week, about my little problem?' At his friend's murmured agreement he continued, 'That's why I need to see you.'

'You haven't done anything stupid, have you?'

'Probably. But it's worth it.' More than worth it, he corrected himself mentally, his cock hardening at the thought of the naked and bound woman in his spare bedroom. 'See you just after lunch?'

'Okay.'

'Great. I'll explain everything then.'

Marc made two more calls, then took a bowl from the kitchen and headed back upstairs. He took a fresh towel from the airing cupboard, then filled the bowl with warm water, adding a few drops of aromatic bath oil. He'd gone too far, tipping that orange juice over her and knowing that she'd be too stubborn to ask him to clean her up. It wasn't fair to leave Sarah feeling sticky and unpleasant. The very least he could do was to give her a blanket bath. He smiled. Yes. That would be something she'd enjoy – yet something she'd hate, at the same time. She'd feel humiliated at having someone else wash her, yet turned on by it in equal measures: it was the perfect refinement, cranking the tension up a notch.

She'd give in. All it would take was time – and a little help from some of his friends. He smiled to himself and walked back into the spare bedroom.

Sarah stared suspiciously at him as he walked back into the bedroom. 'What's that for?' she demanded, seeing what he was carrying.

'I thought you might like to freshen up a little.'

'So you're going to let me go?'

'I didn't say that. Merely that you might like to freshen up a little.'

She looked at the bowl of foaming water and the towel. 'I can't wash when I'm tied up.'

'Which is why I'm going to do it for you. If that's what you'd like.'

She scowled. 'I'd rather wash myself.'

'That isn't an option.'

She took a deep breath. 'I need to go to the bathroom. Please.'

'Why?'

She flushed. 'You fed me that orange juice. That's why.'

'You mean, you need to pee?'

'Yes.'

'Then why don't you say so?'

Her colour deepened and she muttered, 'I need to use the toilet.'

'Please,' he reminded her.

'Please.'

He placed the bowl and towel on the bedside cabinet. Sarah almost sagged with relief. At last, he was going to release her. To her shock, he did nothing of the kind. He merely sat on the edge of the bed again, reached underneath the bed, and produced a chamber pot. 'Problem solved,' he told her cheerfully.

She stared at him in disbelief. 'You expect me to use – that?'

'You said you needed to use the toilet.'

'I do.'

'Then use this.'

She shook her head. 'I can't. Not in front of you. It's too...' She swallowed. Humiliating. Embarrassing. She couldn't do it. 'I can't,' she said again. At the same time, she was aware of a swelling feeling of excitement, deep in her belly. Hot shame flooded through her. She couldn't be excited by that. Not that. 'Marc, don't do this to me. I can't.'

'Okay. I'll give you your bath then.' He put the chamber pot on the floor, then dipped a sponge in the water – a natural sponge, Sarah noticed suddenly, not some cheap man-made foam thing.

She suddenly remembered something. 'I thought you weren't going to lay a finger on me until I asked you?'

'I'm not. I'm using a sponge,' he pointed out laconically.

She flushed again and was silent while he washed her. He was very good, she had to admit. Almost practised, almost like a nurse – except, of course, Marc Dubois had never been anything to do with medicine, in his professional life. A beautician, maybe: but that was an equally stupid thought. She knew his personnel file inside out. Even his hobbies were decidedly masculine. Squash, rugby, rock-climbing.

Yet the way he used the sponge on her, soothing the stickiness of the orange juice away from her face and her neck, felt fantastic. Then he moved down over her breasts; she couldn't help an involuntary shiver as he caressed her nipples with the sponge, using slightly more force than was really necessary, so that the tiny holes in the sponge created a delicious friction against her nipples.

He continued to tease her, rubbing the hard tips until she was close to asking him to use his mouth on them, ease the ache she knew he was deliberately creating; but before she could open her mouth, he moved on, sponging her ribcage and her abdomen. He pressed on her lower belly, making her gasp; she really did need to urinate. There was no way she would shame herself by soiling the bed. She would use will power to hold on until he finally released her. At the same time, she acknowledged that the pressure against her bladder made her sex feel even hotter and wetter.

You devious bastard, she thought. You must have played these sort of games before, to be this good. This subtle. Well, I'm not going to give in so easily.

The next thing she knew, the teasing sponge had moved between her legs. There was nothing she could do to stop him; the way she was tied meant she couldn't clamp her thighs together and refuse him access.

'You're sticky here, too,' Marc told her, his voice slightly throaty. 'Sticky from me.'

She didn't need to open her eyes to know he was hard. She could tell from his voice. He was remembering what they'd done together, the previous night, the way they'd come at the same time, her quim rippling round his cock as he pumped into her. The memory stirred her, too: that, combined with the way he was using the sponge on her. He brushed up and down her musky cleft, exploring her folds and hollows, then pressed down hard on her clitoris, pushing it against her pubic bone. He brought her nearer and nearer to a climax, using an insidious circling motion designed to make her sex soft and wet and ready for him. Any minute now he'd throw the sponge aside and kneel between her thighs, unzip himself and push his beautiful thick hard cock into—

She opened her eyes in shock as he stopped sponging her, but didn't move to enter her. He'd climbed off the bed, too, and looked as if he were about to head out of the door. 'Marc?'

He turned to face her. 'Something you want to say?'

She wouldn't give him the satisfaction of begging him to take her again; and she knew it was pointless, telling him to let her go – or even asking him. As for the bathroom:

she knew that that, too, was a pointless request. He'd only offer her that bloody chamber pot again. 'No,' she said quietly.

'Sure?'

'Sure.' She lifted her chin. 'Sure.'

'Okay. I'm going to get a paper. See you later.' He smiled. 'By the way, it's pointless crying out for help. Apart from the fact that I'm way off the beaten track and no one's likely to pass, the windows are double-glazed. No one will hear you. So you might as well save your breath.'

'Bastard,' she growled savagely as he left the room, closing the door behind her. If she hadn't been tied she would have thrown something at the door. Preferably something breakable. But if she hadn't been tied, the question of calling for help wouldn't have arisen in the first place. She grimaced. He was subtle, and very clever. But he wasn't going to win.

Chapter Six

When Marc eventually walked into the bedroom again, this time carrying one of the Saturday broadsheets and a mug of steaming coffee, Sarah was relieved to see him. Her will power wasn't going to last for much longer.

'Hello.'

He smiled back at her, obviously pleased with her response. 'Hello.'

'Marc – please may I use the bathroom? I can't hold out any more.'

He took a sip of coffee and looked at her for a moment. Her distress must have shown on her face, she thought, because he nodded. 'All right.'

'You're going to let me go?'

'I didn't say that. Just that you could use the bathroom.' He set the mug down on the bedside cabinet, dropped the paper on the floor, then rummaged in a drawer for a moment, producing a set of handcuffs.

'You're going to *handcuff* me?'

'Mm-hm,' was the laconic response.

Her brain worked fast. 'You're going to handcuff me to you?'

He sighed exaggeratedly. 'Why all the questions? You're intelligent enough to work it out for yourself.'

'You're going to be in the bathroom with me?' She stared at him in shock. 'But—'

'But nothing,' he said, snapping one cuff round her wrist and the other round his. Then he untied her wrists, gently easing her into a sitting position so that he could untie her ankles, too.

Her muscles screamed a protest. As if he knew, Marc gently massaged her arms, easing the ache in her muscles. 'Okay?' he asked softly.

'I... I just need to use the bathroom.' She was almost in tears. Why did he have to take it so far? Why couldn't he allow her some privacy? Yes, she liked him pushing her to her sexual limits, but this was something else entirely. It wasn't sexy or funny, and she didn't like it at all.

'Come on.' He gently swung her legs round, helping her to her feet. Her legs felt wobbly. She stumbled and he caught her, sliding his arm round her waist for support. 'The bathroom's not far,' he said softly. 'You can make it. Hold on, sweetheart, hold on.'

The sudden kindness, after his earlier offer of a chamber pot, made her feel even more tearful. He said nothing during the short journey to his bathroom. When they were inside she stared at him.

'Marc, I—'

'I know. Shh.' He bent his head to kiss her very lightly on the lips, then lifted her up and stood her in the bath.

'But—'

'But nothing. You want some privacy; I want to keep you tied up. Unless you want me to handcuff you to the radiator – which wouldn't be very comfortable for you – this is the best compromise.'

She stared at him, not understanding. When he clicked the cuff from his wrist and attached it to the shower rail, she suddenly realised. 'You mean – you want me to – *to do it – here*?'

He smiled and pulled the shower curtain across.

'You're not going to stay there and listen, are you?'

'Nope,' he said, then his hand appeared behind the curtain and he switched on the shower. 'Just to spare your blushes,' he told her, then she heard the bathroom door click shut.

Marc stood outside the bathroom, shaking slightly. In some ways he couldn't believe how far he was going. He knew that what he'd just done was way, way beyond his usual limits. He wasn't into toilet games – and neither, thank God, was Sarah. He'd just wanted to push her, see where her limits were.

But the look on her face had confirmed his suspicion that she was a sexual submissive, behind her control-freak façade in the office. Although she'd protested at the way he'd kept her tied to the bed, she'd been aroused by it. When he'd sponged her, her sex had been hot and puffy, like some exotic flower whose petals unfurled to show the rare beauty at its centre. He'd brought her almost to the point of climax, deliberately brushing her clitoris again and again and again; but he'd stopped before the crisis, knowing that if she'd lost control it would have had embarrassing consequences for both of them.

He took a deep breath. Now that situation would be averted. But he'd still need to dry her from the shower, then carry her back to the bedroom. The only way he could think of to do it without her struggling was to bring her to a short sharp climax – but he'd promised not to lay a finger on her until she asked him. She was too stubborn to ask. So...

His lips curved. There was always a way round these things. Whistling, he knocked on the door and walked back into the bathroom.

'Finished?'

Sarah scowled. 'Yes.'

'Good.' He reached behind the curtain to turn off the

water, then pushed the curtain back again. He was holding a thick fluffy bath towel. 'The question is, do I dry you in or out of the bath?'

'Does it matter?' she asked coldly.

'Probably not. But if you have any idea how good you look, stretched up like that, your body in a perfect arch...' His voice was faintly husky. Sarah glanced involuntarily at the crotch of his dark trousers. He was definitely aroused: and the knowledge sent a shiver of anticipation through her body.

She was furious with herself. The man was keeping her captive, for God's sake. She should hate him, not want to feel his body against hers, skin to skin. The little voice in her head reminded her that she wasn't an entirely unwilling captive: and that Marc Dubois was probably the most attractive men she'd met in years. Not to mention the most sexually inventive. The more she resisted him, the more she stretched his imagination – and her own boundaries. And he had at least had the decency to leave her alone in the bathroom, not insisting on watching her urinate. His limits were obviously close to hers.

In the end she clenched her jaw, not wanting to betray herself by talking to him.

'Okay. So you're leaving the choice up to me. That's good.' He deftly wrapped her in the towel, transferred the handcuff from the shower rail to his own wrist, and lifted her out of the bath.

'You said you weren't going to lay a finger on me until I asked you,' she reminded him as he began to dry her.

'I'm not,' came the annoying reply. 'There's a towel between my hands and your body.'

He had an answer for everything; Sarah couldn't help admiring him, albeit grudgingly. He thought on his feet, and she liked that.

She also liked the way he was drying her: patting the droplets of water from her skin, cherishing her. She closed her eyes, luxuriating in the feel of the soft cotton against her skin. As if he sensed the change in her, he changed the way he was drying her, moving the towel in tiny circles over her back and her buttocks. Tiny erotic circles. Now her muscles had recovered from the cramps of being in one position for so long, her body felt fluid and relaxed. The gentle massage was just what she needed.

He moved round to dry her breasts and her belly, then dropped to his knees so he could dry her legs. Almost without realising it, she parted her thighs, allowing him access. She could feel his warm breath against her delta. It would take such a tiny, tiny movement for his mouth to make contact with her sex, for his tongue to slide the full length of her musky furrow, to delve in her furls and hollows and tease her clitoris from its hood. Such a tiny, tiny...

She was suddenly aware that she was holding her breath, waiting for him to move. She knew he'd notice. How could he not? And yet he merely continued to dry her, in a sexual way – unlike the way he'd sponged her. That had been a distinct tease, calculated to make her beg him to touch her. And he'd stopped just when she was on the point of giving in. She had a feeling that he'd known it, too.

She swallowed hard. What was he going to do now? The towel was gradually moving up her thighs. Was he going to push her legs more widely apart, explore her properly with his clever fingers and his mouth? Was he going to make her wait? Or would he snap the handcuff from his wrist and force her to bend over the edge of the bath, while he closed the handcuff round the taps, wrapping the chain round them so she couldn't move? And then, while her rear was exposed and defenceless, would he break his word and lay his hands on her? Would he raise his hand, bringing it down hard on her warm and still-damp skin, leaving the imprint of his fingers in a fiery red mark on the soft white globes of her buttocks?

She could imagine it so easily. Herself, bound and unable to do anything, straining against her bonds as Marc's hand struck her again and again in perfectly measured blows, each one calculated to sting without doing any permanent damage. Each one would land on a fresh area of white skin, turning it pale pink and finally bright red, a livid blush which matched the corresponding darkening in her swollen sex.

And then he'd bend forward, touch his lips to her reddened buttocks, soothing the sting with his tongue. He'd kiss her gently, reverently. Then he'd part her legs slightly wider, giving him access to her sex, and slowly lap at her intimate flesh, arousing her still further. When her whole sex was fluid and weeping, and she was nearly at the point of coming, he'd push one finger into her, easing it back and forth, taking it slowly. She wouldn't be able to hold back: she'd climax, her internal muscles flexing hard around his intrusive finger.

He'd wait until the aftershocks of her orgasm had died away, and then he'd build her up again, slowly and sweetly. He'd add a second finger, and a third. He'd rub his thumb against her clitoris, setting up a rhythm in counterpoint to his thrusting fingers; and then, he'd dip his head and touch his tongue to the puckered rosy hole of her anus. Just as he'd done the previous night, introducing her to the hidden delights of something she'd previously not even dreamt of. A deep, dark need she was only just beginning to acknowledge...

'Sarah?'

His voice broke into her thoughts. She flushed, horrified

at just how far she'd become engrossed in her fantasy. 'I...'

'I think I can guess.' He stood up and kissed the tip of her nose. 'It was written all over your face.'

Her lips tightened. 'What have you done to me?'

'Dried you with a towel.'

'Don't be smart with me.'

'I merely answered your question.'

Those beautiful eyes were laughing; but they were laughing with her, rather than at her. Teasing and affectionate. If she weren't careful she could grow addicted to this man. Addicted to the way he touched her, the way his mouth curved. That beautiful, vulnerable mouth, which she'd fantasised about in the past – and now knew exactly what it felt like on her skin...

She had to stop this. Right now. 'Let me go.'

'That was the whole point of you being in the bathroom.'

He'd deliberately misunderstood her; she scowled at him. 'Release me, Marc.'

'Release is what you want, hm?'

Again, the misunderstanding was deliberate. Sarah was even more furious because he was answering a deeper need. Release was exactly what she needed. Her fantasy had aroused her to fever pitch, and she was uncomfortably aware that moisture was seeping down her leg. Thank God he wasn't kneeling down and drying her legs and feet, or he would have noticed. Though she had the nasty feeling that he knew, anyway.

'Stop playing games with me, Marc.'

'Do you really mean that, I wonder?' He dabbed at a non-existent bead of water with the towel. 'I've thought for a long while that power games turn you on. That's half the problem in the office. That's why you and I fight so much: because you're playing power games. In the office

80

you're in charge; here, I am.'

'Like hell.'

He smiled. 'Apart from the fact that this is my house – the proverbial Englishman's castle – you told me quite distinctly last night that I was in charge.'

'Today's another day.'

'But the rules are the same. If you really want me to let you go, you know what you have to do. What you have to say.'

'That's blackmail.'

He shook his head. 'Blackmail would be if I were threatening to reveal something secret about you. Which I'm not. This is something else, Sarah – and you know it.'

She was silent, not wanting to admit that he was right.

He dropped the towel. 'Bend over.'

Sarah was shocked by the images that slammed into her brain. He wasn't going to do what she thought he was... was he? What she'd dreamt about, fantasised about, never experienced...

Her stomach lurched.

'I said, bend over.' His voice was firm and commanding, brooking no argument. Not sinister, not spiteful: just coolly and calmly hinting that if she didn't do what he told her, things would be even harder. A perverse desire leapt inside her, a desire to test him and see just how far she could push him, how far he would take her. Yet, at the same time, she knew she wouldn't.

Not this time.

Silently, she bent over the edge of the bath. Just as she'd fantasised, he snapped the handcuff from his wrist and closed it round the taps, wrapping the chain round them. She tugged experimentally at her bonds, but they held fast. There was no way she could back out now. No way she could stop him – except the one way they both knew she wouldn't use.

Because she wanted him to do this.

Her sex grew hotter and wetter at the thought. She knew what he was going to do to her now. 'You said – you said you weren't going to lay a hand on me.' Her mouth was dry with anticipation and excitement.

'Perhaps I've changed my mind. Not that I need explain myself to you – do I, Sarah?'

'I... No.' She could barely force the words out.

'Wet skin stings,' he said conversationally. 'But I think you know that, don't you?'

Her face flamed. 'Are you suggesting that I... that I?'

'That you've played these games before? No, but I think you've wanted to. You've just not met the person who'd indulge you. Until now.' He stroked her buttocks, as if deciding which area of skin to tackle first; and then, without warning, he lifted his hand and brought it down sharply in the centre of her left buttock, leaving a fiery red mark on the soft white skin.

She couldn't help crying out. 'You bastard!'

'You asked for it,' he said softly. 'Not in so many words – but your thoughts were written all over your face, Sarah.'

She flushed deeply, the vermilion of her cheeks matching the handprint on her buttocks. 'I hate you.'

'Good.' Again, without warning, he brought his hand down on her right buttock, leaving an identical fiery mark on it.

The pain shocked through her; as he'd said, wet skin stung. A lot. Yet as the pain receded, it blurred into pleasure.

'How many should I give you, Sarah, I wonder?' he asked. She knew she wasn't supposed to answer the question. He'd already decided. Just as he'd obviously decided, even before he brought her to the bathroom, that he'd do this.

Again his hand landed on her exposed rear, turning the pale skin to a livid red. Again. Again. Again.

She closed her eyes, bracing herself for another... but nothing happened.

She waited. And waited. And waited. Her buttocks were suffused with a warm glow and her sex was weeping, its flesh dark with arousal, redder than her spanked bottom. Surely he wasn't going to stop now? Either he was waiting for the pain to subside before he dealt her another six hard smacks, or he was going to fulfil the rest of her fantasy, soothing her reddened skin with his mouth, and taking her to a series of orgasms that would leave her slumped and satiated for hours.

To her shock he simply leant forward and unclipped the chain, transferring one of the cuffs back to his wrist. She stared up at him in surprise, a hundred questions written on her face. He simply smiled. 'What's the matter, Sarah? Expecting more, were we?'

'I...' She swallowed hard. 'No.'

'Later,' he promised. 'Later.'

The thought was deep and dark and incredibly exciting. Sarah was shocked to realise just how turned on she was by the thought of Marc fulfilling the rest of her fantasies. Spanking her again, blurring the line between pain and pleasure – and then taking her on to new experiences, new feelings.

She allowed him to pull her to her feet again.

'Come on.' To her surprise he dropped the towel and led her out of the bathroom.

'Where are we going?'

'I don't think I need answer that, do I?' He stopped before the bedroom door.

'I'm not going back in there.' She lifted her chin. 'No

way.'

'Would you rather use my bed, Sarah?' he asked huskily.

'I...' Her throat dried.

'I thought not.' He gave her an odd smile, then opened the bedroom door and led her through it. 'Now, we can either do this the easy way, or the hard way. It's up to you.'

'How do you mean?'

He sighed. 'If you really want me to spell it out for you. All right. The easy way, you climb back on the bed and stretch out for me.'

'And the hard way?' she tested.

'The hard way gives me licence to do whatever I want. Your choice.'

There was something dangerous in his voice, something that thrilled her. She remembered what had happened in the bathroom, and shivered. If she gave him licence to do whatever he wanted, he might just do that. Haul her over his knee and spank her until she was shrieking for mercy, and then thrust his cock into her wet and aching sex, taking her to a higher peak than she'd ever achieved...

'You'll do what you want, anyway.'

'Maybe. Maybe not. Your choice,' he repeated.

She was silent, and he grinned. 'Silence indicates consent,' he said softly. 'I think, Sarah, that you'd like me to force you. You'd like me to bend you over my knee and redden your cheeks again, wouldn't you? Smack you like a naughty girl, bring my hands down on your buttocks until you're squirming on my lap, your bottom red and your sex hot for me.'

She gasped in shock. How the hell had he guessed what she'd been thinking? 'No. No. That's not what I want at all,' she lied.

'No?' His smile showed that he didn't believe her.

'No,' she insisted.

'Then you're free to choose the easy way.'

She stared at him. 'You bastard. Either way, I lose.'

'Not necessarily.' He took her hand. 'Last night you enjoyed what I did to you. You liked the way I touched you. Your body responded to me, Sarah. Your nipples grew hard when I touched them, when I tasted them. You liked the feel of my mouth on your breasts, sucking and licking and biting. Except I think you would have liked me to take it a little further – like I did today. Deep inside, in such a secret place that you've even hidden it from yourself, I think you like those sort of games. There's a part of you, Sarah, that wants to play the submissive whore. You pretend to be shocked – or maybe even bored – by tales of women in leather and chains, but secretly you identify with them, don't you?'

'No.'

'No?' He drew one finger into his mouth and sucked it. 'Imagine, Sarah. Imagine yourself as one of these women. A woman in a film, in a magazine. Dressed in a black leather harness, thin black leather straps bound tightly round your breasts to lift them up and display them better, with shiny platinum rings round your erect nipples, like little collars.' He traced the outline of the harness he was describing on her skin, making her shiver. 'It would be criss-crossed over your stomach: there would be a jewel in your navel. An ice-blue sapphire to match your eyes. And then it would cross again here, just above your mons.'

His fingers traced the top of her delta; involuntarily, she tilted her pelvis, and he smiled. 'Oh, yes. You can see it, can't you? And the leather would come down between your legs, here.' He described the movement of the leather between her thighs. 'Every time you moved it would rub against your clitoris, teasing you, making you want to be

85

filled. And here, the leather would be wet from your sex, hot and wet.' His fingers skated the length of her slit, pausing at the entrance to her vulva. 'And it would taper off, become like a tiny g-string,' he said, brushing the cleft of her buttocks. 'Finally, it would attach here, where it had criss-crossed you previously.' His fingers fluttered in the small of her back. 'Can you see it, Sarah?'

'No,' she lied. She could see it, only too clearly. Part of her was appalled, but the greater part of her thrilled at the idea.

'Your hair would be up. On top of your head, in a sophisticated chignon. But one twist of my fingers would have it down in seconds, cascading over your shoulders like silk.' His voice was caressing, tempting her. 'You'd be wearing a black domino.' He traced the outline of a tiny mask on her face. 'A black silk domino. And you'd be wearing red lipstick – not an obvious colour like scarlet, but a deep blood red. You'd be wearing a platinum collar, here, to match the little shiny collars on your nipples.' His fingers caressed her neck. 'Black hold-up lace-topped stockings, and black patent leather stilettos, much higher than you'd normally wear, so that you could only take tiny steps and had to thrust your beautiful bottom out for balance.'

She swallowed. 'No.'

'No?' His breath caressed her ear; he licked her earlobe, sending a shiver of desire down her spine. 'I think you're lying to me, Sarah. Because you like the idea – particularly if you were then forced to walk across the floor towards me in those impossibly high heels. Say... across your office floor.'

'My office floor?' She was shocked.

'Yes. With the blinds drawn. Just you and me. But whenever I chose, I could lift those blinds and let all the other men outside the room see you like that. They'd be hard instantly, Sarah, their faces pressed against your window and their cocks throbbing. They'd want to be there, like me, able to touch you and taste you and slide into your delectable body.'

She shivered again. The way he spoke to her, she could visualise it all too clearly. And the worst thing was, he was right. The idea excited her. The idea of being every man's wet dream, yet untouchable by any of them. The blinds and the plate glass were the perfect barrier. See, but don't see. Look, but don't touch. At her whim – or his.

'I'd be standing by the blinds, and you'd be walking towards me. You wouldn't know when – or even if – I'd decide to raise those blinds, and who would see you through the window. It might be your boss; it might be the training manager; it could be anyone. And they'd recognise you behind the mask, Sarah. Just like I recognised you behind your mask. Hands off, don't touch. Miss Prim-and-Proper. But you're not like that at all, are you Sarah? You're more like the woman I've just described, the sensualist who'd wear a black leather harness and be proud to walk towards me, with your sex weeping and your clitoris throbbing and your nipples tight and your heart pumping madly.'

She didn't answer – couldn't answer. She could barely think straight. The vision he was painting was clearly etched in her imagination. And yes, he was right. She'd be proud to walk towards him wearing that outrageous outfit. She wouldn't care if or when he raised that blind. Whoever was on the other side of the window didn't matter.

'And once you reached me, I'd kiss you. I'd kiss you hard, exploring your mouth, pushing my tongue into you, the way you'd like me to push my cock into you. I'd kiss you until your breasts were swelling, the nipples hard and aching for my touch beneath their little collars, and the leather grew tighter round your breasts, pinching you slightly. I'd kiss you until your clitoris was chafing against the leather strap between your legs. And then I'd pull back and make you walk back to your desk so I could watch the proud sway of your buttocks, the curve of your back, as you moved.'

Sarah moistened her suddenly dry lips. The way Marc was talking to her – she could almost feel him making love to her, feel her body reacting to his touch. And yet, since he'd mentioned the blinds he hadn't touched her once. She was hot for him, just from his words: she wasn't sure whether that made her feel more ashamed or excited or afraid. Marc Dubois could have a lot of power over her, if she wasn't careful. He could—

'Sarah.' His voice interrupted her panic-stricken thoughts. 'Sweet Sarah. And once you were at your desk, I'd command you to bend over and display yourself for me. And you would. You'd lean across your desk, gripping the far edge tightly, your legs splayed wide. And I'd be able to see everything. The leather strap between your legs, with the small bulge of your clitoris pushing against it. The place where the leather was wet from your sex. All the shades of red in that hot musky furrow, betraying your arousal. I'd be able to see it all.' His voice dropped slightly. 'Just as you'd be now, if I asked you to lean over that bed and display yourself for me. Glistening, the pearly sheen of your arousal coating your sex.'

'I...'

'Do it for me, Sarah. Lie on the bed and spread your legs. Let me see you.'

Slowly, very slowly, she did what he said. It was as

though she had no will of her own, or as if her will had become his. She climbed onto the bed, settled back against the pillows, closed her eyes and splayed her legs. He came to sit next to her on the bed, so she didn't have to stretch out her arm.

'Beautiful Sarah. Have I told you how beautiful you look? Even without that outfit, you're stunning. Your skin's so pale, so beautiful. I love the way you curve, so soft and inviting. It turns me on to see you like this. Stretch your arms up, Sarah. Arch your back, let your breasts thrust up. So beautiful, so soft and warm and delectable...' His voice relaxed her, made her feel desirable and drowsy. She did what he said, stretching her arms up. Then, without warning, she heard a soft click.

She opened her eyes and stared at him in horror and disbelief. He'd tricked her into putting her arms up by the headboard – and he'd handcuffed her to it. All the while he'd been talking to her when her eyes had been shut, he'd unclipped the cuffs from his own wrist, wound it round the headboard, and pinioned her other hand in the cuffs. And he'd moved fast, shifting to pin down her legs so she couldn't kick out at him.

'You bastard.'

'Now, now. I didn't do anything against your will. I didn't drag your arms up, did I?'

'You might just as well have done.' She gave him a look of pure hatred.

'Sarah. This is for your own good, you know.'

'Like hell.'

He smiled. 'Maybe it's for my pleasure, too. But it's also for yours. Because you liked what I did to you, last night. You liked the way I used my mouth on you, kissing you all over. You liked the way I licked you. And you liked it when I slid my cock into you.'

There wasn't a trace of gloating in his voice; he spoke matter-of-factly, quietly. It defused her anger. She listened to him as he continued.

'You said I was in charge. And that's how you wanted it – leaving it to someone else to make the decisions, for once. Letting me choose how to pleasure you. You liked it when I tied you up, made you helpless. And when I blindfolded you – yes, you were shocked for a moment or two, but you loved the idea. Especially when I told you someone else was in the room, watching us. It gave you the chance to act out your deepest fantasies without having to ask or be made to feel ashamed. Just like a few moments ago, when I suggested what you and I could do in your office. Because that's who you really are, Sarah. All woman. All sensual. And submissive.'

Her eyes met his. 'Marc. You're so sure of yourself. What if I tell you you're wrong?'

'Then you'd be lying,' he said simply. 'You need this, Sarah. You need it like breathing. You might have denied it to yourself for a long while, but it's true. Right now, handcuffed to the bed, you feel more alive than you've felt in years.'

She swallowed. 'You're a chauvinist pig.'

'Am I?' He tipped his head on one side. 'Hand on your heart – metaphorically, anyway – do you really mean that?'

She hung her head. The accusation simply wasn't true, on any level. 'I...'

'Shh. Let me pleasure you, Sarah,' he commanded. 'Just like I did last night. Touching every inch of your skin with my mouth, tasting your pleasure.'

His words made her shiver with longing; she couldn't answer him. He smiled, and deftly retied the silk scarves round her ankles. 'Sarah. Sweetheart. I can see your sex, and you're aroused. Very aroused. Your quim's all the shades of red and scarlet and vermilion, and your clitoris is hard, peeping out from its hood and demanding attention. Your sex is glistening and beautiful, like some exotic orchid.' He paused. 'Don't you want me to touch you, Sarah? Don't you want me to bring you pleasure, take you up and up until you're not sure which planet you're on and what day it is?'

'I...'

He smiled. 'Fair enough. We'll leave it at that then, shall we?' He stood up, picked up the paper and the mug of cold coffee, and walked towards the door. Sarah stared at him in shock. Surely he wasn't going to leave her there, tied up and aching? His earlier fantasy had aroused her more than she would admit – and the way he'd described the appearance of her sex, he knew exactly how turned on she was. Surely he wasn't going to leave her unsatisfied?

The soft click of the bedroom door behind him confirmed that he was.

'You bastard, Marc. Well, you're not going to win,' she vowed softly. 'Do what the hell you like – but you're not going to make me submit.' Though at the same time, she knew she was going to enjoy him trying.

Chapter Seven

Some time later, Marc breezed back into the bedroom. 'Lunch,' he announced, depositing a tray on the bedside cabinet.

'Supposing I'm not hungry?'

He shrugged. 'That's up to you, isn't it?' He picked up a knife, and her eyes widened for a moment in panic, until he took a peach from the tray.

God, how stupid of her. Of course he wasn't going to use a knife on her. He wasn't a maniac. She knew she was perfectly safe with him. She wasn't sure quite what the limits were to the game he was playing, but they certainly wouldn't include anything that would actually hurt her. Not permanently, anyway.

Again, those unbidden thoughts surfaced. She could imagine Marc hauling her over his knee and spanking her soundly, the flat of his palm cracking against the smooth white globes of her buttocks until the burning sensation spread to her sex, then changed subtly into a deeper and warmer pleasure...

She closed her eyes, not wanting him to guess what she was thinking.

'Sarah.'

She felt something drip onto her mouth, the little rivulet of moisture running down her lips and cheek. She opened her eyes again, frowning. 'What the...?' Then she saw what he was holding: a slice of ripe peach. Expensive, out-of-season peach.

'Open your mouth, Sarah.' His voice was very soft, but

still commanding. She responded instinctively – particularly as she had a sudden and very vivid picture of him saying the same thing in a very different situation. A situation where she was on her knees in front of him, he was standing, and he was holding the tip of his beautiful erect cock to her lips.

He slid the slice of peach between her lips, and she took a bite. It tasted good – very good. Sweet and succulent and juicy. Then she suddenly realised what he was playing at. Making her eat something that would spill juice over her face, make her sticky again – and he would offer to clean her up.

'Good, is it?' he asked softly.

'Yes.'

'Sweet and aromatic. Just like you, Sarah. Eating a ripe peach, for me, is like using my mouth on you. Tasting something sweet and musky, something meltingly soft under my tongue. And all the while I can smell that delicious scent, that spicy musky scent that drives me insane with wanting you.'

She shivered at the mental picture he was painting. She could imagine all too easily what he saw, what he felt, when he touched her intimately like that.

'Can you see it, Sarah?' His voice was still low, almost hypnotic. 'Can you feel how it would be to taste a woman's sex, to feel that beautiful nectar flowing into your mouth as you aroused her?' He deliberately squeezed the peach, making the juices drip into her mouth. 'Such a sweet, exotic taste.'

A pulse in her sex began to beat rapidly. What he was suggesting to her... it was something she had never done. She'd never even once been tempted; as far as she was concerned, she was a hundred per cent straight. But the way he was talking, she could almost imagine what it would be like to kneel between another woman's thighs, placing the flats of her palms against the other woman's legs to widen her stance, and then bend her head to draw her tongue down the full length of her sex.

'That's right, Sarah. You can see it, can't you?' He stroked her cheek. 'And it feels so good, doesn't it? Licking her and lapping her, teasing her in just the way you like to be teased.'

'I...' With an effort, she focused on her surroundings. 'No. Marc, I'm a hundred per cent straight.'

'Sure you are, honey.'

'I am,' she insisted.

'There's a theory that no one is a hundred per cent straight,' he told her, matter-of-factly. 'That everyone has at least one single-sex experience, even if they won't admit it.'

She looked at him incredulously. 'Are you telling me that you – that you've...' Her voice faded. She couldn't quite imagine Marc with another man. Would he be the dominant partner, or the submissive? Submissive, just like she was at that moment, doing whatever his lover told him to do?

'No, I haven't,' he said, breaking her thoughts. 'I haven't really thought about it much – other than that I can see why the women in my department like to have pictures of their favourite men around.'

She should have known he'd bring that back into the conversation. That was the whole purpose of her sojourn in his cottage, wasn't it? To make her agree to his demands, to leave his scruffy department exactly as it was, with tatty pictures stuck to the walls. Then she registered what he'd just said. 'Do you mean that you fancy some of those men, too?'

He grinned. 'No. But, aesthetically speaking, I can see

what attracts the girls to those pictures. And when they're happy with their surroundings, they work better.'

'More like they spend half their time fantasising about what they'd like their heroes to do to them,' Sarah said acerbically.

He raised an eyebrow. 'Are you saying that that's why your office is so anally-retentive neat? Because if you had a picture of your favourite hunk on the wall, you'd keep looking at him until you ended up closing your blinds and masturbating?'

'I'm a professional,' she reminded him icily. 'I don't act like...' Her voice faded. Who the hell was she trying to kid? She'd almost ended up touching herself in the office, thinking of the very man who sat next to her feeding her ripe juicy peach slices. The memory shamed and excited her at the same time.

'Don't act like what, Sarah?'

'Like that.'

'Are you telling me you never masturbate? Because I don't believe you.'

'Not everyone has sex on the brain.'

'True. But everyone thinks about it, at some point. Aren't there statistics showing that men think of sex every ten seconds, or something like that?'

'Statistics. It's easy to bend them to suit yourself.' Her voice was filled with contempt.

'I know. I've done it myself. But we weren't really talking about statistics. We were talking about masturbation. And you haven't answered my question.'

'What question?' she prevaricated.

'Were you trying to tell me that you never masturbate?'

'That's none of your business.'

'Perhaps.' He fed her another slice of peach. 'But then again, you're in my bed.'

'Your spare bed.'

'It's still mine though. And we've shared it together. Last night,' he reminded her.

She didn't answer, and he smiled. 'Okay, so you're not going to admit it. Tell me what you fantasise about, instead.'

'What I fantasise about?' Her voice came out almost as a croak. She certainly wasn't going to tell him that. Especially the fantasies she'd had since she'd been in his cottage. They were way outside the usual realms of her fantasies. It scared and excited her at the same time.

'Tell me, Sarah.'

'I... Oh, just the usual things.'

He fed her another slice of peach, deliberately letting the juice spill down her throat. 'I'm not a woman, Sarah. I don't know what "the usual things" are.'

'Just a man making love with me.'

'Doing what in particular?'

'Just making love.'

'*Just* making love?' he mocked. 'Come on. You can do better than that.'

'What do you want me to do – talk dirty to you?'

He laughed. 'Not necessarily. I'm just interested. I'd like to know what kind of scenarios turn you on.'

'It's none of your business.'

'Maybe.' He paused. 'I wonder, Sarah. Have you fantasised about being held captive and tied up? Am I making your dreams reality?'

'That's arrogant.'

'I didn't say I was your dream man,' he pointed out, 'just that I might be acting out your dream scenario.'

'And what do you think my dream man is like?' she fenced.

'Someone,' he said very quietly, 'who's dominant. Who

takes control. Completely the opposite of the kind you deal with in your day-to-day business life.'

'Which excludes you.'

'Probably.' He didn't sound in the least bit concerned; Sarah felt suddenly hurt. She'd thought her barb would wound him, at least; or maybe she meant less to him than that. Maybe he didn't care what she thought of him.

'Why are you doing this?' she asked.

'Doing what?'

'Keeping me here like this.'

'We've already been through that. It's because I want you to admit that you're completely in the wrong, and you'll let me run my team the way I want to run it. I want the office to go back to normal – a lively, happy place, full of gossip and laughter and teasing, with people being there because they want to, not just because they need the money to pay their mortgage or their car loan or whatever. I hate the idea of it turning into a slick, soulless place, where nothing's personal any more and no one feels they have a stake.'

'A place where they spend more time chatting than working, and the amount of tat on the walls makes the place look scruffy and disorganised. Disorganisation means slack working patterns,' she told him.

'So it's stalemate. For now.' He fed her another slice of peach. 'You're covered in juice, you know.'

'That's your fault.'

'You know how it is. Disorganised, sloppy boss bringing his work practices home,' he mocked.

She flushed as the barb hit home. 'There's no need to be snide.'

'I'm merely using your terms. You think I'm sloppy, don't you?'

'No.'

'Right. So if I'm not sloppy and I don't make a mess unintentionally, then I must have done this deliberately, mustn't I?' he asked, tracing one of the rivulets of juice with his fingertip. 'And if I make a mess, I need to clear it up. Or make someone else do it for me.'

'I can't exactly wipe my face.' She waggled her fingers, drawing his attention to her handcuffs. 'Unless you're going to let me go.'

'Not yet. I've hardly started on you, Sarah. By the time I've finished...' He smiled. 'Well. We'll see.'

Her eyes widened. 'You're not... Look, what are you going to do to me?'

'That's for me to know, and you to guess.' He bent his head to lick the juice from the side of her throat.

Someone else. She couldn't get the idea out of her head. Someone else. Was he going to let someone else make love to her, to make her drop her opposition to his plans for the office? And if so, who? A man? Another woman? He'd been very insistent about the way that eating a peach reminded him of using his mouth on a woman's sex. Had that been a veiled hint? That, and his comment that no one was a hundred per cent heterosexual?

'Relax,' he said softly. 'Don't look so worried. I won't make you do anything you don't want to, Sarah.'

'You said I was submissive. That means you think I have to do what I'm told.'

'Not necessarily. You have boundaries, Sarah, limits. I might stretch them, but I won't go beyond them. That's the whole point. Being submissive means having total freedom. You don't have to worry about what's going to happen and whether you're going to be faced with a decision you don't want to make.'

'I'm not submissive.'

'No? Then tell me, would you like to beat me?'

'*What?*'

He grinned at the shock on her face. 'Of course you wouldn't. Like I said, you're not the sexually dominant type – certainly not a fully fledged dominatrix. But I think you might like me to beat you. Not now, but at some point in the future. I saw your face when I suggested it. You'd like me to haul you over my knee and chastise you: and then spend the next few hours making you forget the sting in your pretty little rear.'

She stared at him in dislike. 'You bastard.'

'Too accurate, am I?'

'No. Not at all. Far from it.'

'You're blustering, Sarah. Just like you were when I asked you if you masturbated. It isn't a sign of weakness, you know. It's a strength – trusting someone enough to give them complete control over you, and knowing they won't betray that trust by making you do something abhorrent to you.' The tip of his tongue touched the pulse in her neck. 'Learn to be kind to yourself, Sarah. Give yourself what you need.'

'I don't know what you're talking about,' she said stiffly.

'No?' He continued to lick the peach juice from her skin, taking tiny erotic bites as he did so.

'Marc. You're not playing fair.'

'All's fair in love and war,' he quipped.

Yes. And this was war, Sarah thought.

Then she thought of the other half of the quote. Love. Was he telling her he was in love with her? Or that he thought she was in love with him?

'Stop thinking,' he told her, smoothing one hand over her forehead. 'When you concentrate, there's a tiny dimple in your forehead, just above the beginning of your right eyebrow.'

She was shocked that he'd noticed such a small detail.

Either Marc Dubois was incredibly observant, or he'd been focusing on her. The question was, which?

And then she stopped thinking as his mouth travelled downwards and he began to lick the hollows of her collarbones. She closed her eyes, murmuring with pleasure as he continued southwards.

His mouth teased her already erect nipples, licking and nipping at the sensitive flesh. When he used his teeth, very gently grazing her skin, she couldn't hold back her gasp of pleasure. He moved downwards, taking his time, exploring every inch of her skin… and then, finally, she could feel his breath against her quim. She tilted her pelvis impatient, wanting him to lick her properly. He'd been teasing her for so long, talking to her, arousing her, making her face things she would rather have kept buried in her subconscious; now, it was time for her reward. She remembered how skilled he was with his mouth, how he'd had her writhing and moaning in pleasure the night before. This, she thought, was going to be—

Nothing. He sat up.

She opened her eyes in shock. 'Marc?'

'Sorry. I forgot myself. Now, where were we?'

She stared at him in disbelief. How cruel could he get? Arousing her to the point where she needed him to fill her, to bring that warm rolling pleasure to a fast boil that bubbled over – and then stopping? It was too much 'I—'

'We were talking about fantasies,' he cut in. 'Masturbation. And you were trying to make me believe that you never masturbated.' His lips quirked. 'I'm half tempted to take off those handcuffs and make you do it now. Because you're hot, aren't you, Sarah? Your pretty little quim is hot and wet and aching, wanting to be touched and filled. If I unclipped those handcuffs now you wouldn't be able to help yourself, would you? You'd have to slide your hands between your thighs and touch yourself, bring yourself to the climax you need.'

She flushed. 'There is such a thing as self-control.'

'Yes. And sometimes it's more of a turn-on to force yourself to wait, making the anticipation keener. I know.' He nodded. 'But sometimes you go past that point. You need to climax and nothing's going to stop you. You don't care who might be listening or watching; you just have to do it, right then and there.'

She licked her suddenly dry lips. 'Talking from experience, are you?'

'What do you think?'

'I...' She shook her head.

'Tell me, Sarah. Do you think I masturbate?'

'I... I don't know. It's none of my business.'

'It is now. Tell me.'

She avoided his eyes. 'Probably.'

'Probably,' he repeated, his voice mocking. 'That's a bit of a cop-out. What happened to the marketing director Sarah Ward, she of the sharp tongue and even sharper brain?'

She lifted her chin, trying to look dignified. 'Go to hell.'

He wasn't in the least put out. 'We were,' he reminded her, 'talking about masturbation. Haven't you ever been tempted, Sarah, in your office? To pull the blinds, lock the door and slide your hands between your legs?'

She flushed. How close she'd come to it, that day, when she'd started thinking about him. 'No,' she lied.

'No?' His disbelief was obvious. 'Or maybe you'd have preferred to keep the blinds open. Adding spice to it: the danger of being caught with your skirt up and your hand down your knickers, rubbing like a maenad.'

Her flush deepened. 'Why don't you change the subject?'

'Caught a raw nerve, have I? Now, what could have made you feel like that? Or, more pertinently, who?'

'You're being ridiculous.'

'Am I?'

She sighed. 'What do you want me to say, Marc? That I want to fuck someone in the office and spend half my time dreaming about it with my hand between my legs, wanking myself silly?'

'If you're trying to shock me with your language, you've failed,' he said quietly. 'And if you think I'm turned on by a woman talking dirty... well, it has its place, but I think your vocabulary is a little richer than that.'

The rebuke stung. Sarah glared at him, tears of mingled rage and misery glittering in her eyes. He smiled at her, stroking her cheek. 'I wasn't intending to upset you. Just pointing out that I think you'd know how to turn a man on with other words, that's all.'

She said nothing.

'But yes, I'm interested. I'd like to know. Tell me, Sarah, have you ever been so turned on in the office that you've touched yourself – or been close to it?'

It was almost as if he could read her mind, as if he'd been there on that heart-stopping occasion when she'd realised she was about to touch herself. Though he had been there, only moments before. He'd been the whole reason why she'd wanted to do it: to bring herself to a climax, fantasising all the while that it was him. His hands on her quim, her breasts.

God. There was only one way she could think of to head him off the subject. 'Have you?'

He smiled. 'Yes. Actually, I have. There's this woman in the office. I see her every day: and ever since I first met her I've fantasised about her. Of course, it's strictly look and don't touch. You know the rules. Never sleep with a colleague – it's unprofessional and affects your relationship in the office, even if you both say it won't.' He spread his hands disarmingly. 'Anyway. I think about her a lot. I imagine what it would be like to touch her, to run my fingers through her hair. To dance with her, holding her close to me. To take her clothes off, very slowly, kissing every inch of skin as I reveal it.' His face grew slightly wistful. 'I'd worship her with my hands and my mouth. And yes, it's driven me over the edge in the office. One night I was working late and, all of a sudden, I imagined her there with me. I could imagine pushing all the papers from my desk and making love to her on it, there and then. I was all on my own in the office... and before I knew it my zip was undone and I was touching myself, thinking of her and remembering her perfume.'

'You... you made yourself come? At your desk?'

He nodded. 'I didn't care if one of the cleaners came in late and caught me, or anyone else in the office. I was past the point of no return. Thinking of her smile – her very rare, very beautiful smile. She doesn't smile enough. It makes her look completely different: much softer, more alive.'

Sarah was shocked to feel a sudden twinge of jealousy. Whoever this woman was, Marc Dubois more than lusted after her from afar. He was in love with her. It showed on his face, that wistful and yearning look. 'Who is she?'

He shook his head. 'That's strictly between me and my fantasies.'

She ran through a mental list of all the women he could come in contact with. One of his team? He worked with a department of women. It could be any one of them. Or someone in Training, in Personnel? 'Is she married?'

'She's unobtainable. Off limits.'

Jealousy twisted again inside her; she tried to ignore it.

'And you masturbated over her.'

'Not literally.' There was a ghost of amusement in his smile.

'I can't believe you did that. In the office.'

'Haven't you been tempted?'

'We're not talking about me. We're talking about you. You actually... in the office?'

'Why the questions? Are you shocked, Sarah?'

Considering how near she'd been to it, herself – no, she wasn't shocked. But she was aroused. She could imagine him sitting at his desk, stretched out in his chair with his head tipped back and his eyes squeezed tightly shut, an expression of bliss on his face as he rubbed his cock, and the very idea made her wet. Very wet. 'Show me,' she said softly.

His eyes met hers. 'You've guessed, haven't you?' he asked, equally softly.

'Guessed?'

'Who she is. The woman I was dreaming about. The woman who's driven me crazy ever since I first met her. I fell for her right from the start, but it took me quite a while to admit it to myself.' He smiled wryly. 'I suppose I must be wearing my heart on my sleeve.'

'Maybe.' She didn't know at all, but she decided to play him at his own game. 'Show me.'

'Show you what?'

'What you did in the office.'

His face was serious for a moment. 'You really want to know?'

She nodded.

'Okay.' Slowly, he stripped down to his boxer shorts.

Sarah took a sharp intake of breath. He was just as beautiful as she remembered from the previous night. His body was perfectly sculpted; and for the first time she noticed a dimple in his chin. It made her want to reach out and touch him, trace his jaw and press her finger into his dimple, teasing him, before tracing his lips and letting him draw her finger into his mouth, sucking on it.

She licked her lips as he finally removed his boxer shorts. She'd almost forgotten how beautiful his cock was, too, rising from the cloud of dark hair at his groin. Long and thick, uncircumcised, perfectly proportioned – and already erect. Marc was obviously turned on at the thought of masturbating in front of her. It was something she'd always thought taboo, never wanting to touch herself in front of her previous lovers – never wanting them to do it in front of her, either. But with Marc it was different. She wanted to watch him – more than that, she wanted to touch herself while she watched him. Being tied was incredibly frustrating. She felt her sex grow wetter and her nipples tauten as he curled his fingers round the shaft and began to rub it, using short light strokes.

His glans darkened and his pupils expanded; those beautiful grey-green eyes were almost black with desire. Was he thinking about her? Sarah wondered. Or was it the woman of his dreams, the woman he'd thought about in the office as he'd performed exactly the same actions?

His strokes quickened, and she could see he was gripping himself harder. He changed the rhythm again, teasing himself with long slow strokes, then speeded up again. She could see how turned on he was: his breathing was fast and shallow, his cheeks were flushed, and he was biting his lower lip. His beautiful reddened lower lip; she itched to sink her own teeth into it, make him open his mouth so she could explore him with her tongue.

Involuntarily, she tugged against her bonds. Watching him was one thing – something she found very arousing – but she wanted to join him. She wanted to kneel in front of him, ring his cock with her thumb and forefinger and rub the shaft as she slid her mouth over the glistening tip. She wanted to cup his balls, just as he was doing, massage them and stroke the soft smooth skin of his perineum, tracing the seam. She wanted to suck him while she had one hand working between her thighs, pushing into her sex and rubbing her clitoris hard.

All the time she was aware that he was watching her. Why didn't he have his eyes closed, thinking about the woman he'd dreamt about? But it didn't matter. Suddenly all that mattered was that he was there before her, masturbating to her command, concentrating entirely on her.

'Is this what you wanted to see?' His voice had dropped a couple of tones – yet another sign of how aroused he was. 'Is it, Sarah?'

'Yes.' She was aware that her voice was as husky as his.

'So you like the thought that I masturbate when I think of you?'

It took a moment for his words to sink in but, when they did, her eyes widened in shock. *She* was the woman he dreamt about? *She* was the one who'd caused him to lose control in the office? 'Marc.'

'Well?'

'I.... yes.' Yes. It turned her on even more, to watch him stroking his cock and know he was concentrating entirely on her. To know he was so turned on by her he couldn't stop touching himself, even in the office. She swallowed. 'Have you... do you...'

'What do you want to know, Sarah?'

'Was it just in the office, that you masturbated over thoughts of me?'

He grinned. 'That'd be telling, sweetheart.' His smile faded, replaced by a gasp of pleasure; deliberately, he squeezed just under his frenum, delaying his climax.

'I want to know. Was it just in the office?'

He shook his head. 'And in the car, on the way home.'

'When you were driving?' She was shocked.

'I'm not that reckless. No, I pulled off into a gateway.'

'And you... you did that? In a public place, where anyone could have seen you?' She nodded at the way he was still stroking his cock.

'Yes. Shocked? Embarrassed?' he challenged.

'I... No. No.' Her quim flexed. Again she tugged at her bonds, wanting to slide a hand between her legs, bring herself to climax at the same time as him. She wanted to watch the pearly liquid spurt from the tip of his cock, splattering over her body at the same time as she worked her sex. It was so close to her earlier fantasy of the men in her office masturbating over her body, then scooping up the sticky mixture and forcing her to lick their fingers clean, that she almost came at the thought of it.

'So have you?'

'Have I what?' She was aware that her voice was slightly slurred, and was furious with herself for betraying her weakness: but then again, she comforted herself, he was hardly in a state to notice.

'Masturbated in the office.'

'No.'

'No?'

'Nearly,' she admitted.

'It's nothing to be ashamed of. Pleasure.' His eyes held hers. 'And if I released you now, would you?'

'Would I what?' Deliberately, she played dumb.

The smile on his face showed that he knew it. 'Would you touch yourself, Sarah? Would you slide your hand between your legs and rub your clitoris while you thought of me?'

She swallowed. 'Yes.'

'I can't hear you.'

'Yes.'

'Yes, what?'

'Yes, I'd touch myself,' she admitted, her cheeks burning.

'You'd touch yourself while you thought of me?' he insisted.

'I'd touch myself, while—' she could hardly get the words out, her throat was so dry '—I thought of you.'

'It's so easy,' he whispered. 'We could do this. Watch each other come – or even better, touch each other. It'd be so easy. Wouldn't you like to do that, Sarah? To touch me while I touch you? To rub my cock while I push my fingers deep inside you, thrusting them like a tiny cock? To fondle my balls while I rub your clitoris? To open your mouth against mine, kiss me hard, just as I want to kiss you?'

She shivered. 'Yes.' She paused. 'Untie me Marc. Let me touch you. Let me use my mouth on you.'

'And what would you want me to do?'

'The same to me. Touch my breasts. Suck my nipples. Lick me. Lick me while I suck you.' A pulse was beating hard in her sex; desperately, she wanted him to touch her. To give her the release she craved: fantasising about him then watching him masturbate had pushed her very close to the edge.

'Then you know what you have to do. Tell me,' he urged.

'Tell you what?'

'That you're submissive, at heart. That you'll let me run my team the way I want to, with no interference.'

She shook her head. 'I can't do that, Marc.'

'So it's "no" to both?'

Her silence was eloquent; he shrugged, removed his hand from his cock, and dressed swiftly and in silence.

'Marc?'

He shrugged again. 'What's the point, Sarah?'

To her shock, he turned on his heel and left the bedroom. She was near to tears. How the hell could he do that? Admit that he fantasised about her, that thoughts of her drove him to touch himself; make her admit the same; and then leave without giving either of them the release they both needed?

He was right. It would have been oh so easy to tell him what he wanted. To admit that yes, she was submissive at heart, that she liked him making decisions for her, in a sexual way. To tell him he could do what the hell he liked with his bloody team. It wasn't that important.

And yet it was a point of principle. She was his boss. So she was in control – wasn't she?

Annoyed, she gritted her teeth and tried to ignore the ache between her thighs, the tension in her nipples. She wasn't going to give in. No way.

Chapter Eight

'Christ, you look rough,' Simon said as Marc opened the door.

'Yeah.' Marc rubbed a hand through his hair. He felt it. More than rough. It had been the hardest thing he'd ever done; to dress while he was still aroused and while Sarah so obviously wanted him, and leave her. It would have been so easy to release her, climb onto the bed beside her and do what she'd wanted, moving so that he was straddling her shoulders and his mouth was clamped firmly on her sex, while she reached up to take his cock into her mouth. But she had to say the words first – and she hadn't. 'So would you, if you'd spent the past few hours like I have.'

'I'm not sure I want to know.' Simon followed his friend into the house. 'Marc, are you sure you know what you're doing?'

'No.' Marc shrugged. 'But it's too late now.'

'So what's going on? From what you said on the phone I thought you were...' His voice faded as he walked into the sitting room and found it empty. 'Where is she?'

'Upstairs.' Marc sighed. 'I might as well tell you the whole story.'

'I think you'd better.'

'Beer or coffee, first?'

'Coffee,' Simon said feelingly.

Marc made them both a mug of strong black coffee, then brought it through to the sitting room and gave Simon a potted version of what had happened between him and

Sarah.

When he'd finished, Simon whistled. 'You're crazy, do you know that?'

'You put the idea into my head.'

'I said spend a weekend with her and get her out of your system, not tie her up and...' Simon shook his head. 'Ah well. So what was it you wanted me to do?'

'I'm playing it by ear,' Marc admitted. 'But I need to make her admit it, Simon. I know I'm right about her. I can see it in her face.'

'What if you're not?'

'Maybe my judgement's off.' He sighed heavily. 'Just now, she more or less admitted that she feels the same way about me.'

'So what went wrong?'

'She's stubborn. I want her to tell me explicitly. I want her to admit her true nature – and she's testing me just as hard, seeing how far I'll go.'

'And just how far are you going to go?'

'That's just it,' Marc said softly. 'I don't know. Every time I think I've reached my limit she says or does something, and it goes further.' He raked a hand through his hair again. 'I thought we'd start by you reading her a bedtime story.'

Simon nodded. 'Fine. Anything in particular?'

'This.' Marc walked over to his bookshelves and removed a leather-bound book. He flicked through it rapidly, then handed the open book to his friend. 'It's called *Fine*.'

'Are you sure she won't mind – well, me seeing her naked and handcuffed to the bed?'

A ghost of a grin flitted over Marc's face. 'Too bad if she does. But no, I don't think she'll mind. She might say she does.'

'And if she means it?'

'Then we'll have to think of something else. But I think it's something she's secretly fantasised about. I can see it in her eyes.'

Simon wasn't completely convinced, but when he'd finished his coffee he followed his friend up the stairs, holding the book.

'Remember – act as if it's completely natural to see her like that,' Marc reminded him in a low voice.

Simon nodded, and Marc opened the door.

Sarah looked up as she heard the door open. Her eyes widened as she realised Marc wasn't alone. There was another man with him – a man she didn't recognise, or at least hadn't seen around the office. He wasn't quite as tall as Marc, and had wavy blond hair, a strong jaw and deep brown eyes. His shoulders were broad and his waist was narrow. Physically, he was attractive, but he couldn't hold a candle to Marc.

Marc.

Her face coloured with mortification. She was handcuffed to the bed, completely naked, her wet and swollen sex on full display, and Marc had brought another man in to see her. To view her. The humiliation almost choked her, yet at the same time it made her nipples and her sex tingle. It was as if Marc had read her thoughts – or had realised why she'd been so turned on by his fantasy of standing by the blinds in her office, able to display her naked body to anyone he chose at one pull of the cord. Maybe that's why he had stopped – because he'd merely been warming her up for the next stage. Being taken by a stranger.

'This is Simon,' Marc said. 'Simon, this is Sarah.'

'Hello, Sarah,' Simon said quietly.

112

Marc looked at Sarah. 'Manners,' he reminded her.

Her flush deepened. 'Hello, Simon.'

'That's better. Now, Simon's going to read you a little story,' Marc said.

Sarah was amazed at the way Simon acted: as though it were perfectly normal and natural to see a woman he'd never met before naked and handcuffed to the bed. Was he under strict instructions from Marc? Or was it a normal state of affairs in Marc's house? Did he make a habit of keeping women tied to the bed? It would certainly explain why he kept the handcuffs and the silk scarves in the bedside cabinet.

Before she had a chance to work it out, Simon smiled and sat down on the bed next to her. Marc remained at the foot of the bed, just watching her. Sarah's sex pulsed. What was going to happen now? Was Simon going to make love to her while Marc watched? Or was Marc going to continue where he'd left off, stripping and rubbing his cock until he came, splashing her body with creamy white fluid while his friend watched and read her a story?

She was lulled by the softness of Simon's voice. 'The story's called *Fine*.

'"Sorry isn't good enough. Someone else could have been waiting to use that book." Alicia frowned at the man standing before her desk.

'"I'm only a day late," Jake protested.

'"A day's a day. If I had my way, people who returned things late wouldn't be allowed to borrow anything else – that way, they wouldn't inconvenience other people. As it is, that's a pound."

'"A pound? That's a bit steep for a day's overdue fine, isn't it?"

'"Library rules," Alicia said crisply, her blue eyes hard behind her glasses. "You're obviously new around here.

My rules are straightforward. If you break them, you pay the price."

'He looked at her, nodded, and paid his pound. Then he turned on his heel and left the library without another word. Outside, in the bracing January air, he leant against the sculpture in the courtyard. No doubt she would have fined him for that as well, if she'd caught him.

'He smiled wryly to himself. Alicia Thornley, the deputy librarian, was a complete stereotype of her kind. She even wore horn-rimmed spectacles and had her hair in a bun. He'd heard rumours about her, that she terrorised the students and the staff alike: which was why he'd deliberately returned a book late, to judge her for himself.

'She was sharp. She'd sussed that he was new around there. But she wasn't sharp enough. She hadn't guessed who he was precisely. He smiled. He'd deal with her the next day. Yes, he was going to get his own back on her. And how. Because Alicia Thornley, behind her prickly exterior and her deliberately dull clothes, was very attractive indeed. Ice blue eyes, fair hair like spun silk, and a body which he suspected was fantastic. He was going to enjoy taming this particular dragon.

'The following afternoon, Alicia headed towards the manager's office. All the staff were supposed to meet the new library manager, Jake Ellis, and she was the first. She had no idea what this Jake would be like; hopefully he would do the same as Alan, who'd just retired, and leave her to run the place as she usually did. Efficiently and properly.'

Sarah looked at Marc. He'd chosen this story deliberately, she knew: about a new manager interfering with the way his subordinate ran the office. It was a direct parallel to their own situation, only with their positions reversed. Even the main female character looked a bit like her, with ice-blue eyes and fair hair.

'She rapped on the door and walked in without waiting for a summons,' Simon continued. 'Then she took in who was sitting at the desk and did a double-take. It was the man she'd fined for returning a book late. The day before, he'd been wearing typical lecturer's garb: a pair of faded denims, a baggy Aran sweater and desert boots. Today he was wearing a well-cut dark grey suit, a starched white cotton shirt and an understated silk tie. He looked fabulous. She was horribly aware that her nipples were growing hard, just from looking at him, and her sex was decidedly wet.

'"Miss Thornley." Jake leant back in his swivel chair, putting his hands behind his neck. "So." His grey eyes challenged her. "What do you have to say for yourself?"

'"About what?"

'"About your behaviour yesterday."

'She rolled her eyes. "If I'd known who you were—"

'"Who I am has nothing to do with it. I'd heard that one or two of the staff could do with a lesson in customer relations. Rumour had it that you were one of them, and I was testing a theory. As far as you were concerned, I was just another person who'd returned a book late."

'"And infringed library regulations. That's why I fined you."

'"You weren't exactly friendly towards me."

'She flushed dully. "I was doing my job."

'Jake stared at her. "There's doing your job and being over-zealous."

'"Look, Mr Ellis, if we slacken off on fines, people won't bother bringing books back on their due date. That's going to inconvenience anyone else who wants to borrow the same copy. And we can't afford the extra funds to buy more copies of the more popular books, just to pander to people who think they're being clever in breaking the rules."

"'You have the right to impose fines – but what you don't have is the right to act like a fascist dictator. I'm in charge now, and I want to change things around here. I want people to use our services and know that they're going to be treated well, not served by surly desk staff."

"'I'm not desk staff." She lifted her chin. "I was merely helping out because we had some people off sick yesterday. I'm the deputy head librarian."

"'Then act like one. Have a bit of dignity – and learn to treat people properly."

"'Or else?"

'He smiled. "If you don't like it, you can leave."

"'Cracking the whip?" It came out as a sneer.

"'Yes, I do have something like that in mind, actually."

'To her surprise, he stood up and walked over to his office door, locking it. His next words shocked her. "Lift your skirt and bend over my desk."

"'What?"

"'You heard. Lift your skirt and bend over my desk."

'Alicia looked at him in disbelief. What the hell did he have in mind?

"'Do it."

'Something in his voice made her decide it was a good idea to do what he wanted. Slowly, she bunched up her tweed skirt and bent over his desk.

"'And your petticoat."

'She bunched that up too, revealing underwear very at odds with the clothes she wore. Instead of the practical big white knickers and tan-coloured tights Jake could have expected of a stereotype dragon librarian, Alicia was wearing very feminine clothes: tiny white lace knickers, teamed with hold-up lace-topped stockings.

"'And now pull down your knickers. Leave them at your

116

knees. And don't move or speak until I give you permission."

'She lifted her head, about to protest, but the steely glint in his eyes silenced her. Part of her was furious with him for putting her in such a humiliating position. She knew she ought to just walk out and report him for harassment. On the other hand, part of her was thrilled by it, by the command in his voice. It made her body leap, her sex moisten and her nipples harden.

'Well, if he wanted a show, a show he'd get. She did what he demanded, pulling her knickers down to her knees. She could imagine him standing behind her, his trousers down to his knees and his cock pressed against the furrow of her buttocks. He'd tease her, slide the tip of his cock all the way along her sex to brush against her clitoris, then back to her entrance, pushing slowly until he was in her up to the hilt. And then—

'The volley of slaps to her buttocks took her by surprise, cutting off her thoughts. "What the hell do you—?"

'He cut her off mid-sentence. "I'm teaching you a lesson in manners, Alicia Thornley. This one's for being rude to me." He slapped her hard. "And this one's for being surly." Another slap followed. "And this one's for stalking into my office as if you owned the place." He delivered another stinging blow.

'Alicia was so surprised she did nothing to defend herself; then to her shock she realised her sex was decidedly hot, her clitoris tingling and her nipples so hard they hurt. She'd never thought she was the sort to be turned on by a spanking – pain had never been one of her kicks – but this...

'Jake delivered one last stinging blow and went to sit back behind his desk.

'Alicia stared at him. "I don't believe you just did that."

'"You had it coming to you." He met her gaze levelly. "Perhaps you'll be pleasant to people in the future." His lips curved into a smile. "Although from the view I had you looked as if you quite enjoyed it."

'She met his challenge head-on. "And what are you going to do about it?"

'"Nothing."

'Shame flooded through her. He despised her. He didn't even think she was worth touching. Or maybe he wanted to prove his power by making her return to her desk in such a state, with her buttocks stinging and her sex empty and aching.

'She was about to pull up her knickers, restore order to her dress and leave, when he stopped her. "I told you not to move – or to speak – until I gave you permission. You've done both."

'"What?"

'"I make it one stroke for every word." He paused, as if counting. "That's seventeen. And one for moving without permission. That's eighteen." He looked thoughtful. "Maybe I ought to make it a round two dozen."

'Alicia didn't dare to protest, knowing that every word would earn her another stroke.

'"I'll leave it at eighteen," he decided finally, "provided you count every stroke and thank me for it."

'Alicia wanted to tell him to go to hell, that there was no way she'd do that – but there was a ripple of excitement running down her spine. She knew she was going to take her punishment, as she deserved. And maybe, just maybe, there would be a reward afterwards.

'He rummaged in his desk drawer, and brought out an old-fashioned wooden ruler. Alicia's eyes widened.

'"And if you cry out instead of counting, we go back to the beginning," he told her as he walked behind her again.

"So, Alicia – you know what you have to do."

'She nodded.

'"Good."

'The first stroke caught her by surprise. She hadn't expected him to start so quickly – or for it to be so painful. She gulped back the tears. "One. Thank you, Mr Ellis."

'"That's good," he said softly, caressing her exposed buttocks.

'The second one landed on the opposite buttock, in exactly the same place. Jake Ellis was a master of the game, she thought. "Two. Thank you, Mr Ellis."

'By the time they got to twelve, her buttocks felt as though they were on fire. Each stroke had been precisely measured, so that none had overlapped, yet every inch of skin on her buttocks had been covered by the sharp sting of the ruler. The remaining six were applied to her upper thighs. She almost sobbed, but managed to keep her voice steady and counted each one, thanking him afterwards.

'"Do you think you've learnt your lesson now, Miss Thornley?"

'She nodded, not trusting her voice – and not sure if he would count her punishment as the end of his prohibition on speaking without his permission.

'"Good." He caressed her stinging buttocks, the coolness of his hand giving relief to her burning skin. "I hope I've taught you some manners."

'Again she nodded. He laughed softly. "You may speak, Alicia."

'She straightened up, and he coughed. "I did not give you permission to move."

'Miserably, she bent over again. Her bottom stung, yet at the same time she was conscious of a subtle pleasure spreading over her skin. Her sex was decidedly wet, and she was sure he could smell her arousal; the musky scent was so strong.

'He was still caressing her buttocks. His hand drifted between her thighs, and she gave a small moan of pleasure as she felt his finger sliding between her moist and puffy labia. She jerked as he reached her clitoris; the little knot of nerves spasmed sharply, reacting to his touch.

'"Well, well," he said softly. "I think you've just learnt another lesson: after pain, comes pleasure. There's a very fine line between the two, Alicia."

'She didn't trust herself to speak. Her legs felt like jelly and the warmth in her backside had spread to her sex. A different kind of warmth, this time: the deep, intense warmth of arousal.

'"So what should we do about it?"

'"I... I don't know."

'He pushed one finger against the entrance of her sex. It slid in easily and her muscles tightened involuntarily around the invading digit. He chuckled. "No? I think you do. At least, your body does. Why don't you tell me, Alicia? Tell me what you'd like me to do." His voice had changed; there was still that commanding note, but the timbre was huskier, as though he, too, were aroused.

'Alicia could imagine the sight she presented. How lewd she must look with her skirt and petticoat hitched up to her waist and her knickers at her knees, and her upper thighs and the white globes of her buttocks striped with red from his ruler.

'"Tell me, Alicia."

'Her throat was dry. She could barely force the words out. "I... I want you to touch me."

'"Not good enough."

'Her cheeks heated, the blush matching the fiery stripes on her buttocks. "What do you want me to say?" she fenced.

"'Just tell me what you want." He continued teasing her clitoris with his thumb, while his finger slid slowly in and out of her wet sex.

"'I... I can't."

"'Would you like me to spank you again? This time using my hand? I could gag you with your knickers," he mused, "so you wouldn't have to worry about crying out."

"'No!"

"'Then tell me what you want," he repeated, still working her sex.

"'I... I want you to make me come. Please," she added, mindful of his earlier insistence on politeness.

"'How?"

'Was her humiliation never going to end? He knew what she wanted. They both knew it. Why did he have to make her tell him?

"'How?" he repeated.

'She didn't dare prevaricate. "I... I want you to touch me. Finger my sex. Put your cock in me."

"'So many words, when three would do. Four, if you're being polite."

'She swallowed, knowing what he wanted to hear. Knowing he wanted the ultimate obscenity from the prim-and-proper deputy librarian. She hated the coarseness of the words but, at the same time, she silently acknowledged their power. "Fuck my cunt. Please."

"'That's better. You only had to say."

'He withdrew his finger and she heard the rasp of his zip. Then she felt the tip of his cock slide down her quim, lubricating the tip with her juices. Then there was a slight pressure on the entrance of her sex and, at last, he eased his length into her. She remained bent over with her eyes closed, loving the feel of it as he set up a slow and deep rhythm, pushing into her to the hilt, and then withdrawing until he was almost out of her.

'Involuntarily, she began to rock back and forth, her movements increasing the pace and the friction of his thrusts. He grasped her hips, urging her on; she winced as the heels of his hands touched her hard-earnt stripes, but then relaxed again as he tilted his pelvis, changing the angle of his penetration to give her maximum pleasure. She could feel his lower belly pushing against her buttocks as he penetrated her fully, but the pain was eclipsed by the pleasure he was giving her.

'She bit her lip to stop herself crying out. Somehow he realised, and murmured gently that she need not be silent.

'Part of her was hideously embarrassed. Anyone could hear her, then walk into his office and see what was happening. His secretary, another member of staff – and it would be obvious what had happened just before, from her reddened buttocks. But as her pleasure grew she stopped caring. It didn't matter. The only thing that mattered was the way he was pleasuring her, the way he'd quickened his rhythm to short sharp thrusts that drove her way over the edge.

'As she felt the beginnings of orgasm she let out a low moan. Her sex began to ripple around his cock, the movements growing harder and fiercer as she reached her climax. She cried out his name at the height of her pleasure – but he didn't stop. He continued thrusting, taking her to a higher peak. She was almost sobbing with pleasure by the time he came, his cock throbbing deep inside her.

'He remained where he was until the aftershocks of her orgasm had died down. Then he withdrew and dropped to his knees behind her, cleaning her sex of his emission with his tongue. The realisation of what he was doing made her climax again: she'd never met a man who was relaxed enough with his own sexuality to take such care of her.

'Finally, he pulled up her knickers, restored order to her petticoat and skirt, and allowed her to straighten up. He spun her round to face him. "So, Alicia. Now you know what I mean by good manners."

'She smiled, acknowledging the sensual glint in his eye. "Yes."

'"And you know what my rules are – and what happens if you break them."

'Her smile broadened. "Oh yes."

'"And you'll abide by them in future?"

'"Of course." Though they both knew that Alicia wouldn't. She'd continue to collect fines in her way – and let Jake collect his from her later...'

Simon closed the book and looked at Sarah.

She swallowed hard. She knew the story had been Marc's choice – and that it had been very deliberate. So what was he trying to tell her? That he was going to discipline her? That he was going to spank her as Jake had spanked Alicia? But that was crazy. Jake, in the story, had been Alicia's boss. She was Marc's boss. So did he mean he wanted her to discipline him?

She couldn't see herself in the role of dominatrix. Yes, she was tough in the office – but she couldn't imagine being dressed in impossibly high black leather thigh boots, cracking a whip over Marc's naked buttocks. No. If anything, she could imagine herself more in Alicia's role, bent over his desk, with her skirt round her waist and her buttocks bared for him. Or, more likely, over her own desk, in the privacy of her office. Mark had taken the open-door policy one step further, and his desk was right in the middle of the team. She didn't want an audience for that kind of game... or did she?

Her nipples hardened at the thought, and she flushed. What had he done to her? Before she'd met Marc she'd never thought about this kind of thing. But since she'd been in his cottage she'd had the most obscene fantasies. Men masturbating over her body. Being spanked. Being taken by several men at once. Having an audience witness her as she climaxed, completely out of control. What the hell was going on?

'So, Sarah. What do you have to tell me?' Marc asked, his voice soft.

'I...' She licked her lower lip. 'Nothing.'

'The story turned you on, didn't it?'

'No.'

'Liar.' His voice was still soft, and there was a mingled note of exasperation and admiration in it. 'Your nipples are hard, Sarah. Hard and rosy, as if they're aching to be touched or kissed.' He walked round to the foot of the bed. 'And your sex is glistening, Sarah. Your labia are swollen. You're aroused – and you can't do a thing about it. If Simon and I walked out of this room now you'd be virtually screaming with frustration. Just like you where when I walked out a few minutes before. We can ease all that, Sarah. We can touch you and kiss you and fill the empty spaces. Ease the ache. All you have to do is tell me.'

She knew exactly what he was talking about. It had become a battle of wills between them, and she was determined to win. 'No way.'

'If that's what you want.' He shrugged. 'I did say I wouldn't lay a finger on you, until you begged me to.'

'I won't beg you.'

He smiled. 'But then again, there's always a solution to every problem, if you think hard enough.'

Her eyes widened. What was he going to do? Command his friend to touch her in his stead, direct his every move? The worst thing was, she acknowledged silently, if he did she wouldn't be able to protest – and she wouldn't want to, either. Marc's friend was attractive, in a more conventional way. He didn't have that faint air of vulnerability about him, his brown eyes were filled with mischief and his mouth was well-shaped. No doubt his cock—

Sarah flushed at the thought. Christ. She didn't do this kind of thing. She'd never been a crotch-watcher. She'd just concentrated on her career. And now she was turning into some kind of nymphomaniac. She didn't even know the man's full name, and here she was fantasising about what it would be like for him to touch her intimately, to slide his cock into her.

She'd been so caught up in her thoughts that she hadn't noticed Marc opening the drawer of the bedside cabinet and extracting something – until she felt the mattress give slightly and turned to look at him. He was kneeling between her thighs, and the smile on his face set alarm bells ringing.

'I said I wouldn't lay a finger on you. I didn't make any promises about anything else.'

She craned her neck, trying desperately to see what he was holding, but she couldn't see. She scowled at him. 'What are you going to do?'

'Simply this,' he said, brushing her labia.

She suddenly realised what he was holding. Some kind of feather – like a quill pen, or something similar. She shivered. 'You bastard.'

'Methinks the lady doth protest too much,' he said, obviously enjoying himself. 'Because your sex certainly likes what I'm doing.'

The way he was brushing her, she was opening like a flower to him, her sex swelling and pulsing in rhythm with each stroke. He continued to brush her, using light yet firm strokes. He teased her clitoris, brushing rapidly across the little nub until it had uncowled and Sarah's jaw was clenched in an effort not to moan with pleasure.

'Definitely turned on,' he observed. 'My beautiful quill pen's damp from you, Sarah. Every time I use it, after this, I'll be able to smell your arousal. You've soaked the feather with the most aromatic nectar.'

She scowled at him, and he grinned. 'Sarah. Don't lie to me – or yourself. You're enjoying it. Otherwise your sex wouldn't be all soft and wet and pouting at me, would it?'

She flushed deeply. Did he have to be so explicit in front of his friend? She risked a glance at Simon. The bulge at his crotch showed that he was turned on by the tableau he was watching – and maybe by the story he'd read her, too. So was Marc going to give him free rein with her? Would Simon take over when Marc had finished teasing her? Would he strip, kneel between her thighs and slide his cock into her sex – or would he kneel astride her and feed the thick hard shaft between her lips?

The combination of her thoughts and Marc's ministrations with the quill pen were enough to tip her over the edge. She shuddered, her quim rippling and flexing against the feather, and Marc laughed softly. 'Sarah. Beautiful Sarah.' He brushed the feather across her lips, coating them in her juices. 'Tell me. Tell me your true nature. That you like what I'm doing to you – that you like me making the decisions for you. Tell me Sarah.'

Although she was still in the aftermath of climax, she had enough strength of mind to shake her head. 'No.'

'So you're still insisting on your regime in the office? Even though it's going to halve productivity and make the place hell to work in?'

'Make it less of a tip, you mean…' she sighed, 'and

'more efficient.'

'Well. You have a long way to go yet.'

'What do you mean?'

He didn't answer; he merely climbed off the bed, threw the feather back into a drawer, and ushered his friend out of the room.

Sarah watched the door close, a mixture of fury and despair welling within her. Why did he have to be so bloody unreasonable?

Chapter Nine

Sarah was left alone for what seemed like hours. She lay there, occasionally tugging at her bonds in the faint hope that she'd find a weak point in the cuffs, and thinking about what had happened. She was furious with Marc for leaving her tied up and being so bloody stubborn. But then again, she was being just as recalcitrant, refusing to give him a chance to do things his way.

She still found it hard to believe what he'd just done. He'd persuaded one of his friends to read her an incredibly lewd story, with characters in a work situation so close to hers and Marc's, and then brought her to orgasm with a quill feather. And then he'd left her to think things through!

She sighed. She was growing tired of being kept prisoner like this. She was almost tempted to give in, to tell him what he wanted. It was true, after all. She'd discovered, during her sojourn in his cottage, that she was indeed a submissive – that fantasising about being dominated sexually turned her on in a big way. On the other hand, she didn't feel like giving Marc the satisfaction of knowing he was right, and she was enjoying their battle of wills, seeing how far she could push him.

Had she reached his limits now?

She was still wondering when the door opened. She turned her head automatically to face the door, expecting to see Marc and maybe his friend Simon. Colour drained from her face when she saw who was actually with Marc.

Amanda Keyes, one of his team leaders.

Sarah was speechless with shock. How the hell could

Marc do this to her? Humiliate her in front of one of *his* subordinates? And Amanda was one of the worst people he could have chosen. Sarah was well aware that most of the men in their company fancied Amanda; she'd often overheard snatches of conversation about Amanda's voluptuous figure, the men sharing their fantasies about what it would be like to go to bed with her. The brunette was vivacious and friendly, always willing to help organise a departmental night out, and she was good at her job. She was always courteous to Sarah, but Sarah suspected that Amanda thought her a frigid bitch. Sarah was just a tiny bit jealous of the brunette, of her popularity and her ease with her sexuality.

You bloody, bloody bastard, Dubois, she thought angrily. Turning the mental thumbscrews another notch. Well, I'm not giving in to you now. I'll fight you all the way.

'Hello, Sarah. Had a chance to think things through yet?'

'How many other people know about what you're doing to me?' Sarah spat furiously.

He spread his hands. 'That's for me to know, and you to guess.'

'You – you...' She shook her head, too angry to get the words out. Was he intent on making her a laughing-stock in the office?

'If you want me to let you go, you know what you have to do. It's a simple choice.' He paused, waiting for her response; when she said nothing he shrugged. 'You know Mandy, don't you?'

A muscle tightened in Sarah's jaw. 'Yes.'

'Good. I won't bother with formal introductions then.' He walked over to the CD player and changed the disc. He fiddled with the controls for a moment, as if programming a selection of tracks, then pressed the 'play' button. The first notes of a George Michael ballad flooded into the room. He returned to Amanda, holding out his arms, and they began to dance.

Hadn't he said he preferred classical music? she mused. Or maybe this was Amanda's choice. Maybe he was humouring the woman – just as he would have humoured Sarah, if she'd been willing to play on his terms.

Sarah turned her face away, not wanting to watch them smooch together; but she couldn't help seeing their reflections in the cheval mirror which stood against the wall. She felt insanely jealous, watching Marc kiss the brunette – yet at the same time she was annoyed with herself for feeling jealous. It wasn't as if she and Marc were married, or even going out with each other. It was none of his business who he took as a lover.

Though hadn't he said it was a personal rule about never sleeping with a colleague? Either he'd been lying to her, or she'd pushed him so far he was starting to break all his own rules. If it were the latter... just how far would he go? And how far would he try to push her?

He was already loosening Amanda's hair from the silk scarf she'd used to tie it back. Amanda's dark curls tumbled over her shoulders; she looked like a model from a Rossetti painting, with that glorious hair, dark soulful eyes, and her full mouth. No wonder all the men in the office fancied her. Just seeing her hair like that would make them fantasise about her wrapping her hair round their cocks – and then following up with her mouth.

Marc and Amanda continued to dance, their hands stroking each other through their clothes; it was obvious what was going to happen next. Too obvious. Almost as Sarah thought it they began to undo each other's clothes. She was unable not to watch them – she'd already discovered that closing her eyes wasn't enough, as she could hear them and her imagination was more than willing to supply pictures to match the soundtrack. But she wouldn't suffer the humiliation of letting them know that she was watching; she kept her head turned away, and watched them in the mirror.

But it was as if Marc had guessed – or had placed the mirror there for that very purpose – because he made sure they were always in her view. She could see him unbuttoning Amanda's shirt, pushing the material away from the other woman's shoulders and letting it drop to the floor. Then he unclasped her navy lace bra, letting her breasts spill into his hands, squeezing them and caressing them and circling the areolae with his thumbs. Just as he'd done to Sarah...

She swallowed as she felt the familiar throb in her sex. God, no. This was so unfair. She couldn't be turned on by watching what he was doing to another woman. She couldn't be. No.

Yet, as Marc dropped to his knees before Amanda and undid her skirt, easing it down over her hips, Sarah's quim started to moisten again. She could imagine him doing that to her. Easing her clothes down, so very slowly, caressing every inch of skin he revealed with his lips and his fingers. Just as he was doing to Amanda: stroking her skin, cherishing her. A prelude to the ultimate intimacy.

Amanda stepped out of the skirt, kicking it to one side, and widened her stance, placing her hands on her hips. She was wearing lace-topped hold-up stockings, with matching lacy knickers. The navy lace was in sharp contrast to her creamy skin; despite herself, Sarah couldn't help staring at the other woman in the mirror, thinking how good she looked. How firm her breasts were, soft and round, tipped with dark rosy nipples. She knew her own figure was just as voluptuous, but she couldn't help feeling another surge of jealousy – that Marc was making love to Amanda, not to her.

She knew that all she had to do was speak, whisper a few words, and he'd stop. Yet she couldn't bring herself to do it. She didn't want to lose. And, an insidious voice in her head murmured, she was excited by what was going on next to her. She shook herself. Of course she wasn't. She wasn't a voyeuse... was she?

Slowly, very slowly, Marc slid one finger under the edge of Amanda's knickers. He pulled the material to one side and she widened the gap between her thighs, giving him access. He bent his head, and Sarah had to bite her lower lip hard to stop herself gasping aloud. She could remember what it had felt like when Marc had used his tongue on her own sex; he was extremely skilled, and it had felt *so* good, the way he'd teased her clitoris and explored her with his mouth. Just as he was doing to Amanda; from the expression of bliss on the other woman's face, and the way Amanda was touching her own breasts, tipping her head back in abandon, Sarah could tell his mouth was working its familiar magic.

She continued watching them in the mirror. Marc's hands cupped Amanda's buttocks, squeezing them and stroking them. He pulled her closer as his mouth worked faster on her sex, bringing her nearer and nearer to a climax. Amanda's breathing grew faster and shallower. Suddenly she cried out, a harsh guttural sound so unlike her normal voice. Even without that, Sarah knew that the other woman had come: there was an obvious rosy mottling that spread over her neck and breasts.

Marc stood up and turned to face the mirror. She could see his lips glistening from Amanda's juices. He gave her a broad wink, and her skin heated. Bastard. He knew exactly what he was doing. He'd planned the whole thing with complete precision.

He helped Amanda remove the rest of his own clothing. His cock reared, hard and heavy, from the thatch of hair at his groin. Sarah swallowed hard. Hadn't he embarrassed and humiliated her enough? Surely he wasn't going to...

But he was. Gently, he turned Amanda so she faced the bedside cabinet, and guided her forward until she grasped the edge of the cabinet for balance. Then he stood behind her, stroking her buttocks. He adjusted her position slightly, then curled his fingers round his shaft, fitted the tip of his cock to her sex, and eased in.

Sarah could only see his body and the curve of Amanda's buttocks in the mirror, but it was more than enough. She stared in horrified fascination as Marc began to move, pushing smoothly in and out. His shaft glistened in the light, betraying just how excited Amanda was. Sarah's sex gave an answering throb. She remembered what it felt like to have Marc inside her. Now she was actually watching him make love and he looked as good as he had felt.

Again she bit her lip to stop herself crying out. She was aware that she was aroused – and that it would have been obvious to the man and woman next to her, if they'd cared to look – and she was furious with herself. She squeezed her eyes tightly shut. He couldn't do any more to her.

She was wrong.

'How does it feel, Mandy?'

'Good. Very good.' Amanda's voice had dropped a couple of tones, and sounded husky with excitement. 'I love the way you're filling me. I've fantasised about this a lot, at work.'

'Have you now?' His voice was amused and sexy at the same time.

'Mm. I've wanted you to do this to me over my desk. I've wanted you to order me to pull my skirt up and bend over my desk, and for you to rip my knickers off, displaying my sex for you. And I wouldn't have cared who watched us.'

'Like Sarah's watching us now.'

'Yes. Sarah.'

Sarah swallowed hard. What was he playing at? What was *she* playing at? Had this all been arranged beforehand, or were they ad-libbing?

'You've wanted Sarah for a long time, haven't you Marc?'

'Yes,' he admitted. 'And this is just what I've wanted to do to her. Slide my cock into her warm sweet depths, feel her sex rippling round me and gripping my cock as she comes.'

'Then why not do it? She's ready for you. Look at her. See how hard her nipples are. They must hurt. I think she'd like you to use your mouth on her, suck her nipples and ease the ache. I think she'd like you to touch her breasts, stroke her skin and squeeze those beautiful soft globes.'

'I promised not to touch her.'

Amanda laughed quietly. 'Then you'll have to do it to me instead, won't you? A surrogate Sarah.'

'Not in this position,' he teased. 'But later, yes. I'll lick your breasts and suck your nipples. I'll use my teeth, just hard enough to bring you pleasure. And then I'll go back to work on your warm sweet sex. I'll push my tongue into you as deeply as I can, tasting the way your body changes as you grow more aroused, feeling your nectar flood into my mouth as you come, all vanilla and nutmeg and honey.'

Sarah quivered. He was making love to Amanda with his body – but he was making love to her with his voice. What he said he was going to do with Amanda was just what he wanted to do to her.

'Sounds good,' Amanda purred. 'Though there are three

of us in this room.'

'True,' he acknowledged.

Sarah's eyes widened. What did Amanda mean by that?

'Can you imagine,' Marc continued, 'what it would be like if the three of us were on that bed?'

'With Sarah untied, of course. I'd like her to be able to use her hands. Ohhh.' Amanda's gasp of pleasure was caused by Marc reaching one hand round to cup her mons; his fingers strayed to rub her clitoris, matching the rhythm of his thrusts into her.

'I don't think she'd like that very much,' Marc mused. 'I think she's a hundred per cent straight.'

'Indeed?' Amanda's voice was filled with disbelief.

'So she claims.'

'Hm. We'll have to see about that. Oh. Oh, yes. *Yesss*.' Amanda moaned as Marc continued to push into her, the short sharp strokes pushing her against the cabinet and towards the verge of another climax.

'So what would it be like do you think? If the three of us were on that bed?' he persisted.

'Mm. We could do a lot of things,' Amanda said.

'Such as?'

'You could be taking me, just like this. And I'd be kneeling between her legs, my palms flat against her inner thighs and my mouth working on her sex, while she touched her breasts and played with her nipples.'

'Or I could be taking her, and she could be tonguing you while you played with your breasts.' Marc said.

Although this latest development was unbelievably bizarre, Sarah's breasts tingled at the thought. She could imagine it all too easily; it horrified her and excited her in equal amounts.

'Or I could be flat on my back with your gorgeous cock buried inside me, and she'd be sitting on my face, letting me lick her while you kissed her and fondled her breasts.'

'Or vice versa,' he pointed out. 'Wouldn't you like to feel her using her mouth on you?'

'Oh yes,' Amanda whispered sexily. 'And we could do it right now. She's in the perfect position, spread out on the bed like that. I could climb over her, straddle her and lower my sex to her mouth, let her lick your seed from me. Let it drip from my sex onto her lips – do you think she'd like that?'

'I think you would,' Marc teased. 'You'd like to watch me fucking her, wouldn't you? You'd like to watch my cock sliding in and out of her – and then have her kneel over your mouth while her sex was still full of my come, letting it drip from her sex into your open mouth. And then you'd take away the tartness, using your tongue on her until her own honey dripped onto your lips.'

'Mmm. Sounds delightful,' Amanda purred. 'Or you could be lying on the bed, with her kneeling between your thighs to suck your cock, while I knelt behind her to use my mouth on her sex. We'd change places halfway through.'

'Or we could make a kind of triangle, with you fellating me, me licking her, and her licking you,' he said. 'So many variations, just from the three of us. We could have hours and hours of fun, stroking and licking and sucking and fucking.'

'Do you think she'd enjoy playing with both of us?' Amanda asked huskily.

'I don't know.'

Sarah's colour deepened. She hated the way they were talking about her as if she wasn't there. It made her feel so worthless, so useless. And yet, at the same time, she could picture exactly what they were talking about so graphically. Their three bodies entwined in pleasure, licking and lapping and sucking and thrusting. It was way, way beyond anything she'd ever done, and it both scared and thrilled her.

'We could ask her,' Amanda said.

'There's no point, Mandy. She'll either refuse to answer, or say no. Even if she means yes,' Marc said. 'Sarah won't admit to her true nature.'

'Pity. I thought she was a tight-arsed cow at first – I've never met anyone so insistent on a clear-desk policy,' Amanda said. 'Usually it's a sign of an anal retentive. But the more I think about it, the more I'm sure it's just a front. That really she's incredibly wild, and she only keeps herself on a tight rein because she knows it, and she's scared to let herself go too far. That's why she never goes on departmental outings: because she doesn't trust herself to keep up the act outside the office.'

'That's what I think too.'

She groaned again as Marc shifted their positions slightly, changing the angle of his penetration. 'Oh yes. That's *so* good, Marc. *So* good. I love it when you push in so deeply, filling me completely.'

'You feel pretty good too. Like warm, wet velvet, wrapped around my cock,' he told her. 'And your skin's so soft.'

Sarah closed her eyes in misery. Why were they subjecting her to this? Why wouldn't Marc just let her go? Why did he have to humiliate her in front of other people? And yet there was a dark excitement deep inside her. What he was doing to her – yes, it was cruel. But she responded to it. Her sex flowered and her nipples tightened and ripples of excitement ran down her spine at the thought.

It was as if he'd tapped into her deepest, most secret dreams – things she'd never even admitted to herself –

and was helping her to live every one of them. If someone had offered to tie her to the bed she would have resisted. But the way he'd talked her into it, and then insisted on keeping her like that, thrilled her.

'Oh. Oh yes. Deeper. Please, please, do it harder. Yes,' Amanda moaned. Sarah didn't have to open her eyes to know that Amanda's forehead was resting on her hands, and she was twisting her head form side to side in an agony of pleasure as Marc continued to piston in and out of her.

'And here? Do you like being touched here, Mandy?'

Despite herself, Sarah opened her eyes to see what he was doing; she still watched them in the mirror, not wanting to admit openly to him that she wanted to see them. He had moistened his thumb and was rubbing the soft pad against the furrow of Amanda's buttocks, pressing down on the rosy puckered hole of her anus.

Amanda's answer was a husky groan.

'Do you want to take it further Mandy? Do you want to go all the way, and then some?'

'Uhhh,' was the brunette's breathless reply.

'Sure?'

'Just do it. Please. *Do* it.' The words were almost ripped from her.

Slowly, Marc eased out of her, then bent forward to nuzzle her buttocks, kissing and licking the creamy globes. Sarah watched in guilty fascination. She saw the tip of his tongue press against the rosy pucker, and Amanda tilted her bottom, giving him easier access. It was just what he'd done to her, that first night, and she could still remember how it had felt: shocking and unbearably exciting at the same time.

Surely he wasn't going to go all the way? Surely it was just a tease? His cock was so big, there was no way a woman could accommodate him in such a tiny and private opening. Her quim flexed in anticipation. If her hands had been free, Sarah knew they would have been lodged firmly between her legs, one rubbing fiercely at her clitoris, and the fingers of her other jammed into her pulsing channel. All four fingers: nothing less would have satisfied her. Although, at the same time, she knew that just one touch would have been enough to make her climax; she was so turned on by what she was watching.

Slowly, infinitely slowly, Marc straightened up. His cock still glistened from Amanda's juices. Sarah swallowed hard as she saw him reach into a drawer and take out a small foil packet. He really was going to do it. He was going to take Amanda up the arse. Even the crude words sent a guilty thrill through her, making her body ache to be filled.

He opened the foil packet, deftly unrolling the condom onto his cock. The rubber was thin and fine, so Sarah could still see every vein and ridge on his shaft, every delicate shading and deepening of colour. The tip of his cock was outlined clearly, straining against the rubber. Then he curled his fingers round the shaft and pressed the tip very gently to Amanda's forbidden entrance. Gently, he eased forward, sliding in millimetre by millimetre and pausing to let Amanda's body grow used to the feeling of his cock stretching her forbidden passage. Sarah licked her dry lips as she saw the tip of his cock disappear fully. Then he fed the shaft into Amanda, still very slowly, until he was embedded up to the hilt.

What would it feel like, to have him bugger her like that? It was something Sarah had never experienced – had never wanted to experience – but now she watched the way he made love with Amanda, taking her further and further, slowly and skilfully, she wanted to know. She wanted to know how it would feel to have him thrust powerfully into her. And she wanted to watch him do it, in the mirror, seeing his cock disappear into her so lewdly.

She closed her eyes again. What had he done to her? She'd fantasised sexually – like most women she knew did – but her fantasies had always been limited to the more common positions and oral sex, nothing kinkier than maybe being blindfolded. This was way, way beyond anything she'd ever dreamt about. The worst thing was, she'd discovered that her limits weren't where she thought they were. Now she wasn't sure just how far she'd go. Or whether Marc could match her.

'You feel so good, Mandy.' Marc's voice interrupted her thoughts. 'So tight and hot. It's unbelievable.'

Sarah opened her eyes; he had begun to move, keeping the strokes long and very slow. Amanda's hand was working frantically between her legs. It was the most obscene thing she had ever seen in her life – and she'd never been so turned on. Her sex felt wet and empty. She longed for him to withdraw from Amanda and push into her own sex, fill her and thrust hard, rubbing her clitoris and squeezing her nipples, until her body splintered into climax. Or even for them to carry out their earlier suggestion, with him continuing to push into Amanda's sex and Amanda tonguing her sex, pleasuring her to the limit while she watched them.

By the time Amanda cried out in climax, and Marc gave an answering cry, Sarah was squirming on the bed, desperate to squeeze her thighs together. The cruel, cruel bastard; making her watch something like that, yet be unable to obtain the slightest bit of relief. She hated him. And yet she wanted him, too, she acknowledged as she continued to watch the tableau in the mirror. Marc was kissing his way down Amanda's spine as he slowly and gently withdrew from her. Then he spun her round to kiss her.

'Thank you,' he whispered softly. 'That was good.'

'For me, too,' she whispered back, returning the kiss and sliding her hands round his neck.

For a moment, Sarah thought Marc was going to lift Amanda up and penetrate her again, make love to her face-to-face while they were standing. But instead, he hugged her and then gently disentangled himself from her arms. He disposed of the condom in a tissue, then took her hand and led her to the foot of the bed.

'What do you think?' he asked.

Sarah closed her eyes, embarrassed. She should have known he'd do this: bring attention to her arousal.

'I think,' Amanda said huskily, 'that she's turned on. Look how wet she is. You can see it. Her whole sex is glistening and swollen. She watched what you were doing to me – or maybe she kept her eyes closed and guessed – and pretended you were doing it to her. Except, because she can't touch herself, she hasn't had the same release that I have. She hasn't felt her sex contracting hard, or your cock throbbing inside her, the warm jets of your semen filling her.'

'So what should we do about it?'

Amanda smiled. 'I reckon you should have a shower – or maybe we should have one together. Afterwards, you can come back and give her what she needs.'

'There's only one flaw in that,' he said thoughtfully.

'What's that?'

'I promised not to lay a finger on her, until she asks me to. She won't ask.'

'We could make her.'

Marc shook his head. 'I need her consent. I won't force her to do anything she's not comfortable with.'

'You forced her to watch us,' Amanda pointed out.

'Actually, no. I gave her the choice: either she could

watch us, or she could close her eyes.'

Amanda whistled in admiration. 'I'll make sure I never get on the wrong side of you. You're a subtle bastard, Dubois.'

'Thank you.' He acknowledged the compliment. 'The question remains: what are we going to do with Sarah, here?'

Sarah fought to keep her face impassive. She hated the way they were talking about her as if she were elsewhere. But she wasn't going to let them see how much it riled her. If this was going to be a test of wills, she'd win. She had the strength, she was sure.

'Well,' Amanda said slowly, 'it's cruel to keep her here like this.'

Sarah opened her eyes in shock. Amanda was on her side?

Amanda's next words swiftly disabused her of that idea. 'Tied up is one thing: but tied up and obviously in need of a climax is quite another.'

'I can't touch her.'

'But I didn't make any promises,' Amanda said.

Marc grinned. 'And you say *I'm* subtle? I wish I'd thought of that myself.'

'Let's go have that shower,' Amanda said.

Sarah watched in disbelief as the door closed behind them. No. Surely Amanda wasn't suggesting that *she* should give Sarah the climax she needed? The idea repelled her. She'd *never* wanted another woman to touch her in a sexual way. She'd looked on women she'd known as friends or enemies, not as potential sexual partners. She'd already told Marc she was a hundred per cent hetero. Surely he would talk Amanda out of the idea?

There was one way, she knew, to stop it. But she couldn't bring herself to give in that easily. Very well, if he was

142

going to let Amanda touch her, she'd submit to that – but she wasn't going to give in.

Chapter Ten

Some time later – time in which Sarah had imagined Amanda and Marc making love in the shower, and had been consumed by a mixture of anger and jealousy and longing – they returned.

'So, Sarah – is there anything you want to say to me?' Marc asked.

She shook her head.

He smiled at Amanda. 'Looks like she's all yours, sweetheart,' he said, grabbing a chair and placing it beside the bed. He sat down, linked his hands behind his head, and leant back to watch them, relaxing. He was still naked – as was Amanda – and his skin was still damp from the shower. His dark hair was damp, too, and droplets of water sparkled in it like diamonds. They'd taken their time about it; no doubt they'd made love under the running water, and Marc had soaped Amanda's body, touching her breasts and her belly and her buttocks and her sex. Just the way that Sarah wanted him to touch her – yet couldn't allow herself to say so. Not in the terms he wanted.

'Hello, Sarah.' Amanda sat next to her on the bed. 'I'm sorry about all this.'

'You're – you're sorry?'

'Mm.' Amanda nodded. 'It wasn't fair of us, was it? To make you watch us making love like that.'

'I...' Sarah's throat dried. She stared suspiciously at Amanda. She had a nasty feeling that as well as screwing in the shower, Marc and Amanda had had a long conversation, and Marc had told her exactly what he wanted her to do.

'It must have been awful,' Amanda said sympathetically. She brushed Sarah's cheeks with the backs of her fingers. 'Such torture. Seeing and hearing everything, yet not being able to move. Feeling your sex grow warm and wet, yet not being able to do anything about it. Feeling your nipples harden, yet not being able to touch them. Poor, poor Sarah.' Her fingers stroked over Sarah's throat. 'And we've kept you waiting, too. Left you here, frustrated and wanting release. And you do want release, don't you?' The question was punctuated by Amanda gently touching Sarah's nipples, tracing the areolae with her fingertips and then rolling the rosy peaks between her thumb and forefinger. 'Tell me, Sarah.'

Sarah shook her head mutely.

'Hm.' Amanda deliberately misinterpreted the gesture as a refusal to speak, rather than a denial of Sarah's need for release. 'Well, they do say that silence indicates consent. I haven't made the same promise as Marc; not to touch you until you ask him to. Beg him to, rather. And I can't leave you here like this, aching and empty and unsatisfied. It just isn't fair.' Slowly, she lowered her head, so that the ends of her hair brushed Sarah's skin.

The light contact sent a thrill through Sarah; at the same time, she was furious. Furious that Amanda could take such liberties with her – and that her body was responding.

'If I were in your position,' Amanda said, 'this is what I'd need.' She lowered her head to Sarah's right breast, making her tongue into a hard point and flicking it over Sarah's nipple. Then she opened her mouth over the hard peak of flesh, sucking gently on it, pressing her tongue against it. She cupped Sarah's breast, kneading it gently as she sucked, then drew back slightly and blew lightly on the wet flesh, making Sarah shiver.

'It feels good, doesn't it? I know you're imagining Marc doing this instead – and yes, I'm privileged enough to know, now, how good he is – but this is the next best thing. Just imagine I'm Marc: I'm his substitute, really. You won't tell him how much you want him to touch you and taste you and fill you – but I can do it all for you. My body works the same way yours does; I like being stroked and sucked and screwed, exactly the same way you do.' Amanda's voice took on a hypnotic quality. 'And it doesn't really matter who does it, Sarah. You can pretend I'm Marc – or you can let yourself be really naughty and know you're breaking another rule. That you're enjoying another woman touching your body so intimately, with her hands and her lips and her tongue. Let yourself go, Sarah. Give yourself up to pleasure.'

Sarah closed her eyes, letting the tension flow from her body. Amanda didn't break the spell by crowing in triumph, but continued to caress Sarah's breasts, squeezing them gently. She moved again, kissing her way down over Sarah's abdomen. Sarah swallowed hard, knowing just where Amanda was heading. She wanted it and was afraid of it, all at once.

Then she remembered that Marc was sitting there, watching them. It was an age-old male fantasy, she knew, watching two women making love. She was damned if she was going to give him the satisfaction of responding, of putting on a good show for him. Yes, she might submit to what Amanda was doing, but she wasn't going to react. She wasn't going to come. She would simply be passive and submit to whatever Amanda did, but she wouldn't react.

Amanda shifted to kneel between Sarah's thighs. Sarah refused to open her eyes, afraid that if she watched what Amanda was doing to her, she might find it all too arousing.

The very thought of the brunette's dark hair spread over her thighs as she bent to her quim was enough to start a wicked pulse beating in Sarah's sex, despite her resolution. Actually watching her do it would surely be too much.

Slowly, Amanda kissed her way along Sarah's thighs, in an almost exact mimicry of the way Marc had done, that first time. Teasing her, making her anticipate what was to come. And then, finally, Sarah felt Amanda's breath warm against her sex. Despite herself, she clenched her hands, tensing herself in readiness for the first contact. Amanda rubbed her face against Sarah's thighs to drive home the fact that it was another woman's soft face between her legs, not a man's stubble-roughened jaw. Sarah's sex gave a guilty throb. And then, so very slowly, Amanda stretched out her tongue, licking the full length of Sarah's quim.

Sarah forced herself to still her sharp intake of breath. No way did she want Marc – or Amanda – to guess how much this was affecting her. Though she had a nasty feeling that the pair of them could tell only too well, from the tense set of her muscles, the hardness of her nipples, and the hot wetness of her sex.

Amanda repeated the action again and again. Each time she pressed down lightly on Sarah's clitoris, then moved away again before Sarah could tilt her hips up. In no time Sarah was shaking and desperate for Mandy to go further; to insert a finger in her aching sex and suck on her throbbing clitoris. But she wasn't going to say so. No way were they going to make her beg. She wouldn't suffer that humiliation.

'How does it feel, Sarah?' Marc asked quietly. 'Do you like being tongued by another woman?'

Sarah said nothing.

'Silly question, really. Of course you do. I remember

147

the way you responded to me, last night. You like your sex being licked, don't you? You like the feel of a tongue pushing into you, and it doesn't matter if it's a man or a woman doing it. If anything, it's probably better for you if a woman does it, because she'll know exactly how you like it: that's how she likes it, herself.'

As if in response to a command, Amanda changed tactics, sliding her hands under Sarah's bottom and tilting her pelvis up slightly, to give her easier access. Then she pushed her tongue against the entrance to Sarah's sex, flicking rapidly, teasing her, before pushing in as deeply as she could.

Sarah bit her lip. This was almost impossible to bear. When would her ordeal be over? Every part of her body screamed out for freedom, wanting to respond to the way Amanda was skilfully working her towards climax – but she couldn't. She couldn't give in. Not now.

'Can you imagine, Sarah? Supposing I'd tied you on your hands and knees instead. That would have been even better, wouldn't it? Mandy and I could both have pleasured you with our mouths. I could have worked on your breasts, while Mandy worked on your sex. Both of us could have licked you, covering your body with kisses. Wouldn't you like that?'

He paused, as if giving her the chance to answer. When she remained silent, he continued. 'Or maybe you'd like more than just the two of us to make love with you. Imagine five mouths, Sarah. One kissing your mouth. One paying attention to each breast, licking the undersides in the way you like, then sucking your sensitive nipples. One working on your clitoris and your vagina, alternating between the two – and one working in a forbidden place. Because it turned you on when I licked your pretty little rosebud, didn't it? It made you feel delightfully wicked. It made you start fantasising about what it would be like to go further – to do what Mandy and I did just now.'

Sarah swallowed. The bastard. He'd got into her mind, somehow.

'Did you fantasise about it while I was taking Mandy? Did you pretend I was doing it to you instead? Did you imagine how it would feel for me to slide my cock into your pretty little arse, to ease all the way in until my belly was resting against your soft buttocks? How deep and dark and scary and exciting it would be, all at the same time, to do such a primeval, forbidden thing?' He chuckled. 'Of course you won't tell me, but your face gives you away, Sarah. You're blushing – but it's not from embarrassment. It's because you want to do it, but you don't want to admit it. Just like you wanted to know how it would feel for another woman to tongue your sex, but you refused to ask Mandy.'

'Go to hell,' Sarah said, through gritted teeth.

'Do you like what Amanda's doing to you, Sarah? Do you like the way she's tonguing you? Do you like the way she's sucking your clitoris?' He sighed. 'Oh, from where I'm sitting, it's such a pretty sight. If only you weren't such a coward, Sarah, you could open your eyes and see it for yourself.'

Coward? Who the hell did he think he was calling a coward? But she knew it was simply tactics, designed to make her open her eyes and look. She wasn't going to fall for that.

'But since you won't look,' he continued, obviously guessing her strategy, 'I'll tell you. You look so good like that, Sarah. You're spread out on the bed, your arms stretched up and your legs spread wide. The black silk is in such sharp contrast to your skin – so similar in texture, soft and warm, yet so different in colour. And the handcuffs: gleaming shiny metal, so hard and bright, linked round your beautiful delicate wrists. Any man who saw you would be instantly erect, and any woman would be wet. You look so desirable, Sarah, lying there captive, with your breasts swollen and aching, your nipples hard and ripe.

'And the way you're tied, your sex is exposed – anyone who looked at you could see how beautiful you are, the soft pale down of your delta and the rich crimson velvet of your quim. Like a deep red rose, rich in scent and pearled with dewy nectar. An angel, even, would be tempted to lust by your sex, Sarah. Who could resist touching or tasting such beauty?

'And now the picture is complete. Amanda's kneeling between your legs, with her buttocks tilted up and her hands cupping your buttocks. Her head's down between your thighs, her mouth working at your sex, and her back curves so beautifully. Her hair's spread over your thighs in soft rippling waves – and although your eyes are closed in denial, it looks more like they're closed in passion. Your lower lip's pouting and inviting, and your nipples look like perfect cones, rosy-tipped and tempting. The way you're tipping your head back among the pillows, it's like you're close to coming.'

Sarah tried desperately not to listen to him. God. He knew exactly the words to use to make her feel even more turned on. The bastard. By the time he'd finished, he'd have her begging to be allowed to tongue Amanda's sex – for Amanda to kneel over her shoulders, lowering her quim to Sarah's mouth, while she continued to lick and suck Sarah's own sex.

The thought made her quiver. She refused to give into it, holding herself taut and tense.

'And that's only from a side view,' Marc continued.

'Now I'm walking round to the foot of the bed. How beautiful you both look. Both with such pale skin, it's hard to tell where one starts and the other finishes. The only difference between you is the colour of your hair.' His voice grew husky. 'I can see how hard and swollen your clitoris is, Sarah, standing up so stiff and proud. Like a tiny cock, almost, begging for attention. I think you'd like Amanda to do that, wouldn't you? To suck it, tease it with her lips and her tongue and her teeth.'

In response, Amanda shifted slightly, fastening her lips round the nub of flesh and sucking. Sarah quivered, feeling her climax begin as a kind of inner sparkling, yet forcing herself to hold off. She couldn't come. Not now.

'And Amanda's sex is so hot and wet, just like yours. A flower unfolding,' Marc said softly. 'I don't know whether I want to bury my cock in her – or whether I should ask her to move, so you can see it for yourself. So you can feel the velvety softness against your lips. So you can taste her sweet musky juices. Would you like that, Sarah? Would you like to lick another woman while she's doing the same to you? Like a living mirror, where you can feel and taste and smell everything she does to you in what you do to her?'

How had he guessed? How had he known what was in her mind? Was he controlling her thoughts in some way? Sarah's attempts to delay her climax were beginning to fail; she could feel her sex starting to pulse and shimmer under Amanda's skilful mouth.

'That's right, Sarah. It feels so good, doesn't it? And her face is so soft, not like a man's. It feels good against your skin, doesn't it? And because she's a woman, she knows exactly what you like – because it's what she likes, too. It's like having someone making love to you, when they can read your mind and guess what you want without you having to tell them. Perfect feminine intuition.' He paused for a moment. 'It makes me hard, watching you, Sarah. I can't help touching myself, too – watching you, and wanting to bury my cock in your warm sweet depths. Or in your mouth. To feel you sucking my cock while Amanda pleasures you so well. And I'd want to come at the same time, to fill your mouth at the same time as you fill Amanda's, flooding her with your nectar so sweet and so rare.'

That final image was too much for her. She cried out, her sex contracting sharply, and she felt the mattress give as Marc sat down next to her, stroking her face. 'Okay?' he asked softly.

'No, I'm not bloody okay,' she snapped breathlessly. 'I'm going to sack the pair of you for misconduct when I get back to the office.'

'Are you now?' Amanda asked, sitting up. There was a strange look on her face, one that made Sarah feel slightly scared and very turned on at the same time. 'Well in that case I'm going to earn my dismissal, and enjoy it.'

Sarah's eyes widened. 'What do you mean?'

Amanda smiled. 'That's for me to know – and you to find out. If you're going to sack me for screwing you, Sarah, then I'm going to make you beg for it first. I'm going to make you admit the truth.'

'I don't know what you mean,' Sarah said stiffly.

'Don't you?' Amanda spread her hands. 'I wonder. Marc. Do I taste like I've just licked an unwilling woman who hasn't climaxed?'

'Come here and I'll tell you.' He held out a hand in invitation. Sarah turned her face away, but she could still see them in the mirror. Marc cupped Amanda's face and kissed her deeply, licking Sarah's juices from Amanda's lips. The kiss went on for a long time, far longer than strictly necessary. When they finally broke it, both of them were breathing more quickly. 'No, you don't,' Marc said. 'You taste like heaven – seashore and vanilla and honey and spice. Like Sarah came over your mouth. And an unwilling woman wouldn't come – isn't that right, Sarah?'

'You bastards. You knew I didn't want you to touch me.'

'Tsk, tsk.' Marc wagged a finger at her. 'If that had been the case, all you had to do was tell us to stop. Or tell me what I want to hear.'

She lifted her chin. 'No way.'

'But because you were silent we had to work on body language. And yours, Sarah, told us you were very, very turned on. So don't lie to us, Sarah. You owe us honesty, at least.'

She couldn't bring herself to answer, contenting herself with a glare.

Marc laughed softly. 'Well, Mandy, they say that silence indicates consent, so I think you've just received permission to do whatever you want with her.'

'Yes...' Amanda walked away from the bed and rummaged in the bag she'd brought with her. Sarah couldn't see what she was doing, as Amanda's back was to her and Marc was standing between them. But from the look on Marc's face, it was something extremely lewd.

When Amanda finally turned round to face her, Sarah gasped. She was wearing a specially designed harness which strapped round her waist and then ran between her legs, before joining the waist-strap again at the back. Between her legs reared an enormous realistic-looking cock. So this was what Amanda had meant.

Part of Sarah was horrified; the other part, the part she normally kept suppressed, leapt with excitement. If Amanda was really going to do what she thought she was, it was way beyond Sarah's previous experience. Just like

153

virtually everything else she'd experienced since arriving at Marc's house.

Amanda approached the bed again. 'Well, Sarah, I think you can guess what I have in mind.' She curled her fingers round the thick shaft and rubbed it, as if she were a man strengthening his erection, and Sarah's quim pulsed with desire.

'I'm going to kneel between your thighs and push this deep into your pretty little cunt,' Amanda told her huskily. 'By the time I've finished you'll have come so many times you'll be begging me not to stop.'

All she had to do was speak. Just a few little words; tell Marc that she was a submissive and that he could do what the hell he liked with his team. If she admitted the truth to herself, she couldn't really have cared less what he did in the office. Not now. But part of her wanted to continue the resistance, to see how far he would go. And how far he would take her.

Amanda climbed on the bed and knelt between Sarah's thighs. 'I'm half-tempted to make you suck it first,' she murmured thoughtfully. 'Yes... I want to see you suck it.'

She moved forward until she sat on Sarah's soft breasts and presented the dildo to her lips.

Sarah shook her head, clamping her lips together. No way was she going to do this. No way.

'Do it, Sarah,' Amanda commanded softly. 'Take it in your mouth and suck it.'

Again, Sarah shook her head.

'Perhaps you need persuading,' Amanda said. 'Perhaps you want me to heat your skin a little first. Would you like me to use a cane on you, Sarah? Or would you like me to spank your pretty little bottom and redden it with my hand? Or maybe you'd like me to work on your breasts. The way your nipples are protruding, they're obviously dying for attention.'

'No!'

At the moment Sarah opened her mouth Amanda pushed forward so the thick dildo slid between Sarah's lips.

'Suck it,' Amanda commanded. 'Suck it.'

Hot shame welled through Sarah. To be in such a position – tied to the bed with another woman wearing a strap-on dildo and forcing her to suck it... Yet her traitorous body revelled in her helplessness. Her sex pooled with the thought of what was going to happen next. And she could still see Amanda, in her mind's eye, fellating Marc, taking that beautiful cock into her mouth.

She sucked.

All the while she pretended she was sucking Marc. And yet the thick dildo didn't taste of him. It didn't have that sharp male tang, the slightly bitter taste of pre-come.

Amanda was thrusting slightly, as if she really were a man wanting to push his cock as deeply as possible down Sarah's throat. But then, at last, she pulled back.

'Good girl,' Amanda said softly. 'Now.' She shifted between Sarah's legs and pressed the tip of the dildo against the entrance to Sarah's sex. 'Doesn't it feel good, Sarah? A nice thick cock, all for you.' She moved her hips to ease the first inch in and began rocking back and forth, very gently, just pushing the fat tip in and out of the narrowest part of Sarah's sex.

Sarah could no longer deny the unbelievable excitement she felt. What Amanda was doing... it was lewd and wicked and wonderful. Feeling a thick cock penetrating her, yet at the same time feeling Amanda's soft and generous breasts brushing her own, the hard tips teasing her own nipples.

'Do you like it, Sarah? Do you like the way I'm penetrating you?' Amanda asked. 'Is it good, being fucked by another woman?' She cupped Sarah's chin with one hand, bringing her forefinger over to brush Sarah's lower lip. 'Though I think Marc's wrong about you. I don't think you're a submissive. I think you're enjoying what I'm doing to you, yes, but you're too stubborn to admit it. And I think you'd like to change places with me. I think you'd like to be the one wearing the cock, with me tied naked and helpless, my sex open to you so you could do whatever you liked to me. I think you'd like to take me hard, until I sobbed your name as I came – and then you could withdraw, push your fingers into me and feel my sex contract round you, feel my juices soaking your fingers and then order me to lick you clean. Or maybe you'd lick them clean yourself. I think you like switching roles, Sarah, to suit your mood – and I think you'd like to take me in exactly the same way I'm taking you.'

Sarah swallowed. 'I...' She couldn't bring herself to say it, but she knew Amanda could sense the sudden pulse of excitement in her quim.

'I'll let you into a little secret, Sarah. It's glorious, the feeling of penetrating your partner.' She smiled. 'Male or female, that is.' Sarah's eyes widened with shock. Was Amanda telling her that she'd used the same implement on a man, pushing the fat tip of the dildo against his anus and easing her way in, thrusting deep inside him? 'And what's even better is being penetrated at the same time.'

'By Marc, you mean?' Sarah just about managed to get the words out: the memory of the way Marc had taken Amanda as she'd bent forward, still sent shock-waves reverberating through her sex.

'In my arse?' Amanda giggled, obviously enjoying herself hugely: she was revelling in the licence to talk as crudely as she liked, in the sure knowledge that the woman beneath her was enjoying it just as much. 'No. I liked what he did to me, and I'd do it again – but I don't need him to do that right now. This little bag of tricks is actually double-ended. It straps on – but I need to slide part of it inside me first. A big, thick black cock, just like the one I'm pushing into you. Every time I push yours in, mine pushes in too. It's wonderful – taking and being taken at the same time.'

Sarah licked her suddenly dry lips, and Amanda bent her head to kiss her, touching the tip of her tongue against Sarah's. Her mouth was skilful, teasing Sarah into parting her lips. At last Sarah yielded and let Amanda kiss her properly, pushing her tongue deep into her mouth in the same way that Amanda pushed the huge dildo into her sex.

Amanda's free hand slid from Sarah's chin down to her breasts, fondling first one nipple and then the other. Sarah arched up as much as she could, tilting her pelvis so Amanda could penetrate her more deeply. If she closed her eyes she could almost imagine it was Marc filling her so delightfully – except she could smell Amanda's sweet musky perfume and feel the softness of the other woman's body against her own.

'Tell me you love it,' Amanda ordered huskily. 'Tell me you love what I'm doing to you.' She changed her rhythm, rocking slowly back and forth so that the dildo penetrated Sarah to the hilt, then slid out again. 'If you weren't tied to the bed, just think how it could be,' Amanda continued. 'Your legs would be wrapped round my waist, your heels against my buttocks, urging me on. Or maybe you'd be the one on top, riding me and fondling my breasts at the same time, feeling how hard and swollen they are, how taut my nipples are. Wouldn't you like that, Sarah?'

'Yes.' The word was almost ripped from her. She hated herself for being so weak and admitting it so easily, so quickly; yet at the same time, the mental picture Amanda had been painting was too much for her.

To her relief, Amanda didn't crow about her success. She merely kissed Sarah lightly on the lips. 'That's good. I'm glad you like it, Sarah. Because it's good for me too. I want to make you come. I want to make your pretty face flush and your breasts ache. I want to make your sex contract so hard it almost hurts. I want to see the dildo sticky and glistening with your juices when I finally withdraw from you.'

She increased the pace, bucking her hips. Sarah cried out. She kept up the fast and furious thrusting, bringing Sarah closer and closer to the edge. Just as she'd demanded, Sarah felt her breasts aching, her nipples tight and hard; then her climax suddenly imploded and her sex rippled sharply round the thick dildo. Only then did Amanda stop moving, letting the dildo rest so that Sarah's sex could tighten round it. Her climax seemed to go on and on.

When the aftershocks eventually died away, Amanda bent to kiss the tip of her nose and withdrew.

'See, Sarah? It's glistening and shiny, from you,' Amanda said, crawling up over Sarah's body to present the dildo, still rearing from between her thighs, to the blonde's lips. She slid the glistening tip over Sarah's chin, coating it with her own juices. 'It felt good, didn't it?'

Sarah swallowed. 'I...'

'Tell me, Sarah.' There was a tiny note of pleading in counterpoint to the commanding tone. 'Tell me.'

That tiny hint of vulnerability got to Sarah more than anything else. 'Yes,' she muttered.

'Good.' Amanda climbed off the bed and unstrapped the dildo. Sarah watched, fascinated, as the thick black tube slid from Amanda's sex, as glistening and shiny as the end she'd just withdrawn from Sarah's own sex. 'So we've established that you liked what I did to you. You enjoyed being submissive, being taken by me.'

Sarah swallowed again. What next?

'And as you were so insistent earlier that you're completely straight, it follows that you must have enjoyed the way Marc took you.'

Sarah shivered. 'I...'

'It's all right. You've as good as admitted it.' Amanda smiled. 'Now, I think you deserve a treat.'

A treat? Just what did she have in mind this time?

Sarah soon found out. Amanda took Marc's hand, urging him to his feet, then dropped to her knees in front of him. His cock was rigid, from watching them and fantasising, Sarah presumed, and Amanda ringed it quickly with her fingers, drawing the tip to her mouth. She swirled her tongue over his glans, then parted her full lips and began to fellate him, moving her head back and forth and setting a contrapuntal rhythm with her fingers. Marc tangled his hands in her hair, urging her on. Sarah couldn't tear her gaze away, remembering how Amanda had used that beautiful mouth on her sex, and how Marc had filled her with that glorious cock.

Marc was groaning when Amanda stopped and stood up, taking his hand and turning him to the bed. 'Finish him off,' she told Sarah.

Sarah stared at her, shocked.

'Finish him off,' Amanda repeated as Marc knelt on the pillows, the tip of his cock nudging Sarah's lips. 'I want you to suck his cock until he comes. Now. Do it.'

There was a long pause. Tension filled the room. Marc and Amanda suddenly looked less sure of themselves, as if they thought Sarah might actually refuse; then Sarah opened her mouth, touching the tip of her tongue to the eye of Marc's cock, lapping up the clear bead of fluid that had appeared there.

Amanda visibly relaxed and stood behind Marc, sliding her arms around his waist and cupping his balls with one hand, while stroking his perineum with the other.

Marc groaned all the more and thrust forward. Sarah tipped her head back so he could ease more deeply into her throat. What she was doing was the ultimate in submissive acts, she knew, but she suddenly wanted to do it. When she'd watched Amanda fellate him, she'd wondered what it would be like to feel his cock filling her mouth; now she knew. And Amanda was right; it was a very special treat. She had the pleasure of having exactly what she wanted, and without having to ask for it.

She continued to suck, using her teeth very lightly on his skin as he pushed in and out of her mouth. He gasped, both at what she was doing to him and at what she guessed Amanda was doing to him. From Amanda's earlier comments about penetrating her lover, male or female, Sarah guessed that Amanda had pushed her finger against Marc's anus, easing the digit in past the tight ring, and was massaging his prostate.

Sarah couldn't help wishing they'd moved to the other side of the bed, so she could see what Amanda was doing to Marc in the mirror. She wanted to see how Amanda massaged him, her fingers mimicking the way his cock slid in and out of her own mouth, and how the plum of his cock made her cheeks bulge.

At last she heard him cry out and felt his cock throb, and suddenly her mouth was filled with salty liquid. She swallowed every drop as Marc withdrew, licking her lips. To her surprise he bent down and kissed her lingeringly, not caring that he was licking his own semen from her lips. 'Thank you,' he said quietly, stroking her hair.

Chapter Eleven

Marc remained looking into Sarah's eyes; she could see longing and admiration and frustration reflected there. If she hadn't been tied she would have reached up to touch his face, to draw her finger along his lower lip. There was something about his mouth that affected her in a big way. But, as she was, she could do nothing.

He glanced at his watch, then turned away from Sarah, speaking to Mandy. 'Dinner's almost ready. I don't know about you, but I'm starving. Shall we go downstairs?'

Amanda nodded and dressed swiftly; Marc followed suit. Neither of them spoke a word to Sarah, and Sarah didn't feel like initiating a conversation.

When they were both full clothed again, Marc took Amanda's hand. 'Come on then.'

The door closed behind them. Sarah gave a long sigh. After he'd eaten, no doubt Marc would return with a tray of food for her, and tease her as he had before. Why did he have to be so bloody stubborn about it all? Why couldn't he just admit that she was in the right; that his department looked a mess and would operate much more efficiently once it was tidy, with clear desks and no posters to distract the team?

She lay there, thinking about what they'd done. He'd taken her way, way beyond her boundaries. Beyond his own, too: not only had he made love with her, he'd made love with a second woman from the office, in her presence. And he'd watched that same woman make love with her, wearing a strap-on double-headed dildo. It was lewd, rude... and very exciting, she had to admit to herself.

Eventually the door opened again. She was shocked and surprised to see Simon, rather than Marc.

'Hi. I thought you might be thirsty.' He was holding a glass of freshly squeezed orange juice.

Sarah suddenly realised her throat was dry. It was hardly surprising, considering how she'd spent the afternoon – making love, then finally swallowing Marc's seed – but she hadn't even thought about it. Now she suddenly needed a drink. She smiled gratefully at him. 'I am. Thanks.'

'Pleasure.'

He held the glass for her; she sipped delicately. Then she swallowed some the wrong way. Her subsequent cough and splutter sent juice dribbling down her chin.

'Easy now,' Simon said, taking the glass from her. Once he'd made sure she was all right, he grinned. 'Oh dear. We've made a bit of a mess. Better get you cleaned up, hm?'

Even before he bent lower Sarah knew exactly what he was going to do. She'd seen the look in his eyes as he'd read her that story: a mixture of desire and surprise and warm appraisal. And now they were alone, and she was still naked: she knew it would be too much of a temptation for him.

She also knew that, at a word from her, he would stop. She'd known instinctively that Simon had an innate sense of decency; he wouldn't force her to do anything she didn't want to do. And that included letting him make love to her.

He licked the spilt juice from her skin, then moved down further, pressing his tongue against the pulse in her neck. She shivered, and he continued caressing her with his mouth, trailing down the sensitive cord at the side of her neck, and then moving slowly to nuzzle beneath her jaw.

Sarah closed her eyes. He was good, very good: but she could remember how it had felt when Marc had done the same, and the memory sent a shudder of desire through her. Was she going to let Simon make love to her, and pretend he was Marc? Or was she going to let him make love to her for his own sake? His build was similar to Marc's; the kind she found most appealing. She'd always preferred dark-haired men to blonds, but she was prepared to make an exception in Simon's case. She found him attractive. She liked him.

'May I?' he asked softly.

She could feel his breath against her skin, just above her nipple. She knew what he wanted to do. She wanted it too. 'Yes,' she said equally softly.

Slowly, his hands cupped her breasts, squeezing them slightly. Then he lowered his mouth to one nipple, drawing its throbbing rosy tip into his mouth and sucking gently. At Sarah's shiver, he sucked harder, drawing fiercely on her nipple until she groaned aloud. He repeated his actions with her other breast, his fingers toying with the nipple he'd just sucked. Sarah stopped thinking and let her body take over, relaxing and enjoying what he was doing to her.

His lips trailed down across her abdomen. She tilted her hips impatiently, wanting to feel his mouth on her aching sex. He teased her, moving to kneel between her thighs and rubbing his cheeks against the soft skin of her inner thighs. His face was slightly roughened with stubble, but Sarah found the slight pain incredibly pleasurable.

'Yes. Do it,' she murmured.

'What do you want me to do?'

Even as her mind registered that Simon was playing one of Marc's games, and no doubt had instructions from his friend to make her tell him explicitly what she wanted, her body rippled with pleasure. 'I want you... I want you to lick me,' she whispered huskily.

'Where?'

'You know where.'

'Tell me.'

If she didn't he would stop: and she didn't think she could bear it. She'd had enough of being teased. She was still aroused from what Marc and Amanda had done to her, and she wanted to come. She couldn't bear to be left waiting again. She gave a small sigh of resignation. 'I want you to lick my sex. I want you to suck my clitoris, to push your tongue right up inside me.'

'Like this?' He stretched out his tongue, drawing it the length of her sex. When she moaned and tilted her hips again he began to lap her in earnest, exploring the furls and hollows of her sex and taking her clitoris between his lips, nipping the little bundle of nerves until she moaned more loudly, jerking her lower body as much as her bonds would allow.

'And this?' he asked, releasing her clitoris and pushing his tongue as deeply into her vulva as he could.

Sarah tugged at her bonds, wanting to tangle her fingers in his hair and push him harder into her sex, to mash her quim against his mouth until she came. She needed more, more. 'Oh, yes. Deeper – please, I need you deeper.'

He withdrew. 'I think you need something more than my tongue,' he said softly. She opened her eyes and he smiled at her. 'How about this?'

'Oh yes,' she sighed, as he inserted a finger and added a second, pistoning his hand back and forth. 'Yes.'

'Enough? Or do you want more?'

Sarah was lost in an erotic daydream of Marc and Simon simultaneously pleasuring her, one pushing his cock up to the hilt in her sex while she sucked the other, letting him penetrate her mouth as deeply as he could. 'More,' she murmured. 'More. Much more.'

She felt him withdraw his fingers and heard the sound of a zip rasping; then there was another pressure against her sex. She gave a sigh of pleasure as his cock pushed into her, and he began to move with long slow thrusts.

'You're   thinking of Marc, aren't you?' he asked softly. 'You're imagining that he's the one penetrating you, not me.'

She opened her eyes in shock. 'I...'

'It's all right. I'm used to it,' he said with a shrug. 'Every woman I know has the hots for Marc. If I had a pound for every time I've been chatted up by a woman, then discovered she was angling for an introduction to him, I'd be rolling in it.'

Sarah flushed. How could they be having a conversation like this, while he was sheathed in her body? And yet she couldn't resist the chance to learn a bit more about Marc. 'You've known him a long time then?'

Simon nodded. 'Since university. We shared a flat at one point; and then both of us ended up with jobs up here. Then he decided he'd had enough of the bright lights, and bought this place. It was a complete hovel – it didn't even have a proper bathroom. He did it up from scratch.'

'You sound like you admire him.'

'I do,' he said simply. 'He's my best mate. Otherwise, I think I'd hate him. He's good at his job, he's reasonably well-off, and he's got women thronging after him. Not that he's bothered with any of them lately.'

'Why?'

'Because he's obsessed with this woman,' Simon told her. 'She's driving him over the edge. I've never seen him in this kind of state in all the years I've known him.'

'Obsessed?' Sarah queried.

'Mm. He can't stop thinking about her. That's why he keeps turning down every woman who approaches him – he says they just won't match up to her, so there's no point. And he says it's unfair to accept a date when he's thinking of someone else. In love with someone else, even – not that he'll admit it.' He looked at her, his brown eyes candid. 'But you already know that, don't you?'

'I...' She flushed again.

'And I think you feel the same way. I'm making love with you – but it's Marc you're asking about.'

She shook her head. 'I was just... intrigued.'

Simon was too well mannered to call her a liar. He simply pursed his lips and continued thrusting, moving his lower body in elliptical circles to change the angle of his penetration and give her more pleasure. 'The problem is,' he said, 'you're both stubborn. And you both like playing power games – in either role.'

Was he telling her that Marc was a latent submissive? That she could have bound him and ordered him to do whatever she wanted, and he'd have done it? Her eyes widened. 'But... I thought Marc was dominant?'

'He is. When it suits him,' was the laconic reply. 'Like you. Right now you're submissive, and you're obviously loving it.'

'I am not,' she protested.

Simon rubbed the pad of one thumb over her erect nipples. 'Better tell your body that, then.' At her silence, he continued, 'In the office you're dominant – and you love that too. Most of the men in your office fantasise about you, you know. They'd all like to see you in leather and lace, stalking through the department and ordering them to service you.'

Sarah smiled wryly. 'Yeah, sure.'

'According to Marc, that is. And Amanda.'

'I'm not a lesbian.'

'I didn't say you were,' Simon said, not put off his stroke in the slightest. 'Just that a lot of the men in your office fantasise about you, and they talk about it to their female friends in the office, too.' He slid one hand between their bodies so he could stroke her clitoris. 'I can see why.'

'Thank you.' Sarah's cheeks coloured further, more from what he was doing to her than from his compliment.

'Marc's right, you know. You're incredibly beautiful when you smile. You get a little dimple in your cheek. It's so cute.'

Her eyes widened. 'I...'

'Shh.' He placed a finger to her lips. 'You don't have to say anything. And I'd rather you didn't tell Marc what I've told you.'

'Why's that?'

'Because... Look, he's a very private person.'

'Oh yes?' A very private person wouldn't have made love so lewdly in front of her with another woman – or watched that same woman screw her. A private person wouldn't give his best friend instructions to read a lewd story to her, then screw her silly. A private person wouldn't even admit to quite liking someone, let alone being obsessed with them.

'Which is precisely why you're different,' Simon said. Sarah's jaw dropped as she realised that she'd spoken aloud.

'He hasn't done this kind of thing before, then?'

'Not to my knowledge. He only ever has a relationship with women he respects, and it's always one at a time. Yeah, he has quite an imagination – if you get the chance to look through his bookshelves you'll see what I mean.' Simon grinned wryly. 'Must be something to do with having a French father, I suppose. He has quite a collection of erotic literature, and half of it's in French. But like I said, in all the years I've known him, I've never seen him in this kind of state. You've pushed him way beyond his limits, Sarah.'

'Why are you telling me this?'

'Because,' Simon said simply, 'he's my best friend, and I don't want to see him hurt. From what he's told me about you – and I virtually had to force that out of him – you like straight talking. I don't think either of you is being straight with the other, at the moment.'

'I can't believe you're telling me this. While you're... you know.'

'Fucking you?' Simon gave her another of those disarming smiles. 'Sorry. Now I've started calling a spade a spade, instead of a digging implement, I don't know where to stop. But yes, I can talk to you like this because this is just our bodies. I don't know you like Marc does; and you don't know me. This is skin to skin, but not mind to mind.'

Sarah nodded. He'd hit the nail on the head.

'So tell me, Sarah – do you make a habit of this kind of thing?'

'No.'

'Let's see if I've got this straight then. You're the boss in the office – very efficient, and scary.'

'Scary?'

'Scary,' Simon emphasised. 'Very scary. You don't ever compromise your professional life by having an affair with a colleague, a one-night stand – or even going out with a crowd and indulging in the odd kiss or cuddle. You certainly don't make a habit of letting men tie you to a bed and doing what the hell they like to you, including getting other people to fuck you.'

Sarah swallowed. 'Correct.'

'And yet you're letting Marc do it to you. Why?'

She closed her eyes. 'I can't answer that.'

'Can't or won't?'

'Did Marc ask you to do this? To interrogate me?'

He stroked her face. 'I'm not interrogating you – and no, he didn't.'

'What did he tell you to do then?'

'To bring you a drink, and entertain you.'

'Entertain me.' Involuntarily, Sarah's quim tightened round his cock. 'That's one way of putting what you're doing to me... And what did you think, when he brought you upstairs and you saw me?'

'Exactly what I'd told him on the phone – that he was crazy.'

'Thanks a lot.'

Simon chuckled. 'You know what I mean. That he's taking things a bit far. When I said to him, last week, that he should whisk you away somewhere and spend the weekend in bed with you, to get you out of his system, I didn't expect anything like this.'

'So it was all *your* idea?'

'Yes and no. I said he should spend time with you, but I meant something like a romantic country house, a four-poster bed and a jacuzzi and vintage champagne and red roses. Not this.' Simon stroked her breast, making her shiver when he began playing with her nipple, rubbing it with the pad of his thumb. 'Mind you, I'm glad he did. You're delicious, Sarah. The way you feel, your sex contracting round me as I push in – it's amazing.' He held her gaze for a moment. 'I don't mind if you fantasise that I'm Marc. If it keeps you responding like this to me, I don't mind at all.'

Sarah couldn't quite believe what was happening to her. If someone had told her, a week before, that she'd be making love with a man she didn't know while she was tied naked to a bed, and that she'd be fantasising about another man even as the stranger's cock was sheathed in her, she would have laughed at them. If someone had told her she would even have invited the stranger to stroke and touch her, begged him to lick her, begged him to enter her... her lip would have curled in disbelief. She wasn't that kind of woman.

At least, she hadn't thought she was. Now it was happening to her she wasn't so sure.

'Close your eyes, Sarah,' Simon whispered. 'Close your eyes and think of Marc. Imagine he's the one kneeling between your thighs, not me. Imagine I'm Marc. What do you want me to do, Sarah?'

Sarah closed her eyes and her sex pulsed hotly. Christ. Simon was even inciting her to fantasise about his friend, to pretend he was Marc.

'I can do anything you want, Sarah. Apart from untie you, of course,' he added quickly. 'Any way you want me to touch you, stroke you – all you have to do is ask me... nicely.'

'Just keep doing what you're doing,' she said. 'Please.' She gave a gasp of pleasure as he quickened his strokes. Her orgasm suddenly shattered through her, making her body tense with the aftershocks.

When her pulse had slowed, Simon withdrew. Only when she heard his zip being pulled up did she consider that he'd been almost entirely clothed throughout. It made her feel like a cheap whore; yet at the same time, it had been *very* exciting.

'You must feel all hot sticky,' he said softly, stroking her forehead.

'A bit,' she admitted.

'Like a bath?'

A bath. Filled with bubbles – a deep, hot, luxurious bath.

'Yes.'

'Okay.'

She frowned when he didn't release her as expected. 'But, don't I need to leave the room to have a bath?'

'Nope.'

She suddenly remembered what Marc had done earlier. He'd given her a blanket-bath. Was Simon going to do the same, and arouse her to the point of frustration?

She soon discovered that that was exactly his intention. He left the room very briefly, and returned with a porcelain bowl filled with scented foaming water, the sponge Marc had used, and a thick fluffy towel.

He even followed the way Marc had bathed her, starting with her face and neck, washing away the sweat and stickiness. He moved down over the swell of her breasts; just like before, her nipples grew tight as he moved the sponge over them, the tiny holes adding to the friction.

Just as Marc had done, he waited until she was at the point of asking him to ease the ache, then moved down to sponge her ribcage and abdomen. He rubbed the sponge in tiny circles over her skin, then patted her dry with the towel. This time, to Sarah's relief, she didn't need to use the bathroom. It would have been way too humiliating for that to happen twice. She didn't think she could have coped with it, not with Simon.

To her surprise, after he'd washed her belly, he moved down to the other end of the bed and sat down. Then he started working on her feet, washing her toes and her soles and the hollows of her ankles. She wriggled slightly as he worked, and he grinned. 'Ticklish, are we?'

'Don't you dare,' she warned.

'You're hardly in a position to make threats,' he pointed out. 'What could you do if I tickled you? Nothing. You're tied. You'd have to submit.'

Her eyes narrowed. 'Was this Marc's idea?'

'No. I was testing out a theory: and I'm right.'

'What?'

'Doesn't matter.'

'Tell me. Please?' she added hastily, remembering his earlier comment about asking him nicely.

'Just that you prefer to be submissive with Marc alone; with anyone else you'd rather be dominant.'

Almost anyone else, she thought wryly. When Amanda had knelt between her thighs and pushed the dildo into her she hadn't been the dominant one. Or when Amanda had commanded her to suck Marc's beautiful long cock. It made her feel uncomfortable to remember how she'd acted with Amanda. She'd always considered herself to be completely straight – but she had most definitely enjoyed her experience with the other girl. She'd climaxed several times, so what did that mean? Was she a lesbian at heart? Was she bi-sexual?

Simon didn't seem to notice her lack of conversation; he merely continued washing her, moving up to her calves and her knees, then up to her thighs. Sarah closed her eyes, luxuriating in the way he moved the sponge over her skin. It was very relaxing – and arousing, she admitted to herself.

He began to stroke the sponge between her thighs, moving it up and down, up and down – exactly as Marc had done earlier. Sarah squeezed her eyes more tightly shut, giving herself up to the pleasure of what he was doing to her. He pressed her clitoris, and she couldn't help a small murmur of pleasure.

Part of her was embarrassed at responding so easily, so obviously, but she reminded herself that even if she'd been silent, Simon would have been able to see how aroused she was. Her nipples were tightening, and her sex was beginning to pout at him.

Simon continued to tease her clitoris with the sponge. As she tilted her pelvis slightly she felt the sponge pressing against her sex. And then he'd eased some of it inside her. She opened her eyes in shock. No. Surely he wasn't intending to masturbate her with a sponge? But he was. As he pulled it back and forth the natural protuberances of the soft sponge teased her sex, making her feel hot and wet and excited.

'Do you like it Sarah?' he asked softly. 'Do you like what I'm doing to you?'

'No.'

He chuckled. 'Such a little word. But your voice betrays you, Sarah. It's deeper than usual, slightly hoarse – because you're aroused. Your mind says it's obscene, being masturbated with a sponge, but your body loves it. Maybe I was wrong about you; get you in the right frame of mind and you'll be submissive to anyone.'

'No way.' Ice-blue eyes opened and stared at him in anger.

'No? Close your eyes, Sarah,' he soothed. 'Just lie back and enjoy. Imagine I'm Marc. If he were here, doing this to you, you'd love it. Though I think you rather love it anyway.' He rubbed his thumb across her erect clitoris, making her shiver. 'Beneath your ice-maiden act, Sarah, there's a very rude little girl indeed, isn't there? A woman with an incredibly lewd imagination. You might not allow yourself free rein – but when you do let your mind slip free, it's there, isn't it? I saw the way you responded to that story I read you. I think you'd like Marc to spank you, wouldn't you?'

'No!'

He ignored her, still moving the sponge in and out of

her sex, and rotating his thumb on her clitoris.

'I think,' Simon continued softly, 'that you'd like him to haul you over his knee, and use the flat of a hairbrush on you. A silver-backed hairbrush with an embossed back – yes, embossed with his initials. And you'd like him to use it on you, so his initials were imprinted on your pretty little rear. Wouldn't you like that Sarah? For him to warm your skin, give you a sound spanking – and then turn the hairbrush round, push it between your smooth soft thighs, and penetrate you with the handle?'

'No!' Sarah choked. She could imagine everything that Simon was saying. She could see it all so clearly in her mind's eye. Herself over Marc's knee, penitent, and Marc being masterful, using the hairbrush and making her count every stroke. And then he'd penetrate her with the handle of the brush. The silver tube would slide easily into her lubricated sex. He'd move his hand back and forth, masturbating her with the instrument of her punishment, just as Simon was doing with the sponge. And he wouldn't stop until her quim was flexing sharply round the handle – just as it was flexing sharply round the sponge...

She cried out sharply and Simon leant forward, stroking her face with the back of his fingers. 'Easy, Sarah, easy,' he said softly. 'It's all right.'

He withdrew the sponge, released her and turned her over onto her stomach, and refastened the bonds before she had a chance to protest. Then he moved to the bedside cabinet and took out a hairbrush. It wasn't the silver one of the fantasy he'd just described; it was a wooden-backed one. Her eyes widened. Surely he wasn't going to...

The mattress gave slightly as he sat down next to her again. Sarah shivered and waited, anticipating the first smack. It didn't come. She held her breath, keeping her eyes squeezed tightly shut. Surely Simon, gentle kind

Simon, wasn't going to do this to her... No, he'd been teasing, that was all. She opened her eyes again, about to turn her head towards him and say something, when she heard a swish and – almost at the same time – felt the hard surface of the brush smack sharply against her vulnerable buttocks.

'Oh!' The gasp of pain and surprise was forced from her lungs.

'That's an extra one for making a noise.'

Sarah buried her face in the pillow as she waited for the next stroke, hoping the thick feather bolster would muffle any sound she might make. A second smack followed... and then a third. Just how many was Simon going to give her? The traditional six-of-the-best, plus one for failing to take the first properly? Or did he have another number in mind?

The fourth smack stopped her thinking. The fifth landed on an already reddened patch of quivering flesh, making her push her face even harder into the pillow, desperate not to make a sound. The sixth made her feel as though her whole bottom was on fire. The seventh, to her shock, sent strange ripples through her quim.

This couldn't be happening, she thought in bewilderment. She couldn't be coming again – not when he hadn't really touched her, when he had only spanked her like a naughty child. She couldn't be coming from... she shuddered as her internal muscles flexed sharply, the pain in her bottom eclipsed by the sheer strength of her engulfing orgasm.

And then the smacks stopped.

Simon smoothed the flat of his cool palm over her buttocks, soothing away the sting. When the aftershocks of her climax had died away he unfastened her bonds, moved her gently onto her back, then tied her to the bed again. He leant over and kissed her lightly on the lips.

'Okay?'

'Okay,' she murmured. Her bottom still tingled, but she felt drowsy and languid and satiated.

'Good.' He gently washed her again.

Chapter Twelve

Just as Simon finished drying her, the door opened. To her relief, Marc was alone; she had been dreading yet another visitor, someone else to see her humiliation. Would Amanda talk about it in the office? Would she tell everyone in Marketing how Miss Prim-and-Proper Sarah Ward had been tied up and made to beg for release – by both Marc and herself? Would she tell them how she'd ordered Sarah to suck Marc's cock, and then watched her do it with abandon, licking the crown and taking the shaft as deeply as she could into her mouth?

And had Marc been listening at the door just then? Had he heard what Simon had said, and then her own sharp cry as she'd climaxed?

She shook herself.

'Dinner,' Marc said softly, coming to sit on the bed beside her as Simon moved away.

'What if I'm not hungry?'

He grinned. 'After all the exercise you've had today?'

She flushed hotly. 'Bastard.'

'I'm perfectly legitimate, I assure you.' He stroked her face. 'Sarah, I thought you might like some smoked salmon. You liked it last night, didn't you?'

She knew he was referring to more than just the meal, but didn't rise to the bait. She looked at the plate he was holding. It was filled with delicious-looking canapés: smoked salmon and soft cheese pinwheels, brie and black grapes on tiny water biscuits, dolcelatte and avocado on triangles of thin brown bread. They all looked as though they'd been prepared by a master chef; he must have spent ages making them, especially for her.

'What if I don't like the rest of it?' she tested.

'A woman of your good taste?' he asked softly. 'I think, Sarah Ward, that you're being deliberately awkward. I'm half tempted to pull you over my knee and spank you for that – although I suspect you'd enjoy it far too much.'

So he *had* heard what Simon had said. He'd been listening at the door – or maybe he'd even told Simon exactly what to say. She tilted her chin, trying to remain dignified. 'Don't be ridiculous.'

'I saw your face when Simon read you that story. I think you secretly liked the idea, Sarah. I think you would have liked to act out the role, with me as the librarian's boss, reddening those creamy buttocks and making her thank him for every stroke.'

'I would *not.*'

'Then why did the story turn you on so much?' He didn't wait for an answer, merely bringing one of the smoked salmon pinwheels to her lips. 'Try this, Sarah. It's good.'

She had the nasty feeling he was talking about something else completely, but did as she was told, opening her mouth and letting him feed her the delicacy. He was right; it was good.

'That's the thing about smoked salmon. The texture and flavour – so delicate, and so like a woman's intimate flesh. Doesn't it remind you of how you ate Amanda?'

Her colour flared. 'I'm not going to dignify that with a response.'

He laughed. 'Another point to me, I think. It's becoming a little too easy to score points against you now. You're slipping, Sarah.'

'Maybe that's because you've kept me tied up for so bloody long I can't think straight.' Her temper cracked.

'When are you going to let me go, Marc?'

'When you've told me what I want to hear.'

'Even though it's a lie?'

He shook his head. 'Oh no Sarah. It's the truth. Isn't it time you admitted it – to yourself as well as to me?'

'Go to hell.'

'Fair enough. If that's what you want,' he returned equably, continuing to feed her dainty morsels.

If she hadn't been so hungry she would have refused to eat; but she acknowledged that she'd be stupid to send him away. What was the point of starving herself and making herself even more uncomfortable?

'Do I take it you're not going to talk to me, Sarah?'

She gave him a mutinous glare. 'What's the point?'

He shrugged. 'We'll do it your way then.' He continued to feed her, but addressed his comments to Simon.

They talked about people and places she didn't know, discussing squash leagues and beer and football. Sarah wasn't sure whether it was more annoying to be ignored or interrogated; she didn't know what Marc had intended her to feel, either. The only thing she was sure about was that it was another strategic move on his part. Was he intending to make her so irritated that she'd talk to him, fight with him – or was he intending her to feel humiliated, of no more importance than a pet dog being fed scraps while its master chatted to a friend? Though the 'scraps' could hardly be called that. Dolcelatte and smoked salmon weren't exactly the cheapest of items.

She savoured the morsels, liking the slightly metallic taste of the dolcelatte, the soft sweetness of the avocado and the tenderness of the smoked salmon. She concentrated on the tastes and textures of the food, and it was a while before she realised Marc and Simon had stopped talking. Both were watching her intently.

'What?' she asked.

'The look on your face, just then,' Marc said softly. 'You were abandoned to pleasure – and you looked so beautiful.'

Her eyes narrowed in suspicion. He was leading up to something, she was sure. Pleasure, abandonment... It was something to do with one or both. 'What do you want?' she asked finally.

'You know what I want.'

She sighed. 'No.'

'Well.' He shrugged and continued feeding her.

Sarah felt the mattress give slightly. She lifted her head from the pillow and looked down the bed, and her pupils dilated. Simon was kneeling between her spread legs, still fully clothed. He placed the flat of his palms on her soft pale skin.

He looked up at her and smiled; the light in his brown eyes was intense and sensual, and she found herself responding to it. He raised one eyebrow, almost in question. When she made no gesture to still him – no frown nor tiny shake of the head nor scowl – he bent his head and drew his tongue along her sex.

Marc placed a smoked-salmon pinwheel against her lips. 'Eat,' he said – and Sarah wasn't sure whether the command was aimed at her or Simon. It felt odd, to be savouring the delicate morsels while Simon was savouring the folds and hollows of her sex – but at the same time she could appreciate the symmetry. Amanda had been right about Marc. He was very subtle when he chose to be.

'Isn't it good, Sarah?' he asked softly. 'Eating and being eaten?'

'Is that what you'd like me to do to you?'

He smiled. 'You're so quick. Yes. I can imagine what it would be like, unrolling one of these and winding it round my cock, then letting you suck it off again.' He spread his hands. 'But that's impossible as we are. So we'll just have to do the next best thing, won't we?' To her surprise he unravelled one of the pinwheels and wrapped it round his finger. He pressed the tip of his finger against her lips and she opened her mouth, giving him the access he wanted. He slid his finger slowly inside, and she sucked on it – all the while imagining it was his pulsing cock, and remembering what it had felt like when he'd knelt on her pillow and Amanda had fed the tip of his cock into her mouth.

She sucked hard, finally eating the salmon off his finger, and was rewarded by a slight dilation of his pupils. She couldn't see him properly – his crotch was masked by the plate of canapés on his lap – but she was pretty sure his cock was swollen to full proportion, constrained by his jeans.

Then she remembered what Simon had said – that Marc and she both liked playing power games, in either role. Had their positions been reversed, had he been the one tied spread-eagled to the bed and she had been feeding him, what then? Would she have stripped, very slowly, anointed her nipples with smoked salmon and avocado and cheese, and made him lick her clean? Would she have taken a breadstick, inserted it in her sex, and made him pull it out again with his teeth?

'Whatever you're thinking, Sarah, it's lewd,' he said softly.

She sighed. 'I don't know what you're talking about.'

'I think you do.'

She shook her head.

'Tell me, Sarah. Tell me what you were thinking.'

'Or else?'

He shrugged. 'I'll decide on a punishment later.'

Her eyes widened. Marc was taking this a step further:

punishment? Would he really do what he had teasingly threatened to do and spank her? Or what the story had hinted at; make her bend over so he could warm her backside and stripe it with a ruler? Or what Simon had suggested; holding her over his knee while he smacked her with a hairbrush? 'I...' She fell silent. Her sex felt warm and wet and puffy, and it wasn't just thanks to Simon's ministrations.

'Nothing to say for yourself?'

She shook her head.

'So be it. I'll add it to the list.'

'What list?'

Marc smiled. 'Don't you work from a list, in the office?'

'A to-do list. Yes.'

'I'm merely doing the same.'

'Writing a to-do list for work? Why?'

'Not for work,' he corrected, his voice low and completely in control. 'For home. A list of all the things I should punish you for – and there's a lot of them, believe me. It'd take me a long time to read it out, let alone chastise you sufficiently for them.'

There was no answer to that. She relapsed into silence. He wound another strip of smoked salmon round his finger, and continued feeding her. She ate nervously; there was a tingling feeling at the base of her spine, a mixture of excitement and fear and longing.

The tingling increased as Simon slid his hands under her buttocks, lifting her up slightly so he could have access to the tiny rosebud between her buttocks. She gasped as she felt his tongue press against her. Despite her attempts to stay in control, her body began to shudder with pleasure as Simon penetrated her more deeply.

Marc said nothing, he merely continued to feed her canapés. When she'd finished the plateful he enquired smoothly, 'Dessert?'

'I...' Sarah gave another soft gasp as Simon deftly swirled his tongue in her forbidden entrance. How could Marc act with such insouciance when Simon was acting so lewdly?

'We haven't had ours yet, have we Simon?'

Simon broke off very briefly from his explorations. 'That's true.'

'What's for dessert?' Sarah asked, knowing even as she spoke that she'd fallen into another of Marc's honey-traps.

'You,' he said quietly. He stood up and left the room. Simon continued to tongue her sex and her anus, switching from one to the other until she was writhing and squirming within her bonds, wanting more. Marc returned with a large bowl.

Sarah didn't ask what it contained; she knew she'd find out quickly enough. A moment later Marc gave her a challenging smile, dipped his finger in the bowl, and smeared some of the contents over her stomach.

'Chocolate mousse,' he told her.

She remembered the creamy confection he'd made the previous night, and looked down, expecting to find her skin covered in white chocolate. She was shocked to see that the sticky mixture was almost black.

'Dark chocolate mousse,' he explained. 'Made with seventy per cent cocoa. I did it this morning while you were... otherwise engaged. Like some?'

She glared at him, and he smiled again. 'Come on. All women like chocolate, according to Amanda.'

Sarah found her voice then. 'So she knows what you're doing to me?'

'Through educated guesswork – yes, probably.'

Did that mean he'd tried it out on Amanda first? The bowl wasn't clear glass and, as he wasn't holding it so that she could see the contents, she couldn't tell whether the mousse had already been sampled. It was none of her business, and she knew it shouldn't matter, but she couldn't deny a sharp twinge of jealousy.

'Sarah, it's good. Try some.' He smeared chocolate on her lower lip. She tasted it; it was as good as the mousse he'd made the night before, but richer and darker.

Like the sex.

The thought came into her mind, unbidden, and she blushed. Marc chuckled softly as if he could read her thoughts, and anointed her nipples with chocolate.

She swallowed. 'I thought you weren't going to touch me again until I asked you?'

He shrugged. 'I've just changed the rules.'

'But—'

'But nothing, Sarah. You're only in a position to make one bargain, and you refuse to do that. So that implies acceptance of whatever I do to you.' He looked at her. 'Unless you have some argument to convince me?'

She shook her head.

'Good.' He traced an elaborate pattern over her breasts and belly, then looked at his creation. 'What do you think, Si?'

'Not bad,' Simon mumbled, glancing up momentarily.

'I know she tastes good, but would you like a little extra sweetness?' Marc asked politely.

Sarah groaned at the way they casually discussed her.

Simon chuckled. 'Women don't have the monopoly on a liking for chocolate, you know. Though you might need to change the sheets,' he warned.

'That's not a problem.' Marc handed the bowl to his friend.

Sarah was expecting the feel of cold mousse against her intimate flesh, but it still made her jump. Then Simon began to massage it into her, rubbing it over her clitoris and her labia, and more into the rose-coloured star of her anal opening. She nibbled her lip anxiously, but it wasn't enough to hold back her groan of pleasure – particularly when Simon began to lick her clean of the dark sticky confection.

Marc bent his head at the same time and licked the chocolate from her flat tummy and soft breasts. As he sucked her nipples, Sarah arched her back and squirmed. She tugged at her bonds, wanting to tangle her fingers in his hair. But she was forced to remain passive and let him make all the moves.

The combined attention of two mouths – lips, tongue and teeth – sent her body spinning into ecstasy. She cried out as Marc bit gently into her breast, and Simon pushed his tongue deeply into her chocolate-covered sex, lapping at the mixture of her own juices and the rich bitterness of the chocolate.

Sarah jerked wildly within her bonds. She clenched her hands and squeezed her eyes tightly shut, pushing her head back into the pillow as her climax rose to a peak. Still the two men did not stop. They continued to lap and lick and suck, driving her to an even higher peak. She cried out as Marc sucked fiercely on one breast, using his thumb and forefinger to draw on her other nipple. His free hand snaked down over her belly, and he rested the palm against her delta, extending one long finger between her labia to brush against her clitoris.

Simon was still licking her sex enthusiastically. He gripped her buttocks, lifting her slightly, and pressed his thumb against her rosebud. With all her major erogenous zones receiving lewd attention, Sarah writhed in abandon, arching up as much as she could to the mouths and hands that gave her so much pleasure. Her sex was rippling round

Simon's tongue, and her nipples were desperate for relief.

Still they kept on, licking and sucking and lapping and rubbing, taking her to a giddy high. She wailed loudly as a second climax exploded within her, making her sex clutch at Simon's tongue and her anus dilate slightly. His probing thumb pushed in a little deeper, and Sarah jerked her lower body, suddenly wanting to feel his cock inside her. She wanted Simon to take her, to thrust hard and fast and deep, while Marc's cock was in her mouth, the tip pressing against her palate. And she didn't care which orifice Simon used: she just wanted to be filled.

She tried to tell them this, but either her words were unintelligible from pleasure or they were ignoring her, because they continued their self-appointed tasks, re-applying the chocolate mousse and eating it from her flesh.

Sarah reached a third peak, and a fourth. Just when she was sure she could take no more and was about to cry out for them to stop, they did – almost in perfect synchronisation – and Marc gently stroked her damp forehead.

'Okay?' he asked softly.

She nodded, not trusting her voice.

'Good. Come on, let's get you cleaned up.' There was a glimmer of humour in his voice. 'We've made quite a mess of the sheets. I suppose I really ought to order you to clean them with your tongue – but I've got something better in mind.'

Something better? Did he mean something more humiliating, or something he thought she'd enjoy more? Sarah knew she could not have licked the sheets clean; she simply didn't have the energy, let alone the inclination.

'But you may clean my face first,' he added with a grin.

His mouth and chin were smeared with chocolate. He brought his face down to hers and she stretched out her tongue, licking the mousse from him. She gave in to the impulse to tease him back; she licked his lower lip clean and then bit it gently, making him open his mouth so she could kiss him hard and explore him with her tongue.

He pulled back. 'I didn't give you permission to kiss me.'

She blushed. 'I'm sorry.' She was tempted to add, 'But you didn't exactly seem to mind,' but thought better of it. She couldn't judge his mood. He kept switching from humour to kindness to this strange dominant manner, and she wasn't sure which was a tease and which was what he really felt.

'You can clean Simon now.'

The blond man moved to sit on the other side of the bed and followed Marc's example, dipping his head so she could lick the mousse from his face. Whereas Marc had tasted solely of chocolate, Simon tasted more spicy – a mixture of the chocolate and her own copious juices. She was embarrassed and turned on at the same time, but Simon didn't make any comment.

'Not bad,' Marc said when Simon lifted his head again. 'But I think we'll need something a little more, to get us properly clean.'

Sarah waited nervously, wondering just what he had in mind. To her surprise, Simon untied her ankles and Marc unclipped the handcuffs from the bedstead, though, she noticed, he kept one cuff firmly round her wrist and the other round his own.

'Can you stand?' Marc asked.

She tried, but her legs felt like jelly, thanks to a combination of the length of time she'd spent in bondage and the number of orgasms they'd just given her.

'Come on, we'll support you,' Marc told her. He unclipped the handcuff from his wrist – obviously realising that Sarah was in no state to attempt escape – and slid one of her arms round his neck. He supported her with his shoulder, and Simon took the other side. Slowly and carefully, Marc and Simon half-carried her along the landing.

Sarah's skin heated as they took her into the bathroom. She could well remember the last time Marc had taken her there – when he'd forced her to relieve herself while standing up in the bath, as he waited outside. What did he have in mind this time?

At a nod from Marc, Simon stripped. Then he supported Sarah while Marc stripped. Finally they lifted Sarah into the bath and climbed in beside her. Marc pulled the shower curtain across and turned on the taps, fiddling with the temperature gauge until the water beat down in a warm and heavy stream.

He took a bottle of shower gel – an expensive honey-based concoction, Sarah noted absently – and squeezed a little into his palm before passing the bottle to Simon and working up a lather between his hands. Simon did the same. Then Marc turned Sarah to face him, so that her back was to Simon. Working as one, Marc and Simon began to soap her body, gently smoothing some of the ache from her muscles.

Marc teased her breasts, lathering the soft underswells and moving down over her ribcage, then stroking upwards again, each time nearly but not quite touching her nipples. Meanwhile Simon worked down her back, over the softly flared swell of her hips, and then moved gently over her tender buttocks.

Of course, Sarah could have easily closed her eyes, giving herself up to the sensual bathing, but she couldn't resist looking down at Marc's taut body. His cock rose rigidly from his groin, and was as beautiful as she remembered it; long and satisfyingly thick. She remembered how it had felt inside her, stretching and giving her such wonderful pleasure. And she remembered how it had felt and tasted in her mouth, and suddenly she wanted to feel and taste him again.

Before Marc or Simon realised her intentions, she dropped to her knees between them.

His initial protest was cut off sharply when she cupped his balls in one hand, ringed his shaft with her other, and slid her lips over the tip of his cock. She glanced up through the spray of steaming water and saw the sudden expression of bliss crossing his face. She smiled inwardly. Marc Dubois might dominate her – but there were some areas where she had total power over him, too. Work was one, and this was most definitely another. When his cock was in her mouth, he was all hers.

She began to move her head back and forth, swallowing him as deeply as she could. He groaned, tangling his fingers in her hair, and she worked him harder, delighting in her ability to make him forget everything.

'Sarah... *Sarah*.'

Her name sounded as though it were ripped from him, and she exulted inwardly.

'Oh yesss. Oh yes, sweetheart.' His fingertips dug into her scalp, urging her on; the pain was a kind of non-pain, because she was so focused on what she was doing. She wanted him to lose control completely; to hold her head still as his cock jerked and throbbed, as his seed filled her mouth and spilt over her lips.

She'd almost forgotten about the other man with them, until she felt a gentle mouth kissing all the way down her spine. For a moment she stiffened, and then relaxed into it.

She made no protest as Simon covered her back and

buttocks with kisses. She continued to caress Marc's balls, setting up a rhythm in direct counterpoint to the way she sucked him. She could tell from his fast and shallow breathing – as well as the pressure against her scalp – that he was aroused beyond the point of no return.

She shivered as she felt Simon dribble the shower gel into the valley between her buttocks, lubricating her. Surely he wasn't intending to...

Her doubts must have shown in the set of her body, for Simon whispered in her ear. His torso pressed against her back, and she could feel his erection nudging between her buttocks. 'Relax,' he murmured, his breath fanning her ear. 'I know you haven't done that before.'

Her emotions swirled. How did he know that? How could he be so sure?

'Besides,' he panted, 'it's not my favourite place.'

What did he mean by that? She felt a guilty throb of excitement in her lower belly. Did he mean that Marc was going to introduce her to that particular activity later? The thing she'd fantasised about, feeling dark and dirty as she did so, but still yearned to experience?

'So relax. I might touch you there, but I won't slide my cock into your pretty little arse. I can feel how hot your sex is, Sarah. It's like a furnace pushing back at me. And I just *know* you'd like to be fucked while you're sucking Marc.'

A ripple of excitement ran through her. That was exactly what she wanted. Pushing her buttocks back towards him, as if to signal her consent, she sucked Marc harder and began to stroke his perineum, each time drawing nearer to the rosebud between his buttocks.

'Oh yesss…' Marc hissed, tilting his hips towards her. 'Yes. Yes Sarah. Do it, sweetheart. Do it!'

At the same time as she pushed tentatively against his

anus, feeling the muscle yield under her fingertips, Simon fitted the tip of his cock against the entrance of her sex and slid easily inside.

What she was doing was incredibly dirty, she knew. Kneeling at the feet of one man in the bath, with her finger massaging his prostate and his cock filling her mouth, while another set about steadily fucking her from behind like an animal. All she needed now was—

She couldn't help moaning, her cry muffled by the thickness of Marc's cock, as Simon did exactly what he'd promised earlier; pushing his finger against her anus and not relaxing the pressure until he'd forced entry there too.

They moved in perfect synchronicity. Sarah's body acted as a kind of lynch-pin between the two men. As Simon withdrew from her, so she slid her lips from Marc's cock, and as Simon pushed into her again, his balls slapping against her quim and sending jolts of delight through her, so she rolled her lips tightly back over Marc's rigid flesh. She lost track of time, and she could no longer feel the strain in her muscles, the pressure on her knees, or the shower-jets beating down on her back. All that mattered were the two rigid cocks servicing her so delightfully, filling her and making her feel complete.

Her climax began to build, a warmth rolling from the soles of her feet and travelling swiftly up her legs, through to her stomach, increasing in intensity until she thought she might black out. Just as she reached her peak she felt Marc's balls lift and tighten. She pushed her finger deep into him, and was rewarded with a hoarse groan and a mouthful of tangy warm fluid. At the same moment she felt Simon's cock throbbing deep within her and the powerful jet of his seed.

She remained exactly where she was, savouring every drop of Marc's seed and keeping him in her mouth until his cock had softened. He gently stroked her face, and she reluctantly released him. Simon's deflating cock slipped from her too, and the two men lifted her to her feet.

'That was incredible,' Marc said softly, cupping her face and kissing her lightly on the mouth. 'Sarah – what you do to me...'

He stopped and pulled back sharply, as if close to the edge of blurting out something he didn't want her to know. Too late, Sarah thought. I already know, thanks to Simon. And she could see the truth in Marc's eyes too.

She let it go – for the moment.

Chapter Thirteen

Marc and Simon washed her in silence, rubbing the soft scented foam into her body and sluicing her clean again. Marc even washed her hair, making sure that none of the suds went in her eyes. Then he climbed out of the bath and grabbed a towel; he wrapped it round her and lifted her out of the bath. He wound a smaller one round her wet hair, turban-style. Then he patted her dry. It wasn't like before, when he'd used the towel as a pretext to arouse her, pretending it was a barrier between his fingers and her body. This time he dried her very gently, very carefully, as if she were made of porcelain, concentrating on her upper body while Simon took another towel and concentrated on her feet, legs and sex.

When they'd finished, they threw the towels into the wicker laundry basket at the side of the bathroom. Sarah waited on tenterhooks. They'd both been so gentle, so sweet. What was it all leading up to?

When Marc turned away for an instant, she braced herself. This was it. Some new and refined torture intended to break her. Something subtle.

She was shocked when he merely took a bottle of body lotion, poured some into his hands, and began smoothing it on her skin. Simon followed suit, and they moisturised her body thoroughly, keeping the actions sexless and soothing.

Still Sarah couldn't relax. It was such a change of tactics from before that she didn't trust him. Even when he placed his hands on her shoulders and touched a kiss to her forehead, suspicion made her stiff and unresponsive. He unwound the turban from her hair, blotting the fine silky strands as much as possible, then combed out the tangles.

Finally, Simon – who had dressed while Marc was combing her hair – held her close while Marc dressed. Then the two of them led her out of the bathroom.

'No,' Sarah said as they led her back towards the room.

'Yes,' Marc insisted.

She struggled, but it was pointless. With one accord, Marc and Simon lifted her feet clear from the floor and carried her into the bedroom. Marc swiftly clipped the handcuffs to the foot of the bed – leaving Sarah half-crouching and furious – while he changed the chocolate-smeared sheet. Then he looked at her.

'We've been here before, haven't we?'

'How do you mean?' She glared at him.

'We can do this the hard way or the easy way. Your choice. But you're going back on that bed, Sarah. I told you the conditions for your release, and they haven't changed.'

'Bastard. I hate you.' She was near to tears, more from anger than anything else. 'What kind of man would keep a woman tied up like this? 'You're a sadist!'

He didn't deny the charge, merely smiled. 'There are degrees of sadism, Sarah – and types. Physical and mental. Like you, I prefer my power games to be mental. But if you want to be disciplined in the traditional sense, I can certainly oblige. What would you like: a cane, a whip or my hand? Maybe a slipper?'

She flushed. 'I didn't mean that.'

'Didn't you?' he enquired politely. 'Funny that. Because the way you're acting you're as good as demanding to be spanked. Simon's my witness to the way you reacted to that story. It excited you, and I think you'd like to bend over, exposing your bare bottom for me to redden your cheeks. And then, after the pain, would come the pleasure. A deeper, stronger pleasure – pleasure like you'd never known before.'

His voice was hypnotic; despite everything, Sarah found herself relaxing.

'In fact, that gives me an idea.'

She looked up, alarmed. His face was impassive, inscrutable. She had no idea what he was thinking or what he was planning. 'How do you mean?' she asked, trying to keep her voice cool and calm and measured.

'I think I've left you in one position for too long,' Marc said. 'I don't want your muscles to seize up. In fact...' He nodded to Simon, who silently came to stand on her other side. Then he unclipped the handcuffs, and he and Simon lifted her up quickly, placing her face-down on the bed.

Before Sarah had time to take in what they were doing, Marc had refastened the handcuffs to the head of the bed, and Simon had retied the silk scarves to her ankles.

'What the hell—?' she began.

'Time for something nice, Sarah,' he told her. 'Something very nice indeed.' He nodded to Simon, who left the room in silence. 'You're going to like this.'

'Untie me you treacherous bastard.'

'Treacherous? No Sarah, I believe in truth. And all I want to do is make you admit the truth about yourself. That you can be wrong sometimes – that everyone can make a wrong judgement, sometimes.'

'Don't you think you might be wrong about me? That I'm not the submissive you've convinced yourself I am?'

'No,' he told her simply. 'When I described that scenario of you in a leather harness, in the office in full view of whoever I chose, it turned you on. It turned you on in a big way. If you'd been dominant you would have laughed, or changed the scenario, told me what you wanted to happen.'

She had no answer to that. The silence stretched for what seemed like a long, long time; neither of them was prepared to break it. Just as Sarah's nerves spiralled to screaming point, she heard the click of the door. She turned her head, expecting to see Simon, and her eyes widened in shock.

It wasn't Simon.

The woman who entered was another of Marc's team, Julia. She was a brunette, who wore her hair in a shiny bob, and who was almost more immaculate in the office than Sarah herself. She was carrying a small case. Sarah had no idea what it contained, but she had a strong feeling it was something to do with Marc's next move.

'You know Jules, don't you?'

The familiarity of the nickname made Sarah feel a sudden surge of jealousy. Ridiculous, she knew; Marc had said he didn't believe in relationships with colleagues, and Simon had said Marc had been celibate for months. She had no reason to disbelieve either of them; of course Marc wasn't romantically involved with Julia. And even if he were it was none of her business. 'Yes,' she muttered, 'I know her.'

'And Jules, you know Sarah. She's a bit stiff. I think she could do with the magic of your fingers.'

Sarah's eyes widened. Hadn't it been enough for him to watch Amanda make love with her? Was he going to subject her to more of the same?

The mingled thrill and dread made her sex pulse, and then she flushed hotly when Marc continued, 'I imagine you've heard, Sarah, that Jules is qualified in aromatherapy massage, which is exactly what I think you could do with right now. You need to relax.'

That was all he had planned? A massage? That was all that was in the box – aromatherapy oils? Not some obscene collection of obscure sex toys? She almost sagged with relief, yet at the same time her suspicions deepened. The way he and Simon had been so attentive to her under the shower, the way they'd moisturised her skin, then Marc had combed her hair. And now this... There had to be more to it than just a straight massage. But then again, Marc had said he preferred his power games to be mental rather than physical. Was he playing an elaborate game of double-bluff, making her think he was going to do something cruel and tighten her nerves in expectation, when he had nothing of the kind in mind?

'I hope you don't mind if I straddle you,' Julia said, breaking into Sarah's thoughts. 'It's just easier to work your muscles if I'm astride you.'

'Right.' Sarah coughed.

Julia chuckled, misinterpreting Sarah's uneasiness. 'Relax, I'm not going to leap on you. Not unless you want me to, that is,' she added wickedly.

Sarah flushed deeply as a pulse quickened in her sex. Christ, what had Marc done to her, to make her so aware of the other woman's sexual attraction? 'I...'

Julia ignored her. 'Marc, if you're going to sit and watch, you can make yourself useful first. I want towels.'

'Towels?'

'Yes. I don't want Sarah's muscles getting cold once I've worked on them. He's a bastard, tying you up like this. If I were you I'd murder him,' Julia continued.

'I feel like it,' Sarah muttered into her pillows. 'Believe me I feel like it.'

'Though you've both kept this very quiet, haven't you? I should have guessed that your rows in the office were a blind. Marc never rows with anyone. He just uses his Gallic charm and they fall at his feet.'

'Do they now?' Sarah was annoyed and embarrassed at Julia's assumption that they were a couple – and that they were both used to these sophisticated games.

Julia didn't seem in the least bit fazed. 'Now, I'm going to use a relaxing oil on you – a mixture of lavender and Roman chamomile, in a base of sweet almond oil. Have you ever had a reaction to oils before?'

'Not that I can think of.' Sarah had no intention of admitting it in front of Marc, but one of her favourite pick-me-ups was an aromatherapy massage. He couldn't have picked anything more likely to please her. Apart from the fact that she was still naked and bound: that rankled. Particularly the fact that she was face down – even though she would have assumed that position, anyway, for a back massage.

'Good. Now, just lie there and enjoy it, as the saying goes. If I'm working you too hard, yell.'

'All right.' Sarah closed her eyes, turning her head to one side and relaxing against the pillows. The next thing she felt was the mattress dipping slightly as Julia climbed onto it, then the soft cotton of Julia's leggings against her back and upper buttocks as the brunette straddled her.

Then she felt Julia's oiled hands smoothing up and down her back, gently gliding against her skin. It was pleasant – very pleasant – but somehow she still had a feeling that Marc was planning something else. She wasn't quite sure what, but no way would he give her a treat like this, with no strings attached.

Julia began to work on the knots of tension in her neck – tension that had been growing steadily, despite Marc's kindness in the shower. 'Hm. You really have had a tough time lately, haven't you?'

'How do you mean?' Had Marc told Julia exactly what

he'd done – or caused to be done – to her? How many other people had he told?

The suspicion in her voice made Julia laugh. 'Calm down. I only meant that your neck is full of knots.'

'So would yours be if you'd been tied here since Friday bloody night,' Sarah muttered.

'Well you only have yourself to blame for that, don't you?'

Sarah opened her eyes and craned her neck as far as she could to look up at Julia. 'Meaning?'

'God, you're so touchy. Anyone would think you've got something to hide.' Julia rolled her eyes. 'Okay, if you want it in simplistic terms – if you don't want something to happen to you, you call a halt to the proceedings. You're tough enough to get your own way. No one's going to force you to do anything.'

'No.' Sarah flushed. 'Sorry.'

'What did you think I meant?'

'Well...' Sarah's voice faded. She didn't want to go into that. 'Forget it.'

'All right. Now, just relax.'

Sarah did her best, but she still couldn't help thinking that Marc was up to something.

'Sarah, what's it going to take?' Julia asked, a tinge of exasperation in her voice.

Here it comes, Sarah thought. The whole point of the charade. 'To do what?'

'To make you relax...' The pressure of Julia's fingers deepened.

'I am relaxed.'

They both knew she was lying.

Julia continued to massage her in silence. Sarah lay with her eyes closed, trying to concentrate on the other woman's slender fingers and the professional way that Julia was

199

touching her. Yet she couldn't. She was still so aware of Marc sitting there, beside the bed, watching her. Watching Julia's fingers travel up and down her spine, watching Julia astride her, soft cotton-covered thighs stretching over Sarah's bare skin, the thin material the only barrier between Julia's sex and Sarah's buttocks.

Her mouth dried. Why had she let herself think of that? She wasn't sexually attracted to other women… was she? She remembered how Amanda had made love with her, and she squeezed her eyes tightly shut, trying to force the memories away. Yes, she'd come. Several times. It had felt amazing, the thick dildo filling her like a real cock, with Amanda's soft breasts pressed against her own. And the way Amanda had licked her, her soft skin rubbing against Sarah's thighs, her knowing tongue and fingers touching Sarah in exactly the way she liked most…

She became aware that Julia had bent forward so that her upper body was pressed against the length of Sarah's spine, and her mouth was next to Sarah's ear. 'There's only one thing I can think of that would make you relax, Sarah – and that's an orgasm. You're so taut, so tense. I need to release some of your energy, or the massage isn't going to work. So you have a choice. Me – or Marc.'

'I don't need anything,' Sarah muttered, embarrassed. No way was she going to let Julia watch Marc slide his cock into her. Or let Marc watch Julia's clever fingers massaging more intimate parts of her body.

'When are you going to stop lying to yourself, Sarah?' Julia continued softly, brushing her lips very lightly across the sensitive areas of Sarah's neck.

Sarah shivered, and Julia slowly straightened up again. Sarah felt tiny drops of oil drip along her back, then Julia resumed the massage. But this time her fingertips were no longer asexual or slightly clinical. This time her fingertips moved across Sarah's skin in a sensual way, in tiny circles that made Sarah arch slightly towards her.

Julia shifted back until she was straddling Sarah's thighs rather than her back, and continued the slow and sensual massage, caressing up and down the whole length of Sarah's spine. The movements were slow and rocking, as though a man were taking Sarah from behind, penetrating her with deep and carefully measured thrusts. Sarah couldn't help responding, pressing her upper body as hard as she could into the bed, and lifting her bottom as much as her bonds and Julia's position would allow.

She knew it would give Julia teasing glimpses of her sex, but she didn't care. She was beginning to be aroused; the softness of the sheets against her hardening nipples was a delicious torment. She wanted to rub herself against the sheet. She wanted to slide a hand under her own body, squeezing her nipples and rubbing the soft undersides of her breasts. She wanted to slide that hand down further, over the planes of her belly. She wanted to wriggle her hand between her thighs, part her labia with her fingers, slide two fingers into her aching sex while her thumb rubbed her clitoris.

A detached part of her wondered just what kind of oil Julia was using; something calculated to increase her arousal, perhaps? But she wouldn't use coercion. Marc wouldn't allow that. Yes, he'd let her drink too much on the Friday night, but only enough to take her over the driving limit. Not enough to make her paralytic and incapable of refusing him, or incapable of knowing what she was doing. And she had been the one who'd invited him to make love to her.

She shuddered as Julia's hands moved down to caress her buttocks, oiling her and smoothing the soft unguent into her skin.

'Tell me what you want, Sarah,' Julia urged softly. 'Tell me. Then I can help.'

'I... I want...' Sarah couldn't do it. She couldn't say what she wanted.

'Then I'll just have to guess. Tell me if I get it wrong, Sarah.'

Sarah shivered as Julia shifted back slightly more, and dripped oil on the base of her spine. The tiny rivulet ran very slowly between Sarah's buttocks, and Sarah shivered again – with excitement rather than cold, because Marc had placed a towel over her upper back to keep her muscles warm.

Julia continued to massage Sarah's lower back, working her way round the spine, and then sliding her hands teasingly up Sarah's sides to touch the soft sideswells of her breasts. She worked up and down, up and down, until Sarah was in torment. Sarah could still feel the oil in the cleft of her buttocks – as yet untouched by Julia – and her quim flexed. Despite all the climaxes she'd had already that day, she needed to come again. She needed to be penetrated, to be touched and licked and rubbed.

She gave a small murmur of longing, and Julia's hands moved down to her buttocks. Slowly, gently, she rubbed her fingertips all over Sarah's bottom, her fingers working in tiny circles. Sarah was almost panting with need by the time Julia finally eased her buttocks apart and smoothed the oil into the soft puckered flesh.

And then, unbelievably, Julia stopped.

Sarah opened her eyes, shocked. How could Julia do that to her? How could she be so cruel, relaxing her like that, touching her until she was wet and open and longing – and then stop?

Before Sarah could protest, Julia placed a finger against her lips. 'I don't think I'm the one you need right now.'

She smiled, climbed off the bed, and swiftly packed her bottles and potions back into the small case. 'See you later, Marc,' she said softly, and closed the door behind her.

Marc came to sit on the bed beside Sarah. 'Is there something you want to say to me?' he asked.

Sarah took a deep breath. There was a hint of longing in his tone: longing he couldn't suppress, no matter how controlled and calm he seemed, outwardly. She remembered what Simon had said, about Marc being obsessed with her. And also what Simon had said about her own feelings.

And it was true. The way she felt about Marc... She'd tried to fight it at work, but she was in no position to fight it now. 'Marc.' Her voice was husky, reflecting his own desire and longing. 'You planned this, didn't you? You told Julia we were together – that you wanted her to give me a sensual massage, something to bring me close to the edge.'

'Something like that,' he admitted.

'I'm right there now.'

'And?'

She knew what he wanted her to say. 'Touch me, Marc. I need you to satisfy me… with your fingers, your tongue, your cock.'

'Any way in particular?'

She gave him a coquettish smile. 'I'll leave that up to you. I'm in your hands Marc. I'm all yours.' She knew he knew what she wanted: she didn't have to be that specific.

'Sarah.' He leant forward to kiss her. She opened her mouth beneath his, letting him explore her. He groaned as he broke the kiss, sliding his hands down her back. 'Sarah. I want you so much.'

'Me too,' she murmured huskily, thrilling to his touch.

Swiftly, he undressed. She watched him appreciatively

as he stripped off his shirt and jeans. She liked the way he looked: those broad shoulders tapering down to a narrow waist and hips, strong arms and sensitive fingers, and his mouth... How she wanted him to use his mouth on her. To do what he'd done to Amanda; taking advantage of her position so he could kiss all the way down her spine – and then go further.

'Sarah.' Her name sounded like a caress, she thought idly. He ran his fingers through her hair, then swept the silky strands over her shoulder, baring the nape of her neck. He climbed onto the bed and bent his head, kissing the back of her neck and making her shiver with desire. Then, very slowly, his mouth worked down her spine, kissing and licking and teasing. By the time he reached the dimples at the base of her spine she was writhing in her bonds, arching her back and pushing her buttocks into the air.

He caressed her smooth cheeks, squeezing them gently and parting them. Then, at last, she felt his tongue against her puckered rosebud. She gasped, pushing back at him, wanting him deeper. She felt him murmur something against her skin, then there was a gentle pressure against the tight ring. She shuddered as her flesh yielded to the insistent probing, and then his finger penetrated her.

'Oh God,' she murmured.

'Okay?' he asked. 'Tell me to stop if I do anything you don't like.'

'No – no, I want you to. I want you to do it.'

'Tell me, Sarah.' His voice was still soft and commanding.

'I want you to take me… there. Like you took Amanda,' she said, not wanting to put it into cruder terms.

He didn't press the point, insisting she use literally four-letter words; he simply continued moving his finger, letting her body grow used to the feeling of being penetrated. He kept the rhythm slow and gentle. Eventually Sarah found herself relaxing and pushing back against him, to quicken the pace and deepen his penetration.

Finally, he leant back over her, kissing her shoulder. 'Are you sure you want this Sarah? I know you haven't done it before.'

'I want it,' she told him huskily. 'I want you every which way, Marc. Like I said, I'm in your hands. All yours.' There. She'd done it. She'd as good as told him that she was submissive. That would be enough for him, surely?

He withdrew, and she took a sharp intake of breath. Surely he wasn't going to desert her now?

'It's okay,' he whispered as he walked over to the bedside cabinet. 'I think you might find this easier if I use something, that's all.'

She said nothing, touched by his concern. Fear and excitement mingled in equal parts: this was it. She was going to live out one of her fantasies – being taken in the most primeval way. She wanted to do it, and yet at the same time she was scared it would hurt, that she wouldn't be able to accommodate him.

'You can tell me to stop whenever you like,' he reminded her, stroking her face. Obviously, she thought, her trepidation showed in her face.

'I'm fine. I want you to do it.'

'I'll make it good for you,' he promised.

Her throat dried as he rolled the condom onto his erect cock, then returned to the foot of the bed. She felt something cool drip into the furrow between her buttocks, and he massaged it into her puckered flesh. Then she felt the mattress give as he climbed between her thighs again. Her heart began to hammer madly. Her sex was hot and aching – and wetter than she'd ever known it. Maybe she should ask him to take her there instead. She was scared it was going to hurt, that he'd be too big for her, that she wouldn't be able to handle it.

And yet she wanted him to continue.

She felt a pressure against her anal opening. Her body tensed, but Marc seemed attuned to her feelings. He stroked her back, caressing her shoulders with his fingers and his lips.

'Relax,' he said softly. 'This is going to be good for both of us. There's nothing to fear. Trust me.'

Slowly, her muscles lost that tense feeling, and the pressure against her rosebud increased. Then, unbelievably, the tip of his cock was inside her. He paused, allowing her body to grow used to the fullness; then he slowly eased his way deeper until he was sheathed completely within her.

'Okay?' he whispered.

Sarah didn't trust herself to speak; she merely nodded.

'Good.' He began to rock his hips, taking it slow and easy. His hand curved round her hip, insinuating between her thighs, and he pushed one finger into her sex. He added a second finger, settled his thumb on her clitoris, and began to pump his fingers in and out of her vagina, in a sharp and quicker counterpoint to the way his cock moved in her rear passage.

Sarah couldn't help crying out. It felt so good to be filled so completely. It was even better than she'd imagined it could be, when she'd watched him take Amanda in the same way.

'Do you like what I'm doing to you Sarah?'

'Ye-es.' She stammered, barely able to speak.

'So you like being submissive – sexually?'

She should have known he'd want her to say that. Part of her wanted to hold out – but then he quickened his pace, sending shafts of exquisite delight through her. 'Yes,' she whispered hoarsely.

He continued to thrust, taking her nearer and nearer to the peak. She felt the inner sparkling of her climax begin in the pit of her belly, growing hotter and wilder. Just as she was about to come he stopped moving, withdrawing his hand from her sex and keeping only the tip of his cock in her anus. 'You've admitted you're submissive. Now will you agree to let me run the office the way I want to?'

Her eyes widened in outrage. How the hell could he raise that topic at a time like this? 'I might be submissive outside the office,' she said, 'but not inside it. No. We'll do things my way.'

'Very well.'

To her shock and dismay he withdrew and climbed off the bed.

'Where are you going?' she asked, panicking as he pulled on his clothes and then adjusted her bonds slightly to give her a little more room to move.

'It doesn't matter Sarah. I don't think there's any point in continuing this conversation, do you?' And with that he left the room, leaving her alone and on the brink of a longed-for climax, and totally unable to do anything about it.

She buried her face in the pillow and sobbed.

Chapter Fourteen

Surely he wasn't going to leave her like that? He couldn't!

But time passed slowly – very slowly – and no one came to the room. There was no clock, and she had no idea what time it was. Just that it was late… and that she was alone. Finally she drifted into sleep, her wrists and ankles still harnessed hopelessly to the bed.

The next morning she was woken by the smell of fresh coffee. She tugged experimentally at her bonds, wondering if Marc might have relented in the night, but they didn't give. When she turned her head to the side she saw no indentation in the pillow next to hers, and she couldn't smell his clean and very masculine scent on the sheets. He'd clearly left her completely alone.

Was it all over? She thought again about his last words to her.

It doesn't matter, Sarah. I don't think there's any point in continuing this conversation, do you?

Conversation, he'd said. Maybe he was just giving them both a breathing space, giving her time to think. Maybe…

When the door opened she tried to mask the eagerness in her face. She must have failed, because Simon looked embarrassed at the sudden change in her expression. 'Morning,' he said quietly.

Sarah was glad he'd left off the traditional 'good'. There was nothing good about this morning. 'Morning,' she said curtly.

He raised an eyebrow and placed the tray on the bedside

cabinet, then fetched the chair Marc had used when he'd watched Julia massage her, setting it next to the bed. 'Marc said you weren't a morning person. Toast and orange juice all right for breakfast?'

She shrugged offhandedly. 'Whatever.' She could have killed for a cup of coffee, but she knew there was no point in asking. Simon wouldn't release her from her bonds, and he wouldn't risk feeding her coffee in case he scalded her with an accidental spillage. Freshly squeezed orange juice was another matter entirely.

To her surprise, he fed her the toast and juice without spilling a drop. It was the complete opposite of her previous meals, when both Marc and Simon had accidentally-on-purpose spilt juice over her, then used it as a prelude to lovemaking. He didn't talk to her either, and Sarah also remained silent, not feeling inclined towards conversation.

When she'd finished eating and drinking, he picked up the tray. 'See you later.'

'Where's Marc?' she asked, suddenly panicking. Surely he wasn't going to leave her here, all day, alone?

'Busy,' was the laconic response.

'Doing what?'

'Things.'

Just as Sarah was about to lose her temper with him, Simon gave her an apologetic smile, then left the room.

She could hardly believe it. What the hell was Marc playing at? Why had he sent Simon with her breakfast, instead of facing her himself? What 'things' was he doing? Her questions were unanswered, and her temper grew nearer and nearer to boiling point as the morning wore on. When he finally showed up, she thought, she was going to have the row to end all rows with the snake.

'Oh, so you've finally decided to show your face?' she snarled, as Marc walked in.

'Yes.' His voice was cold, impassive; and then she noticed what he was carrying.

A whip.

He was carrying a whip.

'What's that for?' she demanded, aware that the remains of her already battered confidence was rapidly draining at the sight of it.

'I thought you needed something to concentrate your mind.'

She stared at him in disbelief. He was going to use the whip on her? He was actually going to... No. He couldn't possibly do that. Not Marc. Not to her. Yes he'd dominated her sexually, but he wouldn't go that far – would he?

She went cold, then hot, as he untied her legs and unclasped one of the handcuffs, clipping it round his own wrist. Even as he helped her to her feet and walked her the short distance to the chair at the end of the bed, she still couldn't believe he was going to do this. No. No way. Even as he bent her across the chair, deftly transferring the handcuff round one of the wooden legs to restrain her wrist, then tied her ankles to the other legs, she still couldn't believe what he was doing.

Finally, as he positioned himself behind her and stroked her buttocks, she found her voice. The words came out in a whisper. 'Marc. You're not really going to whip me, are you?'

'Yes. It's what you need and what you deserve.' His voice was cool and filled with authority. She'd never heard him sound so dominant. Even as she began to shiver with consternation at the pain she knew was coming, something else bubbled beneath the surface; an undeniable tremour of excitement.

It was what the last two days had been leading up to. Gently, from the initial blindfold and silk scarf ties, when he'd made love to her on the Friday night, through to Simon telling her that story and Amanda making love with Marc in front of her, and then to her in front of Marc, using the double-ended dildo. From the way she had made love in the shower to both him and Simon, to the way Julia had massaged her, bringing her so close to the edge, and then Marc had taken over, sliding his cock into that forbidden orifice... Yes, this was the final step.

If she didn't want him to do it, she knew exactly what she had to say. All she had to do was tell him she was submissive, and that she'd let him do what the hell he liked in the office, provided he continued to warm her bed.

That was all.

And yet a tiny voice in her head told her that this was what she'd wanted all along. From the moment Simon had read her that story, and she'd imagined herself in the place of the librarian being spanked by her boss, she hadn't been able to get the scenario out of her head. Herself, bent over Marc's bed, and Marc standing behind her turning the creamy globes of her buttocks a fiery red. In the story Jake had used a ruler on Alicia. Sarah had half-expected Marc to use his hands. But he'd gone one better.

He'd already guessed that leather turned her on. The way he'd described that tight harness, and herself masturbating on her desk, displaying her sex to whoever he chose, had been far too near the stuff of her deepest and barely admitted fantasies. And now he was going to discipline her with the ultimate: a sharp black leather whip.

'I wonder how many strokes I should give you. Has anyone ever whipped you before, Sarah?'

She knew the question was rhetorical. They both knew

the answer; and he was only stroking the whip between the cheeks of her bottom, down across the folds of her sex, to tease her. Of course no one had ever done that to her before. No one would have dared.

'If you're not going to answer me, then that's a stroke for insolence. Another for putting me to all this trouble – that's two. A third for being so bloody stubborn – that's three. And we'll double it because you've been lying to yourself too. That's six.'

Sarah didn't make a sound. If she said anything, she had a nasty feeling he'd double the punishment, or something – just like Jake had done to Alicia in the story.

'So, Sarah, shall I make you count them all, and thank me? Shall I make you beg for each one before I bring the whip down on your pretty little rump?' He was musing aloud, she knew that. Whatever she said would make no difference. He had already decided what he was going to do.

'No, this time I'll spare you that. I'll count them for you.'

This time.

She couldn't stop the shivers from running down her spine. But they weren't shivers of fear: they were shivers of anticipation. Was this to be the first of many times she'd be bent over a chair, her buttocks tipped up and her sex on full display? And in the future... would it be just the two of them, or would there be an audience for her punishment? Would she be spanked or caned or whipped in front of several men, all of whom would have permission to do what they liked with her afterwards, from making her suck their cocks to letting them penetrate her where they—

The leather whistled through the air, stopping her thoughts, and then a line of fire was scored accurately across her buttocks.

She yelled out, unable to help herself.

'Oh Sarah. And I thought you were such a brave girl.' There was a hint of mockery in his tone.

She glowered and bit her lip. Next time she'd be silent.

The second stroke caught her unawares, neatly placed just below the first. It landed just across the fleshiest part of her buttocks. It stung cruelly, but she was determined not to cry out.

'That's better. Three,' he said, and the whip swished down again, with another perfectly placed cut across her flesh.

'Four.'

The whip whistled and the chair creaked as she rocked under the vicious impact. Her eyes moistened, but she refused to make another sound.

'That's good. Sarah, if you could only see what a beautiful picture you make. That beautiful creamy skin, criss-crossed with red. Like a Chinese pillow-book, with the characters written across your flesh... Five.'

The muscles in her toned legs tensed as she absorbed yet more pain from the supple leather.

Last one. Could she do it? Could she make it through without screaming or begging for mercy?

'Six.'

She squeezed her eyes tightly shut as the sixth swept down and bit with a loud crack.

Six... she'd done it!

'Good girl. I'm glad you can take your punishment like an adult.' The mockery was deliberate; yet at the same time there was genuine admiration in his tones too.

She heard the whip drop to the floor, and then she felt oil being smoothed across her buttocks. The lines of fire he'd placed there suddenly cooled to a pleasurable warmth.

213

She didn't know what kind of oil he was using – the scent was unfamiliar – and she didn't want to ask but, whatever it was, it was extremely effective. It took away the stinging pain, and left only a delicious feeling – a deep, warm feeling that she'd never experienced before.

'Now,' he whispered softly, pushing against her sex. He entered her easily, and she was shocked to discover just how turned on and ready she was.

Then she thought about it, and was even more shocked. She hadn't heard the rasp of his zip – and whatever was inside her wasn't thick enough to be his cock. It was too long to be his fingers: so what the hell was he using? Her mind worked quickly, and the answer made her nipples tingle. He was using the handle of the whip to masturbate her.

Her muscles tensed, and he obviously realised that she'd been thinking about it and come to the correct conclusion, because he chuckled softly. 'Ah, Sarah, don't you know that the flip side of pain is pleasure? They're one and the same. Pleasure can be pain, and pain can be pleasure.'

'No.'

'Don't deny it.' His voice was very soft, yet held a note of command. 'I whipped you Sarah. I placed you over this chair, handcuffed you to it so your sex was exposed to me, and I whipped your bare arse. The idea excited you; I could see how your body responded, anticipating what I was going to do to you. You'd never done it before, but you'd thought about it in secret. At night, when you wondered what it would be like, when you touched your own breasts and fingered your own cunt, pushing a finger deep into yourself to ease the ache. You'd dreamt about it, hadn't you?'

'Yes,' she admitted, her voice no more than a whisper.

'You wanted to be disciplined – to walk that secret path

to excitement, didn't you?'

'Yes,' she said again, groaning as he withdrew the handle of the whip.

'And you're as out of control as I am right now. Your limits are stretching further and further and further. You're learning things about yourself you never knew, never even guessed. Am I right Sarah?'

'Yes. Oh!' She pushed backwards as he slid the whip into her, very slowly, and withdrew it again.

'You wanted to feel my hand warming your pretty little rear: but that wouldn't have been enough for you Sarah. That's why I decided on this.' He paused. 'And why I decided that the instrument of your pain should also be the instrument of your pleasure.' He pushed the handle of the whip into her again, and her quim rippled round it involuntarily, pulling it deeper.

'Do you know how lewd you look, I wonder?' he mused. 'Your beautiful buttocks striped, and the whip protruding out of you... It's a sight to warm even the coldest heart, the coldest sex. Let me show you, Sarah. Let me show you how good you look – how lewd and rude and wanton.' He left the whip where it was and stood up, crossing over to the cheval mirror. Then he lifted it, placing it where Sarah could see herself.

He was right. She looked lewd and rude and wanton, her hair mussed and her face red and her lower lip swollen with passion. Her breasts, too, looked ripe and swollen; she couldn't resist arching slightly against the chair, so she could see the hard crests of her nipples. There were six lines across her buttocks, stripes she'd earnt the hard way; and finally, the whip protruded lewdly from between her thighs.

An even lewder thought struck her. It was obvious from the angle that the whip was inserted in her sex. But what if he'd used the other orifice, lubricated the handle of the whip with her own musky juices and then pushed it slowly against her rosebud? Her pulse quickened at the thought and her face flushed hotly.

'Madonna and whore,' he whispered. 'If I could paint, I'd paint you like that. As it is I'm half-tempted to photograph you.'

'Photograph me?' The words came out as a croak.

He laughed softly. 'Sweet Sarah. Don't worry that I'd try to blackmail you with them. That isn't my style. No, I'd keep them for my private consumption. When I'd had a hell of a day at work, and you'd been more unreasonable than usual, then I'd come home and take out my photographs and look at you. My cock would be bursting, and I'd lower my zip, freeing it. Then I'd stroke the shaft slowly, pretending it was your hand pleasuring me… and I'd look at your photographs.'

His voice became huskier as he continued. 'I'd see you, your mouth open and your head thrown back and your teeth bared in passion. I'd see you, your buttocks striped and your sex pouting and wet, begging to be entered. I'd see you with Amanda between your thighs and one end of her dildo pushed into you. Or kneeling in front of me, your hands cupping my buttocks and your beautiful mouth working its way along my cock. Or maybe lying on your back, one hand between your legs – just as you were on Friday night when I brought that glass of water in for you.'

Her eyes widened with shock. How the hell had he known? Had he been watching her through the keyhole? 'I...'

'Don't deny it Sarah. I didn't say anything to you at the time, but it was obvious what you'd been doing. You looked so guilty. But were you thinking of me, I wonder, as you touched yourself? As you stroked your breasts, then placed your feet flat on the mattress and spread your legs... were you thinking of me?'

'That's for me to know,' she whispered.

'I could beat the answer out of you,' he said ruminatively. 'But I think you'd enjoy that too much.'

'I wouldn't.'

'If someone had said to you, last week, that you'd enjoy being whipped, you'd have laughed at them. But now... if you hadn't enjoyed it your sex wouldn't have been wet. I wouldn't have been able to slide the handle in so easily – and you wouldn't have been tilting your bottom back towards me, encouraging me to push deeper. Just like you are now.'

'I hate you.'

'Do you?'

'I...' Her voice faded.

'Well, well. Sarah Ward lost for words? Or are you worried I'll do this, leave you unsatisfied?' He withdrew the whip; Sarah, taken unawares, gave a small murmur of disappointment. He laughed. 'I guess you'd like me to slide it back in?'

'I...' She swallowed, then muttered, 'Yes.'

'I can't hear you.'

'Yes,' she said, raising her voice slightly.

'Yes, what?'

'What do you want me to say? Yes, sir? Yes, master?'

'You don't need to use a name for me. We both know what you are – and what I am,' he told her softly. 'No. I want you to tell me what you want me to do. Nicely, not crudely.'

'I want you to... to use the whip on me.'

'How? To beat you?'

'No.' She swallowed again. 'To... to make me come.'

'I think you can be more explicit than that, Sarah.'

217

He was giving her no quarter. She hated him for it – and yet she admired him, too. She admired his self-control, when her own was so tenuous.

'Tell me, Sarah.' He was commanding and inviting at the same time.

Explicitly, but not crudely. She took a deep breath. 'I want to you push the whip into my sex and masturbate me.'

'Nicely,' he reminded her.

'Please, Marc.'

'Certainly, madam.' His mockery was gentle.

Sarah bit her lip as he urged the leather stem back into her. She would have liked to ask him to use his cock instead, but she knew he'd refuse. This was as far as he would go right now, and it was a hell of a lot further than she'd ever been in her life.

She watched in the mirror as he continued to pump the handle of the whip in and out of her sex. It was the rudest, most exciting thing she'd ever seen in her life. Her bottom still felt hot but, thanks to the oil he'd used on her, it didn't smart too much.

Her climax was unexpectedly sudden and intense. One second she was watching Marc in the mirror, seeing his eyes were dark with desire, and the next her body was shuddering and jerking, and her blood felt as though it were fizzing through her veins. She cried out, her body convulsing, then slumped against the unyielding chair.

'Pleasure and pain. They're the same thing,' Marc said as he undid her bonds, helped her over to the bed, and placed her on her stomach, so that there would be no pressure on her weals. 'The same thing,' he echoed quietly as he refastened her bonds to the bedstead, and then he left the room.

Sarah felt languid and dreamy. She closed her eyes,

settling herself comfortably against the pillows. This time, Marc had left her a little more room with her bonds, so she was able to change position slightly, moving onto her side to ease the ache in her muscles. She could still hardly believe what had just happened: that he'd really gone the whole way, the ultimate in domination.

She smiled – and fell asleep, still smiling.

Some time later, she was aware of the door opening again. She peered groggily at her visitor, and realised it was Simon. She felt a slight disappointment in the pit of her belly. She had hoped it would be Marc. She wanted to talk with him to resolve the situation. They had unfinished business, and neither of them would be able to settle until it was sorted.

'How are you feeling?' Simon asked.

'Okay. Slightly sore, still aching, but fine.' She paused. 'Where's Marc?'

'Busy.'

So Marc had gone back to playing games, keeping her guessing. Well, there was no point in asking Simon for more details. He wouldn't tell her anything that Marc didn't want her to know.

'Do you need any more cream, or something?'

Sarah realised that Simon was staring at the marks on her bottom, apparently fascinated by them. She smiled. 'For what, Simon?'

'I... er...' he blushed. 'You know.'

'No. Tell me,' she invited huskily, amused by his reaction. Obviously Simon hadn't played these kind of games before, and didn't know that Marc played them, either. Then again, maybe Marc didn't usually go that far. Maybe that particular chemistry was just between her and Marc.

'Your... the stripes on your bottom,' he managed at last.

'No. But if you'd like to touch them, be my guest.' It was a weird feeling – the submissive becoming dominant – but she liked it. She also knew that, the moment Marc stepped into the room, she'd switch back again.

Simon's eyes widened, and he changed the subject. 'Would you like some lunch?'

'Depends what it is.'

'What do you want?'

Marc. She smiled. Not that she'd get it. 'I don't know. Anything. Surprise me.'

'I'll do my best.'

He left the room. She wondered if Marc would return in his stead. But then the door opened and Simon reappeared, bearing a tray. 'Hot food's a bit difficult, in your condition,' he said.

'You could always release me. Just for lunch. I won't tell Marc,' she tempted.

'I think not.' Simon sat on the bed beside her. 'Do you want me to turn you over?'

Sarah shook her head, and moved onto her other side. Marc had loosened her bonds more than she'd thought; she had considerably more freedom of movement than before. She propped herself up on one elbow, and Simon fed her the tiny prawn sandwiches he'd brought, followed by bite-sized pieces of fresh melon and kiwifruit.

She was half-expecting him to spill the sparkling mineral water and fruit juice concoction over her, starting the whole erotic cycle off again, but he didn't. He merely waited until she'd finished her drink, then left her.

Suspicion nagged at her. The last time Simon had fed her a meal without following it by an orgasm, Marc had whipped her. So what was Marc planning for the afternoon? Was he intending to lead her further along that erotic path, and if so, just where was their destination?

The afternoon dragged on. She waited and waited, but no one came. Either they'd forgotten about her or Marc was doing it on purpose. No doubt he was giving her time to think. She smiled ruefully. He probably intended her to think about their situation at work; but all she could think about was what had happened between them. He'd taken her so far, stretched all her boundaries. It had started off so innocently, with dinner, then the most gentle love-making – and slowly, it had become deeper and darker, bringing her wildest fantasies to life. Each step had seemed natural, a slow and easy progression; and now, now that they'd gone all the way...

She wanted him. She wanted him so badly. Her sex was slick with arousal and her nipples were tingling peaks; her whole body was taut with longing. If he walked into the room at that moment, she knew she'd crack. She'd tell him how much she wanted him, how much she needed him – and she was willing to accept his terms. Though perhaps that was precisely why he was staying away: because he wasn't sure just how tough she was, and was afraid that he'd be the one to crack.

When the door finally opened Sarah looked eagerly towards it. But it wasn't Marc.

'Hi,' Simon said neutrally.

'Hi.'

He sat on the edge of the bed. 'Dinner.'

Had she really spent six hours on her own, just thinking about Marc and what they'd done together? Had she really spent all that time planning what she was going to do to him, once she'd submitted? 'Thanks,' was all she said.

Simon made no reply. He simply fed her forkfuls of the fluffy cheese and mushroom omelette and salad. There was nothing erotic in the way he fed her, no suggestiveness: he was almost detached and clinical. He asked if she needed to use the bathroom. When she said no, he nodded and left.

So this was the next round, Sarah thought as the door closed behind him. That was Marc's plan. Intense heat followed by intense cold. Strangely enough, Simon's cool and casual attitude didn't upset her. If anything, it stiffened her flagging resolve to win. Her earlier decision to submit totally was reversed. If anything, she'd make Marc submit to her. And how.

Chapter Fifteen

Sarah slept badly that night. Not just because her bonds made it difficult to find a really comfortable position, but because she felt restless, her body unsatisfied. She wasn't used to doing nothing, and she found herself drumming her fingers against each other, growing more and more irritated at being kept captive and bound like this. While Marc had kept her body at the edge of pleasure, she'd been able to forget the rest of the world; just concentrating on him. Now, left to her own devices and without enough freedom of movement to relieve the longing in her sex, she was becoming stir-crazy.

She'd just managed to doze off when the door opened, and she heard a laconic voice announce, 'Breakfast.'

She opened her eyes. Marc. 'You,' she said coldly.

He tutted, annoying her further. 'You're really not a morning person, are you?'

'When are you going to untie me?'

He shrugged. 'That's up to you, isn't it? You know what you need to say.'

She sighed. 'Stalemate again, then.'

'It seems like it.' He sat down and took an absent-minded bite of toast. 'I've just called the office. Human Resources know you won't be in for the rest of the week.'

'You're not going to get away with this.'

'No?'

'All right. Supposing you keep me here for a week. What happens next week?'

'I'll cross that bridge when I come to it.' He raised an

eyebrow. 'I have a week to think up something.'

And he would. She knew that. Marc Dubois thought on his feet. Nothing fazed him. That was one of the reasons why he was so good at his job.

'Is there anything you want to say to me?'

'No.'

'Fair enough,' he said equably. 'Do you want some honey on your toast?'

'No.'

'Just plain toast and butter. Okay.' He looked at her. 'It's better hot than cold and soggy.'

Sarah thought about telling him she wasn't hungry, but her stomach rumbled, giving her away, and she scowled, pushing herself as far up the bed as she could.

'I think you need some support,' Marc said quietly. For a moment she thought he was going to screw her, but he merely lifted her a little more and slipped a couple of pillows behind her. 'Comfortable? In the circumstances, I mean.'

She nodded, not trusting herself to speak. She wanted to yell at him, but she knew that would be a mistake. He'd simply leave her on her own again. She ate the toast quietly, allowing him to feed her sips of orange juice in between bites.

When she'd finished, he left the room, returning with warm sudsy water, a sponge and a towel.

'Another blanket bath?' she asked nastily.

He shrugged. 'That's up to you. If you want to feel clean—'

'I'd rather wash myself.'

'That isn't an option. I can do it, or I can leave you as you are. It's your decision.'

She sighed. 'All right. One point to you.'

'I think all the points are to me, so far,' he said quietly.

224

There was no trace of triumph or mockery in his voice – just a bald statement of facts. Strangely, that annoyed her even more than if he'd boasted or been arrogant about it.

Without another word, he dipped the sponge into the water and began washing her. His touch was cool and impersonal, and she was furious at her body for reacting to it. Her breasts began to swell as he sponged them, and the nipples hardened.

Marc said nothing, but she knew he'd noticed. Particularly when he squeezed a trickle of water from the sponge, making it drip on the rosy peaks.

'Lighten up, Sarah,' he advised, seeing the thunder in her face.

'How can I? When you've got me tied up like this, unable to do a bloody thing?'

He tried – and failed – to suppress a smile. 'That's what's wrong, is it? You're frustrated.'

'Oh, fuck off.'

He laughed aloud. 'Do you know, Sarah, that's the first time I've ever heard you swear at me? Apart from the time I incited you to, of course.'

'So?'

He shrugged again, that Gallic mannerism that looked so natural on him and fanned her annoyance even more.

'When you finally let me go,' she said, through gritted teeth, 'I'm going to... I'm going to...' She nearly screamed with frustration, unable to think of anything sufficiently spiteful.

'Yes, boss,' he said, his lips twitching.

New tactics, she thought suddenly. He was teasing her. He was going to tease her into submitting totally, the bastard. And she'd nearly fallen for it. 'I'm glad you know your place,' she said icily.

He chuckled, as if amused that she'd seen through his

plan. *'Touché.'*

He continued sponging her, paying more attention than was strictly necessary to her breasts, then moved down over her lower belly. 'Open your legs for me Sarah,' he said quietly.

A pulse began to beat hard in her sex. Was he finally going to ease her frustration? 'I...'

'So I can wash you,' he added.

She fought to keep the disappointment from her face, and did as he'd asked. Then she closed her eyes, trying to concentrate on what he was doing and ignoring the ache in her body; the need to feel his cock sliding deep inside her.

'I was thinking about holding a dinner party,' he said. 'Something fairly high-powered. I'd like you to be the guest of honour.'

'Me?' She opened her eyes, shocked.

'Mm. And I'd like to help you dress up for it,' he said. 'I'd like to take you shopping. In London, I think, to some very exclusive shops. Where the price tags are high, and the assistants are discreet. Very discreet. We'd start with a little black dress. Something designed to show off your curves and hide them, at the same time. A kind of *trompe à l'oeil*. Something clever, with black chiffon and lycra. Something smart and short and figure-skimming. And then we'd progress to underwear.

'I quite like the thought of you being with me at a dinner party, wearing a demure little dress, when I'd know that you weren't wearing anything beneath it except that leather harness and the sapphire in your navel. But that's probably going too far. So we'd need something to make you look respectable. "Look" being the operative word.'

Sarah tried not to listen to him. He was using his silver tongue to arouse her again, to turn her on with just words.

She knew that. And yet she couldn't help responding. She could imagine it, too: attending that dinner party, exchanging sensuous glances with Marc across the table, because both of them knew what she was really wearing.

'So that means bra and a g-string, I suppose. I think we'd go for black lace. Yeah, I know it's corny, but I love the thought of you in lace. Covered, and yet not covered. Especially if it was a peep-hole bra. Not the kind of cheap tacky thing you see advertised in the back pages of magazines: I'm talking real quality. Good fabric, perfect fit, expensive. We'd need to go to a discreet shop for that, Sarah. A place where the assistant would let me go in the cubicle with you. I'd watch the assistant measure you, putting that cold tape across your breasts. Your nipples would harden under her touch. She'd know you desired her, but she'd be off limits.

'She'd tease you. She'd bring in half a dozen different bras, in different styles, so you could see their range. Different fabrics too; lace as fine as a spider's web, almost filigree, that would cover your breasts and yet expose them, clinging to your curves and letting your nipples peep through the lace or the tiny cut-out in the centre of the cups. She'd check the fit of the cups. She'd slide her fingers between your breasts and the lace, moving her fingers gently, until you were so turned on you were near to cupping her face and pulling her mouth onto yours.

'She'd do the same with the tiny g-string, adjusting it and accidentally-on-purpose just brushing the mound of your sex each time, until we could all smell your arousal, that sweet heady musky scent. And then she'd leave us to it, let me view you in all the different outfits we'd chosen together. Though she'd know exactly what would happen when you and I were alone. And we'd both know that she knew.

'Can you imagine it, Sarah? You and I, alone in a changing cubicle, with only a thin midnight-blue velvet curtain separating us from the shop? You'd be wearing just the lace underwear, black filigree that left nothing to my imagination, and I'd be wearing... let's see. A black polo-neck sweater and black leather trousers, I think.'

Sarah shivered; the picture he was weaving was way too close to her fantasies. Marc in leather trousers. Yes. She could imagine it, and it made her pulse race. The soft hide would cling to him like a second skin, revealing his cock as it hardened. She'd desire him so much.

'There would be a full-length mirror in the cubicle, and a chair. That would mean so many interesting possibilities, Sarah, because we'd both be aroused. I'd be turned on from watching you pose for me, in the underwear, and you'd be turned on from the way the assistant touched you and the sheer sensuality of the underwear. Just imagine it. And you, as my beautiful submissive lover, would do anything I asked you to...' He paused momentarily, as if checking that she was still under his spell, despite the hated word 'submissive', and then continued his hypnotic commentary.

'I'd tell you to place the chair in front of the mirror. And then I'd make you unzip me, freeing my cock but leaving my clothing in place. I'd be tempted to tell you to kneel and suck me – with both of us watching you in the mirror – but in the end I wouldn't be able to resist the lure of your sweet cunt. I'd tell you to turn round and grip the top of the chair, to stick your bottom out towards me and part your thighs. I'd kiss my way down your spine. I'd caress your buttocks, and then slowly lick the inviting valley between them.

'I'd tease you, so you wouldn't be quite sure where I was going to take you – whether I was going to be lewd or *really* lewd – and then I'd straighten up again, and fit the tip of my cock to your lovely wet quim. I'd ease inside you, so very slowly, feeling the walls of your vagina like warm wet silk and velvet round me. And then I'd fuck you properly.

'You'd have to bite your lower lip to keep quiet: because it would look and feel so good, Sarah, but you wouldn't want anyone in the shop to hear us. You'd see yourself, your breasts spilling out of the lace, your nipples hard and peeking through the centre. You'd see my cock, shiny and sticky with your fluids as I withdrew. And you'd see my hand snake down over your belly, curving between your thighs and pushing the front of the g-string to one side so I could caress your clitoris, so I could stroke that sensitive little knot of nerves in just the way you like it stroked.

'And then you'd come, your beautiful quim rippling round my cock and making me come, too. Can you see it Sarah? Can you feel it?'

She licked her dry lips. 'Yes.'

'We'd have to buy the underwear, of course. Once you'd moistened it with your lovely nectar we couldn't exactly return it to the shelves, could we? So I'd tell the assistant that you wanted to keep it on, to save any embarrassment, and then you'd dress and we'd leave. And all the while you'd be wondering if we'd been caught on closed-circuit cameras; who had seen it, and how they'd reacted to the sight of your beautiful upturned bottom and my cock sliding in and out of your lovely wet cunt.

'You'd wear the lingerie for me, that night, at the dinner party. And every time your dress caught the light, the other guests would look at you and wonder just what you were wearing, or if it was their imagination that they could see your nipples through your dress and your bra.' He smiled.

'The other guests being all male, that is. You'd be the only female guest there. You'd enjoy yourself, Sarah, holding your own in the conversation, impressing them with your sharp brain and wit. You'd enjoy the food, too. But most especially, you'd enjoy the exotic dessert.' He paused. 'Because you, Sarah, would be the exotic dessert.

'When the table was cleared, at a signal from me, you'd stand up. Slowly, very slowly, you'd take off your dress, letting it slip to the floor. Underneath it you'd be wearing the filigree lace peep-hole bra and matching g-string we'd christened in the shop. Your stockings would be the lace-topped hold-up type. And your shoes would have the highest heels possible, so that when you walked your beautiful bottom would be shown to its best advantage.

'Slowly, you'd walk up and down the room, so the others could see just how good you looked. And then you'd sit elegantly on one end of the table and lie down. You'd kick off your shoes and place your feet flat against the polished surface, with your knees wide apart. And then dessert would begin. Remember how much you enjoyed Simon and me eating the chocolate mousse off your delectable body?'

She moaned softly. 'Marc...'

'Shh.' He placed a finger momentarily against her lips, and she had to fight the urge to suck it. 'You liked it, didn't you? Two men licking and sucking you, attending to all your pleasure-spots. Imagine having five men at your disposal, Sarah. Five men – not the paunchy executive types who think their money makes up for their physical shortcomings, but five younger and more sculpted men, five intelligent men who'd appreciate your mind as well as your body. My five guests would be instantly erect when they saw you lying on the table. They'd all want to touch you, to taste you. So I'd tell them that dessert was served...

you.

'They'd cluster round the table, just looking at you at first. Your skin, like peaches and cream; the soft velvety texture of your full ripe breasts, spilling over the lace; the beautiful rosy hardness of your nipples peeping through the cut-outs. Your sex, glistening and half-veiled by the g-string. Looking at you wouldn't be enough though. And when you smiled at them, giving them that utterly seductive look from lowered lashes, they'd reach out to touch you. One of them would pull the lacy cups down, releasing your breasts properly. The electric atmosphere would make you breathe slowly and deeply, and your luscious breasts would rise and fall mouthwateringly as you filled your lungs. Another would stand opposite the one who'd touched you, on the other side of the table, and they'd work on one breast each, squeezing and caressing, then finally they'd dip their heads to take your nipples into their mouths. They'd work in perfect synchronisation, using their lips and their teeth and their tongues to give you pleasure.

'Two more would stand at your feet, lifting your feet and parting your thighs even more, so they could feast their eyes on your succulent sex. And then they'd kiss their way up your legs, from your ankles to the softness of your inner thighs. They'd taste the way your skin changes in texture, and lick you all over. You'd feel their breath, warm against quim, and you'd want them to taste your sweet musky juices. You'd tilt your pelvis in invitation, and one would push your g-string aside and work on your clitoris, while the other pushed his tongue deep in your vagina.'

Sarah's eyelashes fluttered and she found it increasingly difficult to breathe.

'And finally another would keep your mouth busy, first

of all bending to kiss you, and then, when you arched up from the table to kiss him back, he'd break the kiss, unzip his trousers, free his cock and feed its tip between your parted lips. He'd watch the shiny helmet force them to peel wider and then slide into your warm wet mouth. And then he'd stop thinking altogether as you started sucking him, drawing him deeper and deeper into your tight throat.

'I'd watch them feasting on your body, licking and sucking and caressing you until you cried out, your body shaking with the first of a very long series of climaxes. The expertise of your lips and tongue on the cock of the man by your head would be enough to make him come, spilling his pearly-white seed into your mouth and over your chin. You'd lick his cock clean, and then they'd move round one position.

'You'd suck the next cock you were offered, revelling in the way it filled your mouth. One of the men at your side would unzip, and you'd ring his shaft with your forefinger and thumb, rubbing him with a neat and deft rhythm. He'd stroke his balls as he watched you fondling his cock, pulling the foreskin back as far as you could and swiftly bringing him to a climax, at the same time as another sucked your clitoris, another tongued your breasts and another inserted four fingers into your wet and willing quim. You'd come again; this time, the man you were masturbating would spill his seed over your body, letting it splatter onto your skin and massaging it in to your trembling breasts and belly.

'Again they'd change position. This time, one would be brave and kneel on the table, astride your stomach. He'd mould your breasts together around his cock. You'd masturbate another and suck another while your sex was being expertly fingered and licked. The man working his cock between your breasts would come over your beautiful throat, rubbing the creamy liquid into your skin and mixing it with the seed of the man you were masturbating. And, of course, you'd have another tribute in your mouth, just as you came too.

'Another change of position, and this time a different man would climb onto the table between your thighs. He'd slide his cock into your still-shivering sex, pushing it deep inside you, right up to the hilt. So you'd be sucking one, masturbating another, taking another between your beautiful breasts, and your beautiful cunt would be filled, while your clitoris was being sucked. Again, your throat and your lips and your breasts would be anointed with their offerings.

'And then, for the finale, they'd turn you over onto your hands and knees. One would wriggle onto the table beneath you, pushing his cock into your hot wet sex. Another would feed his cock into your mouth. Two more would guide your hands onto their cocks, and support your body while you masturbated them. And finally, one would kiss your anus deeply, lubricating you... and then ease his cock into your vulnerable and willing arse. You'd feel so hot and tight, Sarah, and he'd be able to feel another man's cock in your sex. They'd synchronise their movements so you'd feel one withdraw as the other pushed in.

'Would you like that, Sarah? To be filled in every orifice, to give five men the ultimate pleasure? You'd be acting the supreme slut, your hair mussed and your black lace underwear awry, your face and your body covered in creamy-white fluid, your sex milking them and your lips almost numb from sucking...'

Sarah licked her lips dreamily. She trembled slightly. Christ, it was almost identical to her earlier fantasy of taking five men at once, after they'd made her come in all sorts of different ways. The only difference was in her dress – black lacy bra and g-string rather than a navy silk-and-lace teddy. Did all women fantasise about that? Or was Marc's imagination simply on the same wavelength as hers; a warped and very extreme wavelength?

She couldn't help arching back against the pillows, offering herself to him. She wanted to feel him inside her, buried completely, his pubic bone mashing against hers as he thrust back and forth.

Then she became aware that he'd stopped talking. He wasn't washing her any more either. In fact, he wasn't doing anything at all. She opened her eyes and stared in disbelief as she saw him open the door, carrying the sudsy water. How the hell could he just leave her when he'd detailed such a graphic fantasy? Surely he wanted her as much as she wanted him?

He turned round, and gave her a broad wink. 'Just a little something to think about, Sarah. I'll see you later.'

'But—!' She gave up as she realised she was talking to empty space.

Chapter Sixteen

Sarah spent the rest of the morning thinking. Marc was right about her nature: she had to admit it now. Might he be right about the office, too? He had a good rapport with his team. Amanda and Julia had both trusted him enough to do exactly what he'd asked them to do. No doubt the others would have done the same, if he'd decided to humiliate her in front of the whole department.

Her body was still as taut as a strongbow, close to the edge of climax. He'd certainly stepped up the torture, she thought, arousing her thoroughly but not doing anything about it – and knowing she was in no position to pleasure herself. The fantasy he'd described had excited her beyond measure. Part of her was ashamed of herself, but part of her revelled in it.

Would she really do it? Would she really screw him in public, where they could so easily be caught, and then allow herself to be the focus of an orgy? She didn't know. But then again, there were quite a few other things she had fantasised about but never thought she'd actually do, and had now done with Marc during her confinement. Making love with two men at once, making love with another woman, watching another couple make love, and letting him introduce her to the deepest, darkest sexual act...

She shivered, and closed her eyes.

It was a mistake. With her eyes shut, all she could see was what Marc had done to her, as she'd watched him in the mirror. Again and again and again, she remembered the feel of his body penetrating hers; the way he'd touched her, stroking her breasts and teasing her nipples and exploring her sex so thoroughly with his mouth and fingers; the way he'd bathed her, teasing her with the sponge. The way he'd driven her so completely out of control.

By the time Marc returned, carrying her lunch on a tray, Sarah was acutely aroused. If he noticed, he didn't remark on it.

'Lunchtime,' he said brightly.

She shook her head. 'I don't want any lunch.'

'Sarah, you need to eat. I'm not going to starve you.'

'I don't mean that.' She moistened her dry lips with the tip of her tongue. 'I don't want lunch, because I want... I want you.'

He placed the tray carefully on the floor, away from the bed. 'Run that by me again. I'm not sure I heard it right.'

'I want you,' she repeated softly. 'I need you, Marc. I need to feel you inside me.'

His eyes darkened. 'Are you sure about this?'

Strangely enough, his doubting tone gave her the confidence she needed. 'Oh yes. I've never been more sure about anything in my life.'

'Right.' He stood there, just looking down at her.

'Take me, Marc. I want to you make love with me.'

He smiled then, and slowly stripped off his light cotton sweater and faded jeans. Sarah watched him, thrilling at the look on his face. Simon was right. They did feel the same way about each other, even if they weren't going to admit it. It was more than lust; something deeper, more enduring.

He looked good. Very good. Her eyes lingered on his shoulders and his chest, broad and muscular, then dipped down to his narrow waist and lean hips. She moistened her lower lip again as he pulled down his boxer shorts and she saw his cock rising from the mat of hair at his groin. She wanted him. She wanted him so badly, in every way he'd taken her before and then some. She wanted to explore more uncharted territory with him. She wanted to go further and faster – all the time knowing that she was safe with him. She trusted him completely.

He sat on the bed next to her, then leant over to kiss her. His lips brushed hers very gently. He teased her with tiny butterfly kisses, nipping at her lower lip, then moving away again before she could respond. When she was panting and tugging at her bonds, wanting to pull his head down to hers so he could kiss her properly, he finally slid his tongue between her lips, exploring her mouth and kissing her deeply.

When he broke the kiss, Sarah was shaking. He smiled, stroking her face. 'Let it go, Sarah. This one's for you – and by the time I've finished with you, you'll be completely out of control.'

'Is that a threat?'

He shook his head. 'Uh-uh. A guarantee.'

'What's the penalty clause?'

He grinned, following her train of thought. 'If I don't make you come until you don't know what day it is, then you can do whatever you like with me, for a whole hour. Tie me up, whip me, tease me with your beautiful sex and then stop until I'm begging you to continue, force me to masturbate for you... Anything.'

Her eyes were heavy-lidded. She rather liked the idea of having Marc completely within her power for a while, submitting to her every whim. 'It's a deal.'

'Good. Now, where was I? Ah, yes.' He bent his head, trailing his mouth down the sensitive spots at the side of her neck.

Sarah felt her sex begin to pool. Marc was an expert, his mouth and hands highly skilled. She closed her eyes, tipping her head back among the pillows as he licked the hollows of her collarbones and then moved down to suckle her breasts. He sucked her hardening nipples, using his teeth to graze the sensitive flesh, and she arched against him. Then he blew on her moistened flesh, making her gasp and open her eyes.

'Like it?' he asked softly.

She nodded.

'Good. Because I've hardly started.' His voice was husky, full of promise.

Infinitely slowly, Marc continued to kiss his way down her body, nuzzling the soft underswell of her breasts, licking round her navel, rubbing his face against her abdomen. As he neared her quivering sex, she lifted her pelvis; she wanted to feel his mouth there, cooling the raging heat between her thighs.

He laughed, and swiftly bypassed her quim, moving down to kiss her insteps, and moving very slowly up her legs. By the time he reached mid-thigh, Sarah was trembling uncontrollably.

'Marc?'

'Mm?' He continued nuzzling her thighs.

'I... Would you turn round, please?'

'Turn round?' He lifted his head and looked at her, not comprehending for a moment. Then it dawned on him what she wanted, and he smiled. 'Oh. Right.'

He moved so he was straddling her, his knees by her shoulders. 'How's this?'

His cock was just out of her reach. She stretched up as far as she could, pushing her tongue out, but she was still millimetres away from tasting him. 'Marc. I... I want to suck you. Please. While you're—' she swallowed '—while

238

you're sucking me.'

'Seeing as you've asked so nicely...' He gave her another of those smouldering looks and curled his fingers round his shaft, placing the bulbous head of his cock on her lips. His breath hissed sharply as she peeled her lips apart and reached up, taking the first inch into her mouth and sucking. 'Oh, Sarah,' he murmured, his voice cracking.

Then he breathed against her sex, teasing her until she writhed impatiently and gave him a warning nip with her teeth.

'Playing rough, huh?' he said huskily.

Sarah's reply was muffled by his cock, and he laughed. 'It's very rude to talk with your mouth full, Sarah. I'll have to discipline you for that, later.'

A delicious thrill went through her at the words. What would he do? Would he spank her with a hairbrush, as Simon had suggested, then arouse her with it? Or would he use his hands, just hard enough to warm her rump, before making her forget the stinging pain with his clever mouth and his glorious cock?

Then she gave up on thinking as he began to pay attention to her clitoris; he flicked the tip of his tongue across the sensitive bud of flesh, back and forth, back and forth. She adopted his same rhythm, sucking him hard. Then she felt him take her clitoris into his mouth, sucking it.

It was far too much. She came instantly, filling his mouth with musky nectar. He shifted slightly, moving his cock from her mouth, and she cried out. Her sex contracted sharply over his mouth, and she felt as though some invisible cord between her sex and her nipples had just been pulled tight.

Before the aftershocks of her orgasm had died away, Marc moved until he was kneeling between her thighs.

He fitted the tip of his cock, still glistening with her saliva, to the entrance of her sex; then he eased in, moving slowly until his cock was completely embedded in her. The thick rod of flesh filled her completely. Sarah wanted to bring her legs up and wrap them round his waist, but she was still tied.

He bent to kiss her again, and she could taste her own juices on his mouth. It only served to increase her arousal, and she kissed him back, hard, her tongue pressing against his. He slid his hands under her buttocks and lifted her slightly, changing the angle of his penetration to give her more pleasure. His thrusts were long and slow and deep, just how Sarah wanted them, and she moaned with delight.

'Look,' he said softly. 'See how perfect your body is, how you arch into me.'

She turned her head and stared into the mirror, which was still placed so that the couple on the bed could see their sexes joining. He was right. It looked as good as it felt: Marc's beautiful long cock pulling almost out of her, so that she could nearly see the tip, then easing all the way back in. The shaft was almost pearlescent with her juices, as if someone had painted him with some very rare and rich liquid.

As she watched he quickened his pace, thrusting deep. She felt her body begin to shimmer again, and then her climax ripped through her, a tidal wave demolishing every coherent thought and turning her body into a raging sea of pleasure. She yelled out, her voice almost wailing in bliss. At the peak she felt Marc's cock throbbing deep inside her and heard his answering cry as he, too, came.

When she finally came back down to earth Marc was lying beside her, stroking her breasts and belly and smiling at her. 'Okay?' he asked softly.

'Yes.'

'What day is it?' he teased.

'Monday.' She smiled back. 'But I think we can forget the penalty clause.'

'Good.' He paused. 'So have you thought about things?'

She'd known he was going to bring that subject up again. 'Yes.'

'And?'

She sighed. 'Okay. You're right. I'm submissive, sexually – though not all the time.'

'Love's sweetest part, variety,' he said softly.

'Is that another quote?'

He nodded.

'The same poet you were quoting before?'

'John Donne. Best love poet in the English language – in my humble opinion, that is,' he added.

'Maybe I'll surprise you and learn some, quote him back to you,' she said, stroking his hair back from his forehead.

He rubbed his nose against hers. 'I'd like that. So that's one hurdle out of the way. Now for the biggie. Have you thought about the office?'

She nodded. 'It's clear that you—' she coughed '—have a good rapport with your team. Amanda and Julia were certainly prepared to do anything you asked.'

'Not all of it was my idea,' he said. 'And I do hope you're not intending to sack either of them for misconduct.'

'No. Nor you.'

'Good. So what's the verdict?'

'Okay. You can run your team however you like. No interference from me. Though I have three conditions.'

'Three conditions, hm?'

'Firstly, they can keep their posters and whatever – if you insist, but I want the filing done regularly. Which means weekly, not once in a blue moon when the department's knee-deep in paper.'

'Fine. I'll bring it up at the next team meeting.'

'Secondly, you report to me every Friday night for a performance review.'

'A performance review?' he echoed, sounding shocked.

'A private one,' she told him, with an impish grin.

'Oh. *That* sort of performance review.' He made a mental note to switch his squash matches with Simon to Thursday nights. He had a feeling that Sarah's performance review was going to take quite a long time. Particularly if he had that leather harness made for her, with a sapphire fashioned to fit in her navel.

'Mm-hm. And thirdly, as I'm supposedly sick, I'm going to spend the week in bed. Your bed, in your room – not here.'

'Okay.' He smiled at her. 'I don't have a problem with that.'

'And no bonds, this time.'

'That's a fourth condition.'

She grinned. 'You interrupted me before I'd finished. Marc, I want to touch you when you touch me. I want to spend the week in bed with you, not on my own.'

'This isn't very submissive, you know – all these demands,' he said thoughtfully.

Her grin broadened. 'But I don't think everyone's a hundred per cent submissive, or a hundred per cent dominant... including you.'

'You might be right.' He unsnapped her handcuffs. 'So... to go back to where we started, would you like some lunch?'

'Yes.' She gave him a deliberately sensual look. 'You.'

'I can't argue with that, boss,' he said softly. He untied her ankles and rubbed her aching muscles. Then he rolled onto his back and placed his hands behind his head. 'I'm in your hands, Sarah.'

'And I'm in charge?'

He gave her a lazy grin. 'At the moment – and only because it suits me.'

'Good.' She knelt to cup his face in her hands, then leant forward to kiss him. His mouth opened beneath hers, and she kissed him fiercely, probing him. Then she licked her way down his body; she teased his hard flat nipples with her teeth and tongue, then moved down over his abdomen. She traced the outline of his stiffening cock on his belly with her tongue, making him gasp, then ringed his shaft with her forefinger and thumb, sliding her hand back and forth.

Marc watched her, an amused smile on his face as she explored his body; when she moved to straddle him, the amusement faded, and his eyes darkened with passion. She lifted herself up, positioning his cock at her sex, then slowly lowered herself onto him.

'Oh, yes,' she murmured, half to herself. She leant forward, sliding her hands down the bed so she could kiss him, then straightened up again, arching back to change the angle of his penetration. Slowly, she lifted and lowered herself onto his impaling cock; she moved her body in tiny circles, flexing her internal muscles round him.

'Do it, Sarah,' he said softly. 'Touch yourself. Let yourself go.'

She lifted her hands to her breasts, cupping them and pushing them up and together, and then pulled at her nipples, massaging the taut peaks of flesh.

'Is this what you do when you think of me?' he whispered.

'Yes,' she admitted dreamily.

'And you were masturbating when I came into the room on Friday night, weren't you?'

243

She closed her eyes and nodded.

'Why?'

'Because – because you turn me on,' she said. 'You excite me, Marc.'

'Enough to lose control? To lose it completely?'

She nodded again.

'So the efficient business machine from the office has a deeper, darker side?'

'You know I have. You released it.'

'Show me,' he tempted softly. 'Show me.'

She let one hand drift down to cup her mound, then pushed her hand between their bodies to rub her clitoris. Her other hand still worked at her nipples, pinching and squeezing them in turn, and her rocking movements over his cock grew quicker, shorter.

'Open your eyes, Sarah,' he commanded gently.

She did so, and he was awed to see how her ice-blue eyes blazed with passion. Her lips were parted, reddened and pouting; her hair was mussed; and she looked incredibly wanton.

'Watch yourself,' he coaxed.

She turned her head and their eyes met in the mirror. What Sarah saw surprised her: a woman at the furthest edge of desire, abandoned and touching her own pleasure-centres while she rode her lover, slamming down onto his cock and rubbing her pubis against his. She looked wild. She looked out of control.

'See how good you look?' he asked, his voice still low and husky.

She shook her head. 'See how good *we* look,' she corrected. 'We make a good team, Marc.'

'What about your personal rule, never to mix business and pleasure?'

She continued to raise and lower herself over him. 'Ever

heard of the exception proving the rule? Anyway, I thought you had the same rule. What happened to yours?' she countered.

He raised his upper body to kiss her. 'It went out of the window, when I first saw you. When I first decided to...' He stopped.

She laughed. 'When you first decided to take Simon's advice?'

'You know about that?'

'Except he meant a romantic weekend with roses and champagne and a jacuzzi.'

'That can be arranged,' he said softly. 'Maybe next weekend. Some country retreat.'

'I'll hold you to that.' She ground her hips, making him moan with pleasure. 'This weekend... it wasn't the only rule you broke, was it? Because it wasn't just me. You made love with Amanda. And Julia.'

'Just Amanda,' he corrected. 'But yes, I've broken a lot of other personal rules since Friday night.'

'Are you trying to tell me that I'm a bad influence on you?'

'What do you think?'

'I think it's mutual,' she said simply. 'Like a lot of other things.'

'Things neither of us want to say first?'

Her eyes glittered. 'I swear you read my mind, sometimes. Some of the fantasies you described to me were things I'd been thinking about too.'

'Karma,' he said softly.

She shuddered as her climax began to ripple through her. 'God, Marc. The way you make me feel...'

'It's exactly the same for me,' he told her huskily.

Their bodies fused; then Sarah slumped against him, burying her head in his shoulder. 'You know,' she sighed, her voice muffled against his skin, 'you really made me suffer this weekend. Making me lose my inhibitions—'

'More like, admit to your true nature.'

She didn't correct him. 'And making me wait, bringing me right to the edge of orgasm and then stopping.'

He grinned. 'Serves you right for being so stubborn.'

'I'm going to get my own back, you know.'

He rolled her onto her side, pulling her into his body and letting his fingers explore her curves, tracing the dip of her waist and the swell of her buttocks. 'Sounds interesting.'

'Interesting?'

'Mm.' He slid his hand between her thighs, making her moan softly. 'And I'm completely at your disposal for the rest of the week...'

More exciting titles available from Chimera

All **Chimera** titles are available from your local bookshop or newsagent, or direct from our mail order department. Please send your order with your credit card details, a cheque or postal order (made payable to *Chimera Publishing Ltd*) to: **Chimera Publishing Ltd., Readers' Services, PO Box 152, Waterlooville, Hants, PO8 9FS**. Or call our **24 hour telephone/fax credit card hotline: +44 (0)23 92 646062** (Visa, Mastercard, Switch, JCB and Solo only).

UK & BFPO - Aimed delivery within three working days.
- A delivery charge of £3.00.
- An item charge of £0.20 per item, up to a maximum of five items.

For example, a customer ordering two items from the site for delivery within the UK will be charged £3.00 delivery + £0.40 items charge, totalling a delivery charge of £3.40. The maximum delivery cost for a UK customer is £4.00. Therefore if you order more than five items for delivery within the UK you will not be charged more than a total of £4.00 for delivery.

Western Europe - Aimed delivery within five to ten working days.
- A delivery charge of £3.00.
- An item charge of £1.25 per item.

For example, a customer ordering two items from the site for delivery to W. Europe, will be charged £3.00 delivery + £2.50 items charge, totalling a delivery charge of £5.50.

USA - Aimed delivery within twelve to fifteen working days.
- A delivery charge of £3.00.
- An item charge of £2.00 per item.

For example, a customer ordering two items from the site for delivery to the USA, will be charged £3.00 delivery + £4.00 item charge, totalling a delivery charge of £7.00.

Rest of the World - Aimed delivery within fifteen to twenty-two working days.
- A delivery charge of £3.00.
- An item charge of £2.75 per item.

For example, a customer ordering two items from the site for delivery to the ROW, will be charged £3.00 delivery + £5.50 item charge, totalling a delivery charge of £8.50.

You can now contact other **Chimera** readers and perhaps
find your perfect partner at our new website

www.chimeradating.com

Chimera Publishing Ltd

PO Box 152
Waterlooville
Hants
PO8 9FS

www.chimerabooks.co.uk

info@chimerabooks.co.uk

www.chimeradating.com

***

Sales and Distribution in the USA and Canada

Client Distribution Services, Inc
193 Edwards Drive
Jackson
TN 38301
USA

***

Sales and Distribution in Australia

Dennis Jones & Associates Pty Ltd
19a Michellan Ct
Bayswater
Victoria
Australia 3153